MISTY'S misadventures

KATHRYN TAYLOR

 FriesenPress

One Printers Way
Altona, MB R0G 0B0
Canada

www.friesenpress.com

Copyright © 2021 by Kathryn Taylor
First Edition — 2021

All rights reserved.

This is a work of fiction. Names, characters, places, and incidents are either the product of the author's imagination or are used fictitiously. Any resemblance to actual persons, living or dead, businesses, companies, events, or locales, is entirely coincidental.

No part of this publication may be reproduced in any form, or by any means, electronic or mechanical, including photocopying, recording, or any information browsing, storage, or retrieval system, without permission in writing from FriesenPress.

ISBN
978-1-5255-0773-1 (Hardcover)
978-1-5255-0774-8 (Paperback)
978-1-5255-0775-5 (eBook)

1. FICTION, ROMANCE

Distributed to the trade by The Ingram Book Company

To my husband and children for their love, support, and encouragement. To my sweet dogs, Judy, Princess and Salt, who sat by my side and understood why walk time was sometimes delayed. To my mother, who believed in me and loved to say, **"The world is your oyster."** ... *you have the ability and the freedom to do anything or go anywhere. Thanks, Mom, for giving me that gift.*

CONTENTS

Chapter 1: The Homecoming Queen	1
Chapter 2: Smooth Operator	7
Chapter 3: Mouldy Old Socks	15
Chapter 4: Bedknobs and Broomsticks	21
Chapter 5: The Gulf Crossing	33
Chapter 6: The Phonse	39
Chapter 7: The Bed of Enticement	49
Chapter 8: Win-Win	57
Chapter 9: Up She Comes	65
Chapter 10: Yes, B'y	71
Chapter 11: Blown Away	81
Chapter 12: Tender Moments	93
Chapter 13: A Shot in the Plexus	109
Chapter 14: You Bees the One	117
Chapter 15: Getting Personal	129
Chapter 16: Well-Heeled	139
Chapter 17: If It Ain't Broke, Don't Fix It	145
Chapter 18: Cupid's Arrow	151
Chapter 19: When Love Comes A-Knockin'	169
Chapter 20: Ho, Ho, Ho	175
Chapter 21: Shiver Me Timbers	189
Chapter 22: Yo-Ho-Ho and a Bottle of Rum	195
Chapter 23: Tidal Wave of Love	215
Chapter 24: Smack-Dab	231
Chapter 25: One Big Mistake	245
Chapter 26: Chemistry Lesson	255
Chapter 27: Mixed Messages	263
Chapter 28: Open-Wide	275
Chapter 29: The Right Stuff	289

CHAPTER 1

The Homecoming Queen

"I have to pee, Mom."

"Oh, for gawd's sake, not again." Misty whipped her head around to stare at her five-year-old daughter Vivienne in the back seat. A large plastic container filled with clothes separated her from her sister. "Are you sure?"

"I have to pee. Like last time," said Vivi, a distinct threat in her voice.

Misty didn't need a reminder. She could still recall in vivid detail how long it took to get the smell out of the car seat and her car. "I should have put you on a Port-a-Potty instead of a booster seat. Matter of fact, tomorrow morning I'll sell that idea to Chrysler and retire." Misty was glad no one could overhear this conversation, which would kill her chances of ever winning mother of the year. But it wasn't her fault. The drive was pure hell and compounded with the fact she felt like such a complete failure, well, she was saying stuff she would never nor...

"Mom, if she wets everything again, I'm never getting back in this car," seven-year-old Liberty said.

Misty glanced in the rear-view mirror and realized she had two choices: stop for a pee break or stop for a fight. "Oh, all right, I'll stop. But we're in the middle of nowhere and I'm taking no responsibility if a moose bites your bum." A six-hour ocean crossing that had morphed into a ten-hour ordeal had already frayed her nerves. They had crossed over waters so rough she'd had a hard time convincing herself, let alone her children, that they'd all arrive safely in Port Aux Basques, Newfoundland.

"Mom!" wailed Vivi. Misty flipped on her signal, pulled over and took a roll of toilet paper from the glove compartment. She was prepared for everything. Everything except what was really happening.

She could handle the ferry, the whining, the spats and, yes, she could handle the pee stops. What she could not handle was the fact she was coming home with most of her worldly belongings stuffed into the trunk of her car. It wasn't the way she wanted it. It wasn't the way she'd envisioned a homecoming. Hell, it wasn't even fair. *Damn you, Jake Muldoon,* she thought for the hundredth time since she'd filed for bankruptcy. *Damn you and your gir...*

"Hurry, Mom," said Vivi as she pulled on the door handle.

Viv's desperate plea snapped her back to reality. Misty jumped out and opened the rear door. The wind ripped through her cotton blouse as she struggled with the release on Vivi's booster seat. She looked longingly at her leather jacket draped across the front passenger seat. Her daughter wiggled and pressed her legs together in the now all too familiar pee-pending ritual dance.

"This never works," Misty said as she vented her frustration on the latch. "There!" The buckle finally released and she took her daughter's hand and helped her out of the car. "Just squat by the door." It was bloody freezing. What was she thinking, packing their winter coats in a suitcase in the bottom of the trunk? It was the middle of June, but the temperature was more what you'd expect for October or November.

"Liberty can see me."

Misty shook her head in wonderment. Was there no limit to the number of conditions her kids could come up with? This was like a sanity test and she was running the risk of failing. "Give me a break, Viv. You've got a choice—either Liberty sees you pee or a moose bites your bum." Misty looked over her shoulder at the shrubs encroaching on the highway and wondered what she would do if a moose popped its head out.

Panic washed over Vivienne's face as she fastened herself to one of Misty's legs, her little hands grasping at the fabric of her pants.

"Moose only eat grass and stuff," yelled Liberty from the back seat. "*Everyone* knows that."

Oh, really? "Look, Miss Smarty Pants, one more word out of you and..." Her voice trailed off as she felt a warm trickle. "Vivi, no!" Her daughter had let go right over Misty's foot and one of her sandals. *You aren't paying attention,* she told herself. *You're too busy being a crab-ass.* She pulled her foot out of the way and waited for her daughter to finish.

A few minutes later, as she slipped her foot out of her sandal, she returned Vivienne's uneasy smile with a frown. Then balancing on one leg and the big toe of her pissy foot, she tore off some toilet paper and wiped Vivi's legs. For an encore she slipped her daughter's panties off and held them delicately between her thumb and pointer, then watched calmly as they sailed through the air and landed on a bush. "You're going to have to do without them for now," Misty said, ignoring the rocks that were biting into her unclad foot as she plopped her surprised daughter back into the car seat, all while locking her gaze on Liberty, just daring her to make another comment. Just one word that would give her the perfect opportunity to lose it.

What exactly did I do to deserve this? I was a good wife. A dedicated mother. Maybe a bit too busy but I never complained. And now this? Give me a nasty client. Give me a tainted product. Anything. Anything but... Misty heaved a rock at the panties and knocked them off the bush into the foliage where they couldn't flap like a sign to every mother who followed in her wake. *Anything... but this.* She sat down with her legs hanging out the door to deal with the more immediate problem of her sandal.

She poured the contents of her water bottle over her shoe and her foot and dried them both with toilet paper. As she leaned over to return the roll to the glove box, she glanced at herself in the rear-view mirror. Her normally golden complexion was pale, and the damp air had exploded in her shoulder-length auburn hair, creating a cascade of frizzy waves. Without make-up she actually looked younger than her thirty years, even with the fine lines knocking at the corners of her brown eyes. Still, bad-hair day or not, she knew she looked a whole lot better than she felt. And that was saying something.

She tucked herself behind the wheel and slammed the door, not caring she was leaving behind a pile of toilet paper. *TP is biodegradable, anyhow. Me, however, I'm just designed for catching shit with no hope of disintegration.* She jacked up the heat and waited for some feeling to come back into her fingers before she pulled out, spewing rocks and gravel from her wheels. From the silence in the backseat, she knew her daughters were suitably impressed or scared totally to death. Either one worked as long as they buttoned up and let her stew about the mess she was in.

They'd travelled five hours from Halifax to the ferry in North Sydney. Lined up and waited three hours before boarding. They'd sung just about every song they could think of, from Madonna to Mary Chapin Carpenter. Somehow it just didn't seem right for young kids to belt out lyrics like "Sometimes you're the windshield and sometimes you're the bug" with quite so much enthusiasm, but if it helped them cover the miles peacefully, she was prepared to be liberal. The true irony of the situation didn't escape her, though, especially since she herself was feeling much more like the bug than she wanted to admit. This drive was simply the sequel to a desperate voyage that included bathrooms that smelled like vomit and boats that crossed in the middle of nowhere.

But, Misty consoled herself, *I am not the mother from hell. I'm just a tired mom who's been driving for hours straight across this island on a piddling bit of sleep.*

And that's all she was. Exhausted, broken-hearted and divorced to boot, heading to Charlie's Cove, Newfoundland, to start her life over. And not just over, but over in a minuscule outpost, population 1600 on a good day. Who could blame her for being cranky? Under the circumstances, even Dr. Phil himself would be hard pressed to put a positive spin on this.

As for arriving in Charlie's Cove five hours behind schedule with a piece of toilet paper wedged between the toes of her bare foot, why that wasn't even worth mentioning.

CHAPTER 2

Smooth Operator

"Excuse me," Misty called through her lowered window to the older man on the side of the road. His plaid jacket, green work pants, and rubber boots seemed like they had been well used for a number of years—so did the man himself. There was nothing about him that inspired confidence, other than the fact she felt assured he was local and she needed directions. "Can you tell me where Charlie Cuthbertson's place is?"

"Aye?"

"Charlie Cuthbertson's place. I'm looking for it," she repeated.

"Try the cemetery. He's in with the Presbyterians. There only bees a few of 'em, but you can't miss old Cuthbertson. Got a deal on the marker when Mont Ferguson's cheque bounced. We just ignores the fact Ferguson's name is on it, too."

Misty deadpanned. She thought she understood what he'd said, but it was touch and go. She hadn't heard anyone talk that fast since…well, since a long time. She tried again. "Not Charlie. His place. His house."

"Oh, you wants his house. You're going in the wrong direction for that." He pointed a few-hundred yards away. "What you wants is back there. T'ird road on your left. You can't miss it."

"Great. Thanks very much." She started to close the window and then stopped as the man continued to speak.

"Duff. Duff Murphy is me. What do you want with old Cuthbertson's place?" He rested his hand on the car door and leaned forward.

Misty figured he was entitled to be curious. "Pleased to meet you, Duff." She stuck her hand out the window and was pleasantly surprised by his warm grip. "I'm Charlie's great niece, Misty Muldoon. We're going to spend a bit of time here." She still hadn't come to terms with the phrase "moving in."

"Mom, you didn't tell me he died. I'm not staying in some dead man's house," Liberty yelled over the seat.

Misty smiled at Duff and raised her voice, hoping to smother her daughter's protests. "Thanks for your help. We'll see you around." She waved politely as she raised the car window again, this time all the way.

Turning a car while glaring at a child in the back seat was not the easiest of manoeuvres but since the onset of this trip, Misty was getting rather good at it.

A few minutes later she pulled up in front of the house at the end of the third driveway. Surely this couldn't be the place? Visions of a brightly painted outport home fizzled as she stared at the deteriorating monstrosity before her. She understood now why no one ever visited Great-uncle Charlie.

"Let's get out," she said rather half-heartedly, honestly hoping the key wouldn't fit. What had her life come to? It was unbearable to think they'd be living here. But as much as she wanted to refute it, in her heart of hearts, she knew this was indeed Great-uncle Charlie's castle and now their new home.

"Vivi's going to sleep in a dead man's room," Liberty jeered at her sister, who ran to her mother in tears.

This is it, thought Misty. *This is my breaking point.* With one sobbing daughter in her arms and the other tagging behind, Misty walked up to the front door and tried the key. When it turned, she pressed her face into Vivi's sweater and hoped her own tears would go unnoticed.

The house was shockingly cold. And dark. Vivienne slipped from her arms and stood by her side. Feeling slightly more composed, Misty tried the light switch and was surprised when it worked. At least that was going their way.

Liberty peeked around her and sized up the room. "What's that?" she asked, pointing to a large black stove with a glass door.

"That, my darling daughter, is what's known as a wood stove. Lots of these old houses have them. We can paint it and use it as a planter. I hope," she added under her breath.

"Not exactly the Ritz Carlton, is it?"

A deep voice carried across the room. Misty screamed and grabbed her daughters. She was visibly shaking as she turned, almost expecting to see Charlie's ghost.

"Sorry, sorry. Didn't mean to scare ya." A tall, angular man stood in the doorway. "I'm Hayward Hedges. Duff told me you'd arrived."

Hedges had been Misty's only contact with Charlie's Cove. He was her great-uncle's lawyer and had been the one to track her down after Charlie had died and left the property to her.

It was the strangest thing, really. Misty had never been to Charlie's house, much less to Charlie's Cove. Her great-uncle had been a reclusive man and what she could remember of him wasn't flattering. He had been cranky and not much fun. This house pretty much summed up her first impression of him when he had once visited her mother—decrepit, gray, and humourless.

But at least it was a refuge from the storm that encompassed her life at the moment and for that much she should be grateful. After all, a single woman, recently unemployed, with two kids and only enough money in the bank for the next two weeks might consider herself lucky to have a house. The aesthetics could be taken care of later.

She shrugged off the slight feeling of unease that Hedge's abrupt appearance had stirred up and offered her hand as well as a smile. "Mr. Hedges. You caught us off guard but I'm glad you're here. Maybe you can show us around. It's strange coming into a house you don't know at all."

"And this one, in particular. Your great-uncle didn't part too easily with his money."

"I can see that."

"Ah, he wasn't too bad of a feller. We were all used to him around here. Even kept an eye on him, though he much preferred we left him alone. You knows the way it is, eh? Once people finds out that Charlie's niece has moved in, you're likely to get plenty of visitors yourself. Everyone 'round here wants to help, long as you don't mind them knowing your business." Hayward stared at her with a suggestive smile that never reached his eyes. "You still looks pale; guess I really shook you up."

"I'm a bit tired from the trip and honestly..." she said as she spread her hands despondently, "I was hoping the place might be in better shape." She glanced at Hayward's hand and noticed he was wearing a wedding band. Still, she hesitated. Maybe it was the way he looked at her but her sixth sense was vibrating. It wouldn't hurt to let him know she had no intention of being the hot new piece in town and she knew a great way to start.

"Let me introduce you to my daughters, Vivienne and Liberty. Say hello to Mr. Hedges, girls."

"Vivienne and Liberty. Very pretty names for two very pretty girls," said Hedges.

"Dad says she got carried away." For a seven-year-old, Liberty had a surprising command of the English language, particularly in the sense that Misty never knew what she was going to say.

"How's that, dear?" asked Hedges.

"Our initials spell something."

"They do?"

"Oh, Liberty, Mr. Hedges doesn't want to hear about that," interjected Misty, hoping to get her daughter off the topic.

"No. I do," said Hedges, appearing intrigued by the young girl.

"La vie. The life. Mom named us after that. See, I'm Liberty Alexis and my sister's Vivienne Isabelle Eugenie. Get it?"

"Got it," he replied after a short pause. "That must have been an interesting period in your life, Mrs. Muldoon. Not everyone thinks of that kind of thing." He leaned against the doorjamb and allowed his eyes to wander briefly from her face.

Misty shifted uncomfortably under his scrutiny. "I'm in creative," she replied as she pulled Liberty and Vivienne closer. "You know. Public relations, advertising, media. That kind of thing."

"Not much around here in that line of work, except maybe at our local paper. You are planning to work, aren't you?"

"If we're planning to eat, yes."

Hedges sized her up again. "Money's tight, eh?"

"I'm recently divorced," she replied, wondering how she, the master of Q and A, had let the conversation drift into such a personal area. "I had to close my business rather unexpectedly." *It's called bankruptcy, a term I'm sure you're familiar with.*

"Well, I've a feeling you'll make out all right in Charlie's Cove. Things has a way of working out here." Hedges was still standing in the front porch, neither in nor out, and Misty sensed he wanted a direct invitation to cross the threshold. She weighed the pros and cons of inviting him in but her unfamiliarity with the old house won out against her better judgment.

"How about the official tour?" she asked. As she turned to move aside, she adjusted the zipper on her jacket all the way up, uncomfortably aware of the cropped jeans that hung low on her hips. For once, Misty wished she'd worn her oldest pair of baggy sweats. "And while you're at it, can you assure Vivienne Great-uncle C didn't die in this house?"

"Scared of a few ghosts, is ya? Not to worry. This place isn't haunted. Charlie died down at the wharf. He just up and keeled over. Beats other alternatives when you're ninety-five years old. How old might you be, Mrs. Muldoon?"

Old enough to know better, thought Misty as she and the girls followed him across the room into the kitchen. *So much for listening to my intuition.*

"Mom's thirty," said Liberty. "I'm almost eight. How old are you?"

Misty gave her daughter a threatening look and shook her head in warning.

"Living up to your name, aren't you, dear?" said Hedges. He was speaking to Liberty but continuing to look at Misty in a way that made her skin crawl. "I'm a little older than your mother, young lady, but, a lot younger than your great-uncle." He winked at Misty as though they were sharing an intimate joke.

"Mr. Hedges…" Misty began, wanting to change the subject before it became even more personal. *How had he managed to manipulate the conversation so easily? Smooth wasn't the word to describe him. Creepy would be better.*

"Now, now, Mrs. Muldoon," Hedges interrupted. "We're pretty informal here in the Cove, especially since we're all friends. I'm just plain old Hayward."

"Hayward," she said with forced cheerfulness. "How about that tour, then?" Her grin had settled into what she felt certain looked more like a grimace. *I gotta get this guy the hell outta here. A few words, the tour, and the bum's rush.* "Were you born here in the Cove? This is home for you?" *As if I care, for godsake.*

If the living room had been a shocker, the kitchen was what you would call a total meltdown. The old linoleum floor was lifting at the edges and the colour scheme was non-existent. From the stains behind the sink and on the counters, the place hadn't had much loving care in years. *There's such a thing as pinching pennies, but how could he have lived like this?* She had no idea how she would do it, but they weren't going to live in a place that looked... no, felt... so abandoned. Somehow she would have to fix it up.

The rest of the tour was just as disappointing. No matter the cost, the first things they were buying were new beds and until then, they would camp out on the floor. She shivered but wasn't sure if it was from the dampness or the thought of insects and rodents.

"Ah, Hayward, where's the furnace?"

"In the front room."

"Front room?" Misty was puzzled. "I'm not sure I understand."

"Charlie didn't have a furnace," he continued. "He used the woodstove in the living room. Like I said, he didn't part with his money very easily. I expect you can manage until you get a furnace put in. I know today's a bit chilly, but the weather will improve. It's only June yet."

The chill in Misty's heart far outweighed the temperature in the house. One of the boxes in her car was filled with bills from her failed PR Company. And now she had to buy a furnace?

"Did Uncle Charlie happen to leave any money?" she asked. She didn't care what impression her question left with Hayward. Uncle C's place was an obvious money pit and quelling the panic that was building in her stomach would require more than a pep talk. It would take real, hard cash.

"Not as far as I know. He prepaid my services and did the same for his funeral. If you ask the locals, they'll say Charlie had pots of money, all buried up here somewhere. It wouldn't hurt to turn over any loose floorboards you come across, what?"

Misty could hear the wheels churning. The house of horrors had morphed into Treasure Island for her two daughters. At least it might keep them busy while she undertook what was going to be a monumental cleaning job. Just the thought of what lay ahead made her want to lie down and sleep.

"We'll keep that in mind," she said as she led him directly to the front door. "Thanks for the tour. At least we know there are no ghosts hiding behind the doors." Despite the cool breeze that whirled around them, Misty held the door wide open. *Time to go, buddy-boy. And don't come back any time soon.*

"No need for you girls to ever feel uneasy or lonely, hey?" He winked at Misty again. "You can always give old Hayward a call."

Subtlety was obviously an art that had bypassed Hayward. But his comment did serve one purpose. She needed to get a phone installed and soon. She wanted a fast link to the outside world, especially if Hayward was a sample of the local hormone pool.

Relieved to finally shut the door, she turned and looked at her daughters standing uneasily in the gloomy room. *We're so alone here. I'm just not sure anymore...what if I made a terrible mistake?* She felt her eyes filling with moisture again.

"What's the matter, Mom?" asked Liberty.

"Nothing, honey. All this dust is making my allergies act up. Come here, you two, and give me a hug." She wrapped her arms around her daughters and squeezed them tightly. She wasn't looking forward to their first night in the house, but her more immediate problem was figuring out how to work a woodstove. If it had been anyone other than Hayward, she would have asked for help.

Anyway, they couldn't possibly freeze in June. At least...she hoped they couldn't.

CHAPTER 3

Mouldy Old Socks

Three heavy thumps on the front door roused Misty from her sleep. Her hips ached from lying on the floor in her sleeping bag. What time was it? She looked at her watch. Only six a.m. The banging on the door continued.

"Just a minute," she called as she extracted herself from between Liberty and Vivienne. *Sweet Jesus, it's cold.* She picked up the sweater she had discarded in the night and pulled it on as she padded to the front door. "Who izzit?" she asked as she cracked the door enough to peek out.

"Marnin', missus. Hayward tells me you needs some help with the heating."

Duff—go figure. "What time do you normally get up around here?" was all Misty could think to ask.

"Same time as the sun. I been up and chopped some wood. You wants I brings it in?"

Duff's breath was clouding in the cool morning air. Behind him she could see the infamous sun shining brilliantly in an almost cloudless sky, as blue as ever she had seen. And she was struck by the sound of birds chirping. The day was alive in ways that she would need at least two hours and a strong cup of coffee to appreciate.

Despite the beauty and the freshness of the day, the coolness in the air hadn't improved much overnight. The girls would be up in a few hours and it would help if the house was warm. *Maybe these old homes are like large, live-in refrigerators,* thought Misty. *Did they use even insulation when they built them? My gawd, if Charlie was ninety-five, then this house could be...what, maybe seventy-five years old?* She gave herself a mental slap. This path of thought was a poor way to start the day. Better to welcome in a man who was willing to help her with heating, primitive though it might be.

Misty nodded for Duff to get started. She left the door ajar and jumped back into her sleeping bag, careful not to wake the girls. A few minutes later, Duff traipsed across the room and began carefully stacking wood next to the stove.

"How 'bout I lights it and gets some heat going?" he whispered.

"Promise the whole house won't burn down?"

"This place? I can fix that for you, too, if it's what you wants." A mischievous grin transformed his face, giving him the appearance of a demonic elf.

"Thanks for the offer but at the moment, this piece of heaven is all we have."

"Right on," Duff agreed as he placed wood in the stove. "I seen worse and I seen lots better. She's what we calls a fix-er-upper of the t'ird degree. One and two being more preferable by far."

As she watched Duff, Misty wondered how she was going to cope. She had no idea how to use a wood stove. "Think you can teach me to do that?" she whispered dubiously.

"Yes, my love. You'll manage once we gets the wood in."

Misty wished she shared his optimism. She glanced at her hands and wondered how long her nails would hold up and if there'd be any point at all to ever have another manicure in her life. If they were going to survive, she would have to shake her strong desire to hide in the bottom of her sleeping bag and pretend this was all a dream. *Broken nails are a temporary drawback; happy, warm children are what count.* She could and would do whatever it took to keep her family together.

Once the stove was lit, Duff continued to carry stacks of wood into the house. The logs crackled and popped and the smell reminded Misty of mouldy old socks. She asked Duff if he thought the same thing.

"Yes, b'y. Hung nar socks over the woodstove in me days. Surprised you'd think of that, though, young thing like you, and from the city, too."

Misty felt her sensory experience would make absolutely no sense to anyone who had never experienced wool socks drying over a stove and the fact Duff understood filled her with a new respect for him. She set about to tap his considerable knowledge. "How'd you know I'm from the city?" she asked.

"Hayward." To his credit, Duff seemed a bit embarrassed.

What else had Hayward told him? Her financial and marital status? Whatever happened to client confidentiality? Most folks could put two and two together but still, Hayward might have shown a bit more discretion than that. Misty gave her head a shake. What planet was she on? Even her very short introduction to Hayward left her feeling that he and discretion were polar opposites.

She noticed their conversation had come to a halt at the mention of Hayward, so she picked up the thread and continued. "We had our weekends around the bay and Dad always kept a camp. There were times I thought I'd lose my toes to frostbite, we were so wet and cold from playing by the shore." She paused and looked at the wood crackling in the stove, wondering once again how on earth she was going to manage. "How often do I add wood?"

"Few times a day. You'll be rising early to do the same if you wants heat in the mornings."

Misty panicked at the thought of being chained to a woodstove. She was going to need a job and fast. A furnace would be an absolute necessity by October. September, even, if these cool temperatures were any indication. She fell back on her sleeping bag and moaned.

Twelve months ago her definition of a necessity would have been thong panties, an under-wired bra, and a glass of wine. Things had changed pretty damn fast.

"That bother you, missus?"

"Bother me? What could possibly be bothersome about loading wood in a stove several times a day?" she said, her voice weighted with sarcasm.

Duff shook his head as he watched her wiggle out of the sleeping bag. "Likes camping, do ye?"

"Hardly. This floor thing is more a matter of not liking the look of the beds." She held up her hand as he started to reply. "No, wait... don't stop me," she said as she looked around. "Just look at this place. What am I supposed to do? This house is old, everything in it is old. For that matter, I'm starting to feel old. My back is shot from sleeping on the floor for just one night. Oops, forgive me, where are my manners? I could just morph into Debbie Travis and turn this place into a palace, if I had a budget and a lot more imagination." She dug around for her flip-flops and found them under her sleeping bag. As she shoved her feet into them, she turned to Duff and threw her arms up in exasperation. "I don't mean to complain. I'm not really like that but what am I supposed to do?" Her voice was shrill by the time she finished and the girls were shifting restlessly in their sleeping bags. Luckily, they were sound sleepers. She realized she was only one step from breaking down in front of a total stranger. And she, the expert in crisis management. A fine example she was setting.

"Was hopin' you'd ask."

"What?" Misty said, a tad too sharply. She narrowed her eyes and tilted her head, rather like a dog trying to decipher human conversation.

"Was hopin' you'd ask," he repeated with a warm smile.

And even though Misty decided she liked that grin much better than the demonic one, she plunged on with her reckless outburst. "That's just the point. I can't ask." She took her frustration out on her sleeping bag as she stuffed it into the small sack that was provided for its containment and never quite managed to hold it all. "It's not like it sounds. I'm not too proud to admit I need help. I could use it right now." She continued to fight with the bag and finally gave up and tossed it into the corner, its contents partially spilling out over the floor. "Look at that." She pointed to it. "That's a perfect example of what I feel like. Trying to do the impossible. I appreciate your offer. I really do, but I just don't have any extra money right now."

"Sounds about right," Duff said, undaunted. He had an unusual habit of sucking saliva through his teeth, which he used to punctuate most of what he said.

"What does?" She looked over to where Liberty and Vivienne were beginning to stir, and she was grateful the room had warmed up rapidly.

"I'll help you and you can make it up when you gets work."

"I can't do…"

"Go on and shut yer gob." He dismissed her objections with a wave of his hand. "Jus' tell me what you wants done first."

For the first time in several minutes, she was speechless. Truly. She couldn't expect this man to work for nothing, and the chances of her getting a job in this pea-hole were probably slim to none.

"I don't take charity. I've managed this far and I'll figure it out. Somehow." Her frustration was thinly veiled and she felt certain he knew it. What she really wanted to say was thank you. Thank you and when can you start?

"It's not the way you thinks it is around here. I offers my services and I finds it insulting that you thinks it's charity. I knows money is tight and like I said, you can pay me when you gets a job."

Misty paused and looked at him. "You're serious, aren't you? You'd do that for us? For complete strangers?"

"You isn't strangers, missus. You're Charlie's kin. Now where does you want to start?"

Misty led Duff up the stairs and into the first of three bedrooms. She pointed at the bed. "That's got to go and there's two more in the other rooms."

"Right. Needs some help with that," he said. Then he turned around, walked back down the stairs, and out the front door. No good-byes or anything of that nature. Apparently, Duff could be a man of few words when he wanted to be.

Misty looked at her watch. It was only seven-thirty and she felt as though she'd lived through a day already. She was still uncomfortable with Duff's generous offer, but maybe that's the way things were done in Charlie's Cove. And that comment about being Charlie's kin, what was up with that? She'd never even been to visit Charlie. The fact her life was beginning to resemble an episode of *The Beverly Hillbillies* wasn't lost on her.

But because she couldn't think of any other solution, she shut off the mental verbiage and decided to have a shower and get dressed. The way Duff operated, it wouldn't be long before he'd be back with help and besides, with the heating situation temporarily under control, she had a new problem.

Hunting up twelve easy instalments on a trio of beds had just moved to the top of her to-do list.

CHAPTER 4

Bedknobs and Broomsticks

Misty spent the better part of the morning lugging things in from the car and dragging stuff out from the house. The pile growing on her front lawn was impressive.

By mid-morning she'd cleaned out most of the kitchen cupboards and installed her own meagre supplies in them. She should have felt more satisfied with her progress, but when she looked, the mostly empty shelves left her feeling disheartened.

"Brought a couple of the boys with me," Duff called as he opened the front door, rapping as he walked in. Misty stuck her head out of the kitchen to tell them there was no need to take off their boots and quickly changed her mind. She had never actually seen what looked like fish parts stuck to rubber, but these guys had managed to do it.

"Er, hi," she said weakly as she took in the sight of the two *boys* dwarfing Duff.

"This here's Stinky," Duff said, pointing to the taller of the two. "And this bees Cedric." The boys weren't exactly boys in Misty's opinion. They were definitely men. Stinky, although taller, was the slighter of the two. He wore his hair neatly cropped and were it not for eyebrows that formed an almost straight line across his forehead, given a change of clothing, might have looked fairly presentable. Cedric, on the other hand, was plain furry. His mass of curls wound into a heavy, dark beard and the arc of his massive shoulders reminded Misty of what it might be like to come face to face with a bear.

Appearances aside, Misty had to admire Duff's resourcefulness as she shook their hands. They had paws the size of hubcaps and no doubt were quite suitable to carry a few mattresses and whatever else she could identify for immediate expulsion.

She briefly wondered how Stinky had gotten his name but felt it would be improper to ask. Chances were good she'd find out sooner or later. Sooner if it had to do with personal hygiene.

"Let me take your coa…"

Duff cut her off. "This ain't no social call. Now, you get on up to Tizzard's and pick yourself out some beds. We'll see you in about an hour."

It all sounded so simple, the way he said it.

"But I…"

"Got lots of credit at Tizzard's," he finished for her and winked.

"I do?" She was once again impressed with Duff's ingenuity.

"Dat's right. You do."

Finding the store was easy. She followed Duff's directions, which were quite exact. Turn right at the end of the driveway and go straight. Seemed everything in Charlie's Cove snaked around the edge of the harbour.

Their first good look at the town was surprising. Charlie's Cove was clean and picturesque, nestled amongst rolling hills. The homes were modest, no doubt about that, but they were also charming and colourful.

"Look, Mom. There's Donald Duck," said Vivienne.

"And Mickey Mouse," added Liberty.

"Whaddayaknow about that." Misty smiled. *It isn't everywhere outside of the States that Disney garners such prominent exposure*, she thought as they passed a yard populated with wooden images of the Seven Dwarfs. She had a feeling that Dopey and his kin might actually be laughing at her, but racked her paranoia up to lack of sleep and soon joined the girls in guessing the exact number of lawn ornaments in Charlie's Cove. They were up to twenty-three by the time they saw Tizzard's.

"I love this place, Mom," said Vivienne. "It's way cool."

"There's lots of boys, too," said Liberty changing the subject entirely, which was so typical of her. She was unusually mature for her age and was what Misty often described as a deep thinker.

"Hmmm, you're right about that," Misty replied, wondering where this was going. She didn't have to wonder long.

"Is Duff going to be your boyfriend?"

Misty laughed, feeling a sudden relief. She had never bridged the issue of other men in her life since her divorce from Jake. With Liberty bringing the matter up, it was the perfect opportunity to touch upon what could be a rather sensitive subject.

She parked the car in front of Tizzard's and swivelled so she could make eye contact with her daughters in the backseat. "No, girls. Duff's just a friend. But maybe someday there will be someone who might be my boyfriend." She watched to see their reactions.

"Like Dad has Kelly?" asked Liberty.

No, not like that at all, she thought, surprised at the sudden and violent ache in her chest. Painful memories of Jake's infidelity were ever-present, though hidden behind a cloudy lens in her mind. She figured coming to Charlie's Cove would help her forget. With all her time directed to survival, it would be hard to mourn her failed marriage. "Someone special is what I think you mean, isn't it?" she asked, then nodded her head in agreement along with her daughters.

It was nice to know they expected her to have a boyfriend someday...chances of which were slim to none in this place, she figured. *As if Duff could be the one.* It would take a lot of lonely to turn Duff into a potential suitor. "I think Duff likes to help and wants us to feel welcome here," she continued, not wanting the girls to think any less of him. It was amazing he should show up in their lives. She was still debating his take on life... treating them as though they belonged, as if it was the most normal thing in the world to be helping them. She'd never experienced that kind of honest warmth from a stranger before and having decided that the only person she could ever count on again was herself, she was still uncomfortable with it.

"He talks funny," said Vivienne.

"That's just Newfoundland, honey. People have their own dialect here, especially in the smaller outports."

"I thinks it's neat," said Liberty.

"Think," corrected Misty. "The correct verb is think."

"According to you. I bet Duff thinks he's right."

"That might be true, Liberty. But how about we let him do it his way and we do it ours?"

"I'll thinks about that," she replied.

There were some challenges about moving back to Newfoundland Misty hadn't anticipated. She'd made her living working with the media, writing all the right things, planning, doing, executing perfectly planned projects where grammar was just as important as the intent of the message. What would become of her kids if they picked up the local dialect? To heck with the kids, what if she fell into easy habits? All those years of cultivating a sophisticated image, blown after a few months in Charlie's Cove?

She felt shallow for focusing on something as ridiculous as the dissolution of her kid's grammar. It wasn't something she needed to worry about at the moment, anyway. She had far bigger concerns, such as how to provide heat and buy groceries. And maybe in the big scheme of things, a Newfoundland dialect was perfectly all right. It was distinctive and colourful, a historic blend of cultures and isolation.

The kids would be just fine, and since she wasn't in the media anymore, what did it matter if she started talking at the speed of a jackhammer? Who was going to hear anyway? She could dis and dat, ye and yay, toss away consonants, or speak permanently in the plural and no one around here would even think it was unusual. Yes, b'y. No, my darlin'. She could be whoever the heck she wanted. Misty paused and realized she felt very free about reinventing her life in a miniscule pond as though it was a very clever illusion. Misty Houdini Muldoon. Escape artist. Watch her closely, friends, for the sleight of hand and mind. And keep your fingers on your wallet.

Misty laughed as she opened the rear door of the car. "Let's go in, ladies. I'll bet they have the bed of your dreams." *And maybe the one of mine.* All that talk of boyfriends had left her thinking about her lack of one. She wasn't even sure she was open to having someone in her life at this point. She'd been sleeping by herself for a long time and even though the idea of a man in her bed stirred her imagination, she wasn't ready to consid...

"Mom!" Vivienne punched her in the bum.

"What?" Misty looked down at her daughter as the image of Brad Pitt under her duvet swirled away with a gust of wind that seemed to come out of nowhere.

"Can we go in?"

How long had she been standing there? Misty used one hand to push her hair out of her face and the other to grab the door that refused to budge more than a few inches. The wind had created a vacuum that held the heavy glass entry better than a crossbar.

Misty pulled harder until it gave, swinging wide open and throwing her off balance. She teetered on the edge of the step for a few seconds, holding tentatively to the handle for support. It was a battle she was destined to lose. Just as she released her grip on the door and braced herself for a fall, an arm slipped around her waist and her body collided with a wall of muscle. Behind her the door blew all the way open, as the wind continued to roar by the entrance, blasting at everything in its path.

"My kids…" she yelled looking for Vivi and Liberty. "Where…?" Her words trailed off as she realized they had made it in and were safely behind her.

The man let her go and turned his attention to the door, which proved to be much more of a challenge. Finally, it closed.

"I've never seen wind like that," said Misty. "It's like it came out of nowhere."

"You got that right. Are you okay?"

"I guess. I mean, if looking like Carrot Top is no problem." She removed a hair clip that was dangling by her ear. It had originally been holding her hair in a partial updo. As she piled her mass of waves back on her head, she managed a smile. "Thanks to you, I'm in one piece." Misty took a good look at the man who had rescued her.

He was tall, just over six feet, she figured. And well-built from what she could see, wearing a brown suede jacket, faded jeans, and cowboy boots. A significant improvement from what she'd seen to-date. She found herself staring, wondering why he looked familiar. And then she knew. It was his eyes. They were the same shade of blue as her ex's. But that was where the resemblance stopped. These eyes were kind and the telltale crinkles at their corners seemed to be the product of laughter. He was smiling broadly at her, displaying the greatest set of teeth she'd seen in a long time.

"You have to be new in town to make a statement like that. Anyone seasoned to Charlie's Cove knows there's no explanation for the weather patterns. What we call a stiff breeze off the bay is a Category-3 hurricane in most places." He held out his hand. "I'm Steve Day, somewhat new to the area as well, you could say. I'm from Toronto."

Misty shook his outstretched hand. "Misty Muldoon, and you are correct about us being new. We're from Halifax." She broke eye contact but kept talking, a nervous reaction that anyone who knew her would nail in a minute. "Since we're on the subject of weather, my claim to fame is being named after a pattern on the east coast of the island."

He laughed as he released her hand. For a moment she almost forgot what she was going to say next until Vivienne hit her in the backside again. "These young ladies are my daughters, Liberty and Vivienne."

"Welcome to Charlie's Cove, Misty, ladies. I hope you like it here."

As he crouched down to shake hands with Vivi and Liberty, Misty found her eyes travelling over his back, watching the way his jacket pulled across his shoulders. Realizing what she was doing, she felt her cheeks heating up, the curse of being a redhead. But it still didn't stop her from admiring him and feeling self-conscious when he stood up and looked at her again.

Misty sidestepped behind her daughters. She was glad her hair had fallen over her brow. It was almost a way of hiding from his direct gaze, a screen behind which she could mask her interest. "Thanks again for your help," she said, recovering her composure.

"The pleasure was all mine," he replied.

He held her eyes just a little longer than expected and Misty felt her cheeks graduate to an even deeper shade of crimson. Steve didn't seem to notice, or was too polite to comment, a fact for which she was very grateful. Like anyone prone to blushing, she had endured enough teasing to last a lifetime and then some.

"Hey, Tiz," he called across the store to a large man. "Take good care of these ladies and don't be playing any games with them. We want them to have a good impression of Charlie's Cove. Not like the one you gave me." He punctuated his statement with another round of laughter.

Misty pulled her daughters closer. As if she needed a bigger shield than the igloo she'd already erected around her heart.

"Have fun shopping," Steve said as he turned to leave.

"Thanks, we will," she replied. As the door closed behind him, her words were swallowed by the gale that continued to roar around Tizzard's front entrance.

Misty felt a tug deep in her solar plexus, the second of the day. Only minutes before it had been an ache for the chasm left by her ex, Jake Muldoon, but now it felt different. What she was feeling was poles apart from that. This felt like longing for something missing in her life. And she didn't like the feeling. She preferred anger or at least resentment. As long as she felt like that, there was no confusion about what she was doing next, looking after her kids and getting her life together. It was all she could handle right now. *Sure, and if you keep telling yourself you didn't find that man attractive, maybe the moon will grow a beard.*

"Morning, missus. Welcome to Tizzard's."

Misty looked around, possibly at one of the largest men she'd seen in quite a while.

"I heared youse was looking for a few beds. Well, Harv Tizzard is the man you needs. That's me. Tiz." He took a deep bow. "At your service."

Duff had said he'd paved the way for their line of credit, but she still wasn't accustomed to people knowing her business so quickly. She'd have to be very careful what she said from now on. What if she made a joke of saying she was also looking for a man to go in her bed? And given her behaviour a few minutes ago, maybe it wasn't a joke.

"We are," said Vivi, seizing an opportunity to assert herself. "Nice ones."

"I see," replied Tiz. "Right this way." He pointed toward the back of the store. As Misty tagged behind, she sized up both Tiz and his store. The man was a giant and his mother must have had hips the size of Manhattan. Tiz's head resembled a watermelon standing on its end, and when she caught him in profile his crooked smile was set in a chin large enough to lodge an anchor. He was *almost* as amazing as his store. "Almost" being the key word.

Tizzard's Home Furnishings was all that and more. From what she could see, it was filled with most everything you could possibly want or need in a lifetime. And plenty that you wouldn't. A child's dream, most certainly, and Misty's worst nightmare. She sighed as Liberty and Vivienne raced toward a display of dolls and stuffed toys.

"Not to worry, missus." Tiz stopped and joined her as she watched them. "Kids is always like that first time in and we can rustle up something for them to take home. Old Tiz has got the gear. Now, let's have a look at them beds."

She followed Tiz through a jumble of tables and chairs. When he finally stopped, lined up before them were five different models. Single. Bunk. Double. Queen. And one massive king.

"Would the girls be sharing a room?" he asked.

"None of us is sharing a room," Misty replied, immediately regretting her response.

"Ah, well, you won't be looking at my master king, then will you?" Tiz chuckled and crooked an eyebrow at her. "It's only a floor model anyways. We never sells 'em," he said, lowering his voice. "I just keeps it here for enticement." The last word was almost a whisper.

"Why not?" said Misty.

"Why not, what?" Tiz asked, turning to stare at her as he slowly stroked his chin.

In Misty's opinion, he was looking at her much as he might a thick, juicy steak. "The king," she replied. "I like the king." She was only thirty years old. Why not buy a king? Her heart sped up as she recalled the strength of those hands that had held her and helped her find her balance. *Wouldn't it be kind of nice to wake up and look at a man like Steve Day? Oh, hell, why not Steve himself? He was the real thing, after all. Real, and probably married,* she reminded herself.

"You wants the king?" Tiz repeated, as he looked her squarely in the eye.

Hooking the fish was what came to Misty's mind as her head bobbed up and down like a dashboard decoration. "I think," she finally said.

"Got room for it?" he asked.

In my life? Yes. In my bedroom? That's another matter. Misty did a mental tour of the master room in Charlie's house. It would be tight, but workable. *Who needs a dresser, anyway?* Dressers were for organized old women. Beds, particularly kings, now they were perfect for a vibrant, hopeful, if not somewhat fantasy-driven, heart-sick, love-sick, plain sick of being alone, laughing, loving woman.

To hell with the budget.

"How much is it?" Her mind raced through the list of things she had to buy: clothes, books, food...the bed...and a bead of sweat formed between her shoulder blades.

"Well," said Tiz as he continued to rub his chin with his hand. "Be good to sell that. Been here a while, you know. No one's slept on it, mind you. Not that I knows of, anyhow."

Misty held her breath.

"I can do five."

"Thousand." The word slipped through her mouth so quietly, Tiz strained to hear it.

"Creepers, missus. Hundred. Five hundred. And if the girls likes the one on the end, I can throw in two of them and make it an even eight."

"Eight," Misty repeated.

"Ah, all right. Seven seventy-nine. But that's the best I can do." He folded his arms across his chest.

When Duff and the boys arrived, Misty was sitting on the service dock, her feet crossed and legs swinging in the breeze. Her daughters, perched on either side of her, each held a doll.

"Looks like you did all right, my love," noted Duff as he hopped out and spied the dolls. "Ready, is you?"

Misty nodded. She found it hard to contain the self-satisfied look that reflected her inner state. She hadn't felt this good about herself in months.

Duff pressed a buzzer and a few minutes later Harv Tizzard opened a large retracting door. Misty, Liberty and Vivienne stood up and watched as the three men carted the girls' beds out to the truck.

"Think we got room for the t'ird one?" asked Duff after they'd carefully stacked the mattresses side by side. He started to head back in with Cedric and Stinky on his heels.

"For the love of Jesus, what's dat?" Duff stopped abruptly and looked at her.

Misty pulled herself to her full five foot six inches and tossed her head. "That one's mine," she replied.

Stinky poked Cedric in the ribs, who then started to cough and covered his mouth with his hand. At least Misty thought it was a cough, she wasn't sure. Duff shot them both a scathing look.

"We'll come back for dat one," he said as he gestured for the two men to follow him. "Why don't you girls go get something to eat at Hatty's? We'll look after this." He swatted Stinky in the back of the head as they got in the truck.

As she followed the serpentine road around the harbour, Misty pondered what had transpired at Tizzard's. Duff and his entourage had some strange ways about them. Sure, her bed was large, but with three men to move it, what was the big deal? She shrugged, marked it up to eccentric outport behaviour, and set her attention on finding the next critical landmark to their survival, Hatty's Restaurant.

Hatty's was a charming diner about four minutes farther up the road. Misty was relieved to find that Hatty was of the female persuasion. Their first sighting.

And some sighting it was.

Hatty was six feet, maybe. And that was her girth. She cleared the floor at about four-eight. And she had the most chins either of the girls had ever seen. Misty cautioned them not to say anything.

They soon figured out that Hatty's stature was an honest by-product of her ability to cook. A soup and sandwich on homemade slabs of bread was only four dollars. And then there were the crisp fries and the humongous slices of pie that the girls insisted they could not live without. Hatty was only too pleased to comply, and even threw in an extra slice for Misty. Coffee, too.

Nouvelle cuisine had definitely bypassed Charlie's Cove. From the size of the portions, Misty figured she could feed them for three days on one meal. She'd simply forgotten Newfoundland's reputation for hospitality and good food.

"So, you're Charlie's kin?" Hatty finally asked, leaning her massive bosom on the countertop.

Misty had just stuffed a piece of pie into her mouth, giving Liberty and Vivienne ample opportunity to answer.

"Mom says Great-uncle Charlie was really old. Was he?" asked Liberty.

"Charlie was a fixture 'round the Cove. That's for sure," replied Hatty. "You wouldn't catch him in here. Not Charlie."

"Tight as a frog's arse," said Vivienne with all the conviction only a five-year-old could muster.

Misty choked on the coffee she was swallowing to wash down the pie.

"Vivienne!" she finally managed to say. So much for worrying about Duff; there were more ears in her household than in a damn cornfield.

Hatty laughed. "You got that right, girlie. A frog's arse had nothing on him."

CHAPTER 5

The Gulf Crossing

Following their excellent lunch, Misty and the girls stopped at the grocery store, which was as easy to find as everything else.

Misty knew they couldn't afford to be eating out, even at Hatty's prices. But the absence of any of the ingredients she was accustomed to using slowed the process down some. Back to basics was taking on a new meaning. Apparently, Charlie's Cove's only grocery store didn't stock fresh herbs, organic lettuce, or goat's milk.

Once again, Liberty came to the rescue.

"Hey, Mom," she said despondently as she realized there was no, and probably never would be, any goat's milk. "I've got a good idea."

"You do, hon?" asked Misty, wondering what was coming next.

"We can grow some things in our yard, and you know what? We can even get a pet goat."

"Goats eat your socks," said Vivienne. "I read that in a book. They eat all that stuff."

Misty's heart tightened and for a moment she thought she might cry. Not about the idea of getting a goat. No, it wasn't that, although in a sane moment such a thought could probably reduce her to tears. What moved her so unexpectedly was the hopefulness in her daughter's voice. Her simple willingness to adapt to the changes in their lives without complaint.

Misty was suddenly filled with guilt. Guilt for her behaviour these past few weeks, especially her short-temperedness. Honestly, her attitude had been bad and here were her children setting the example, making the best of things.

Misty threw her arms around her daughters and cradled them against her. "You are so, so wonderful."

"Mom," Liberty squirmed. "It's just a goat. Anyone could think of that."

"No, it's not that. It's you two. I just love you so much."

"So, we can get a goat?" asked Liberty.

"God, yes. We can get a goat and a garden and whatever else we need."

"No goat," pouted Vivienne.

"C'mon, Viv," prodded Liberty. "You can name her."

"Can I?" said Vivienne, becoming more interested. "Can I, Mom?"

"Of course," said Misty, realizing that giving a name to a goat she never, ever wanted to own was probably a bad idea. Somewhere in Charlie's Cove there was likely a goat that would turn up to claim that name. What was she getting into?

Viv pursed her lips for a moment, then said, "Daisy. Daisy the goat. That's a good name."

"I loves it," cried Liberty.

"Lo…" Misty started to correct and then stopped. It wasn't important anymore. What was important were her daughters and their innocent ways of making things right.

imagination kicked in and she figured she wouldn't go there. She had an inkling her long-forgotten heritage was about to surface a lot faster than she wanted it to, especially if she was going to apply for a job at the paper.

Understanding the locals would be a prerequisite, but she could do it. It was like riding a bike. You never really forget; you just have to jump right back on. "Been up the stump myself a couple of times," she said to Duff.

Duff stared at her strangely. "The likes of you? Not the same way as Flossie. She bees holding a lottery to find out who gets the tax deduction. Wouldn't be enough test tubes on the island to do it any other way."

Okay, so it might take a while, but she'd eventually get the hang of it again.

CHAPTER 6

The Phonse

Misty couldn't believe her luck. Maybe things were turning around.

The past year of her life had been like wearing wet underwear on a long drive home—damn uncomfortable with the only solution being to ride bare ass and hope to avoid an accident. Mostly she'd managed, but it hadn't been easy.

First, there was the discovery her husband's extracurricular activity hadn't been racquetball at all. It had been scre...no, she wasn't going to use that word anymore. She took a deep breath. It had been playing a rather unique game of hide and seek. Hiding the truth and seeking her best friend.

Her best friend. Imagine that? What had been going on in her head not to notice something? Anything, really. But no, she hadn't been much better than an ostrich. Only, in this case, her head had been buried in her new public relations company and not the sand. But for all the good it had done her, she might as well have camped out in the back yard and dug a hole.

Misty Muldoon Communications Management. We specialize in getting your message to the public. We're just piss poor at managing our own stuff.

Mrs. Muldoon, when did you first suspect your husband was boffing your friend?

Well, really. It might have been the time I found hot-pink thongs in his kit bag.

Another woman's undies in your husband's kit? Didn't that seem strange to you?

At the time, no. He blamed it on his buddy who was boffing someone.

Birds of a feather, perhaps?

Hey, I was working twelve-hour days. You try starting your own company. And I've got two young kids.

Oh, what was she doing? Re-hashing the events of the past two years wasn't going to help matters. Sure, there were a lot of things she probably could have done better but maybe she would have gotten the same result anyway. After all, not mentioning names, the nature of an asshole is limited. No matter what, an asshole will always shoot the shit.

So leaving her marriage and her company behind wasn't a choice, it was a matter of saving herself and her children from a sinking ship. Great-uncle Charlie's offer (she liked to think about it like that) came at just the right time. She really had nowhere else to go.

Maybe if her name had been Misty Ryan or Misty O'Flaherty, she'd have had some brothers and sisters to call upon. The way it was, Misty Cuthbertson-Muldoon, the product of staunch Presbyterian stock, was lucky to have even a few cousins. Perhaps there was some truth to the tale that your birthright got in the way of sex.

No sisters, no brothers, parents deceased—it all sounded pretty depressing. The Cuthbertson line ended with great old Uncle C. Funny how things worked out. Here she was, back in the old Cuthbertson homestead disguised as Misty Muldoon.

But for some inexplicable reason, things seemed to be improving. Even in her most creative moments, she could never have conjured up a guardian angel like Duff. But that was how she was beginning to regard him. Duff, the guardian angel.

And if anyone deserved a set of wings, he did. What a sight that would be. But as long as he kept sending the luck her way, she had every reason to be very, very grateful.

Luck this morning was taking the form of an interview with *The Yarn*. Duff had shown up to take the girls down to the wharf to see lobster traps, freeing her to call on Phonse Penney. *Could it be any better?* she thought as she climbed the steps leading into the office that housed the local paper. This might simply be a matter of good timing.

"Mr. Penney is in the john," said the receptionist, as though nothing was out of the ordinary in supplying this information. "Give him twenty minutes and he'll be right with you."

"Right." Misty turned away before the woman could see the expression on her face. *Seriously? Did I just hear what I think I heard?* Misty wasn't quite sure what she found most offensive, the fact she'd been told Phonse Penney was in the john, or the picture in her mind when she imagined him passing twenty minutes in there. *Way too much information, thank you very much.*

She sat down on the only chair available in the front reception and picked up a copy of the paper. She had never been so ill prepared for an interview in her life. But from the appearance of the entry with its worn tiles and spartan furnishings, she wasn't expecting too much.

The woman behind the desk was staring at her and Misty met her gaze with a forced smile. There was someone who didn't seem too interested in her job, if open-mouthed gawking was any indication.

Misty turned her attention to the paper and ignored the uncomfortable feeling of being watched so intently. Maybe Mr. Penney's constitutional constipation could be considered an opportunity; she set about reading and gathering the information she might need to land a job with *The Yarn*.

The front-page headline grabbed her attention immediately.

Wife Arrested for Using Husband as Fish Bait

Catchy. She turned the page.

Mayor Dunks Balls in Fish Tank

That must have been quite the fundraiser, Misty thought, a picture forming in her mind. The story itself wasn't too badly written, but she imagined the mayor might be of a different opinion.

She flipped to the personals. She could always judge a paper by its personals—if there were lots of them, there were lots of readers. With headlines like these, the personals should be really interesting.

She found them buried between Boats for Sale and Real Estate.

Seeking: husband, employed, full head, saved.
Missing: wife, full-bodied model driving Harley.
Wanted: marriage, kids, supplied or created.

Where were the bits of magic in these? They were like bullets for a recipe book. Something was definitely wrong. The headlines were more interesting than this drivel. She'd always thought small outport papers were notorious for putting the "personal" in personals.

Misty continued to peruse the paper. Twelve tabloid pages in all. A few ads. A few pictures. Maybe Duff was right. It was a jeesly rag, after all. *The Yawn* would be more apt.

"For Chrissakes, order some arsewipe."

Misty looked up to see a man glaring at the receptionist. He was of medium height and the buttons of his shirt were popping against a distended abdomen that looked like month eight in a bad pregnancy. His neck disappeared into his shoulders, which gave his head the appearance of a field pumpkin with glasses. There were a few sprouts of hair standing at attention like the stem of said pumpkin, and he had a cigarette clamped between his teeth that seemed to provide no impairment at all to his speech. She felt, without a doubt, she was looking at Phonse Penney.

Finished with his co-worker, he turned his radar gaze to Misty. "So you're what blew into town. Misty Muldoon, I suppose. Stand up, I gets a look at you."

Misty dropped the paper and stood up. She felt a flash of fire when her eyes locked with Phonse's, but she attributed her sudden light-headedness to the rapid change in elevation rather than intimidation.

He snorted and walked out of the room. Misty hurried through the door on the heels of Mr. Penney. It was a small building. She could track him down easily enough.

And much faster than she imagined. He was sitting right in front of her at the largest desk in the newsroom. Those eyes bored into her again and this time she did feel, perhaps, just a little less self-assured.

"Mr. Penney," she began.

"Phonse," he interrupted.

"Phonse," she began again. "I'd like to apply for a position with your paper. I'm very well qualified..."

"I got eyes. Can you take a picture?"

"Yes," she replied.

"Knows punctuation?"

"Semi-colons and dangling participles are putty in my hands."

"I pays twelve dollars an hour. I wants thirty hours a week, days or nights, I don't give a coot's ass. We goes to press on Wednesdays. You get your copy in to me by Tuesday four o'clock and we'll get along fine."

"Yes, sir," she replied. Did this mean she had the job?

"Advertising and personals is mine."

That explained it.

"One more thing."

Misty held her breath and waited to hear what he might say next. It was at times like this she realized how terribly her confidence had eroded.

He stubbed out his cigarette and ran his tongue over his lips. "You don't look like you'd need a bed the size of a passenger ferry."

"Excuse me?" Misty raised her eyebrows.

"You heard me. I got no use for floozies at my publication. Sleeping better be what that bed's intended for. I has enough headaches dealing with Flossie, I hardly needs another one up the stump." He lit another cigarette and held the smoke in his mouth for a moment. "The way I sees it, you being a Cuthbertson and all, you probably plans to use the bed for sleeping away."

Misty thought of a lot of things she could say but didn't. Instead, she planted her feet and held out her hand. "Do I have a job or not?"

She watched the smoke ease out of his mouth, his nose, and what looked like his ears, but that could have just been a result of the lighting. And her attempt at forging a handshake was failing miserably. *Wasn't this the part where Superman should show up? C'mon, Lois, we're getting out, you and...*

"Take the desk in the back corner and give Tilly your information. Today's Thursday. I wants three stories by Tuesday afternoon." He stood up and walked out, ignoring her still-outstretched hand.

Misty was in shock. The fact she had a job still hadn't registered.

"Hey."

Misty jumped and turned around. It was the lady from reception. "Welcome to the team."

Her throat was dryer than salted cod, but she managed to smile. "Thanks."

The woman laughed. "You won't be thanking anyone, working for Uncle Phonse. I needs a bit of info when you gets settled. You knows where I am."

Alone again, Misty took a good look around the newsroom. Untidy would be the kindest way to describe it. She walked over to her desk and sat down.

So long, Clark Kent. Take off, Superman. This desk is mine. The official address of Misty Muldoon, cub reporter.

She liked the sound of that. She officially had a job. Not much of one, for sure, but any job counts when you're desperate. *Still, twelve dollars an hour? Let's see, to cover expenses that means I'll only have to work... say...120 hours a week. Just perfect.* Misty took a deep breath and reminded herself it was better than nothing. Not much better, but marginally. And anyway, once she got to know him, maybe she'd even like Phonse Penney.

A short while later, after concluding her business with Phonse's niece, Tilly, Misty parked her car in front of her house and did a little jig across the lawn. "Yahoo," she cried out to Duff and the girls, who were sitting on the front steps. "I got me a *j-o-b*."

"That's what you thinks," replied Duff. "What you got is a piece of work with a piece of work. But it'll do for now. Congratulations. What did you think of Phonse?"

"Crusty." She sat down. "Is he really that bad?"

"Depends," replied Duff. "On whether you bees working for him or married to him."

"What's up with personals and advertising?"

"That. Phonse's wife got saved a few years ago and she don't let him put any juicy stuff in there anymore. As for the advertising, no one wants to waste their money. Phonse's got a grant from the government, what keeps it going. Another squanderous insult on our tax dollars."

"Oh." She could feel her enthusiasm ebbing like the tide.

Duff passed her a piece of paper.

"What's this?" she asked.

"A list of t'ings going on the weekend. Should get you started on your new career." He was careful to emphasize "career", like it was something significant.

"Get out. You did this for me?" She scanned the list. Church dinner, wedding, bingo. Wasn't much to work with. The last one caught her eye. Lynching. She pointed to it. "What's up with this?"

"That's going to follow the wedding."

"You're kidding, right?"

He looked at her and frowned. "No, b'Jesus, I'm not kidding. Fig Hendley's marrying Wilfred Stroud."

"I don't get it," said Misty.

"Fig and Wilfred's both men."

"Get lost. You're telling me that Charlie's Cove is having a same-sex marriage?"

"That's the intention. We'll see what happens." The evil little smirk she'd seen a few times before passed over his face like a shadow across the moon.

The four of them were quiet for a few minutes while Misty crinkled the paper between her fingers and pondered how she might cover a same-sex marriage as her first assignment. Maybe an advance interview would be a good idea. She wondered where she could contact the grooms.

Duff stood up and stretched. He sniffed the wind. "Better bundle up, girls. The temperature's going to drop this afternoon." And he headed down the driveway with a simple wave.

"Duff's cool." Vivi looked at her mother as if expecting her to object.

"Very cool, Viv," Misty replied.

"He could be your boyfriend, Mom," added Liberty. "He does what Prince Charmings do."

"What's that, Lib?"

"He finds the shoe that fits your foot."

Misty stared at her daughter. She wondered seriously about her IQ. Her ability to sum things up succinctly was almost uncanny for someone her age. What was it people said about kids like that? Old souls. That's what it was.

Misty was beginning to understand exactly what they meant. Liberty was unusually perceptive. Maybe there was an old soul in there somewhere. Or, maybe she was just smart. And, maybe she took after her mother. A sense of smug satisfaction washed over Misty. She placed her arms around the girls and gave them a big squeeze.

Perhaps there would be a Prince Charming in Charlie's Cove, after all. But it wasn't Duff. He didn't fit her idea of a Prince Charming at all. He was a lovely, kind old geezer but hardly prince material. Misty sighed. She knew who was, though. And the paper might provide the perfect opportunity for a bit of investigation.

CHAPTER 7

The Bed of Enticement

By Friday night, Misty had wrangled herself an invitation to the wedding of the year, gotten phone service installed, and covered the potluck dinner at the Presbyterian Church. With her budget blown on beds, Duff had helped her find some furniture at the second-hand store and what wasn't available there, he provided. It wasn't perfect by any means, but it was a start.

Phonse had given her a key to *The Yarn* office so she could come and go as she pleased. As long as she tracked her hours and delivered three stories by Tuesday, she had a fair bit of freedom, which worked fine with her since she was used to working independently.

Duff had helped her find some domestic support with the girls, a young woman named Pansy, who was planning to move to Toronto in the fall. Misty hoped she'd change her mind, as she seemed to be quite capable and the girls liked her.

Misty put the finishing touches on her make-up as the phone rang. She wondered who would be calling on a Friday night. She ignored it, knowing one of her daughters would pick up.

"Mom, it's for you," Vivienne hollered up the stairs. Misty closed her lipstick and picked up the extension in her bedroom.

"Hello?" she said.

"What you at?"

"Who's this?"

"Stinky."

Her eyes widened. "Stinky."

"What you at?" he asked again.

What exactly was she at, she wondered. Putting on make-up on a Friday night to watch a movie with the girls. "Nothing," she replied.

"Want to go out for a few beers? Dere's a band from St. John's at the bar."

Go out with someone named Stinky? "Ah...." She hesitated, and she who hesitates is lost.

"Be by in five. Right on." He hung up and the deal was done. Stinky was coming over. She panicked. What had just happened?

"Pansy," she called down the stairs. "I may have a problem."

"Your mom's got a date, girls," Pansy said.

"I do not have a date," Misty countered. "What I have is an inability to say no fast enough."

"Told ya. She's got a date." And she laughed.

Misty raced down the stairs. "What do you know about Stinky?" she asked Pansy. "He's on his way over here. I didn't agree to go anywhere with him but he thinks I did." Her voice had gone up an octave.

"Stinky," Pansy scoffed. "You don't got no worries there. Unless you meets up with Skylene."

"Skylene? What's Skylene?"

"Not what, who. She's his fiancée."

"His what?" She was hyperventilating.

"They been together now for eight years."

There was a knock on the front door. Misty grabbed Pansy's arm and shoved her toward it. "You get it. Tell him I'm sick. Anything. I don't care. Tell him I'm throwing up." It wasn't far from the truth, she thought as she raced up the stairs, straight into the bathroom where she locked the door and sat down on the toilet seat.

A few minutes later a knock sounded on the door. "You can come out now. He's gone," said Pansy.

"You're certain?"

"Look. When I says he's gone, he's gone."

"Was it any problem?" asked Misty as she cracked the door and looked out.

"No, b'y. I just called Skylene."

"You called his fiancée? Why would you do that? She's going to hate me."

"Nah, Stinky does this from time to time. Skylene won't hold that against you, but she'll straighten him out."

The phone rang again.

"You get it this time, Pansy."

A few minutes later Pansy returned with her hand over the phone. She looked at Misty, a hint of mystery in her eyes. "For you. It's Cedric."

"Cedric? What's he want?"

"Same thing as Stinky, I'd say. The band's not bad. You should go on up and have a good time. I can stay for a few hours."

"He's not my type."

"For one night?" Pansy prompted.

"Not even. Tell him I'm working."

"Oh, all right. But you're missing a good time."

"I'll survive." Misty followed Pansy downstairs and eavesdropped on the conversation. Satisfied that Cedric got the right message, she relaxed.

Suddenly, the evening loomed before her like a great abyss. What was she going to do? She couldn't spend the rest of her life locked up with her kids. She was only thirty years old, after all, and if you believed what you read in *Cosmo*, her life was just beginning. Not ending.

At that enlightening thought, she chased Pansy, who had gone into the living room. She desperately wanted her to stay for a while. Not that she was lonely. You could hardly be that with Liberty and Vivienne in the house. She was just craving grown-up company and probably a friend. It had been a long time since she had indulged in a girl's night.

She entered the room and stood quietly, watching her daughters. They had curled up with Pansy in front of the television. Pansy's head of coal-black curls cascaded over her shoulders like a wild bush. She was a very naturally pretty woman. She had luscious curves where Misty's body was more streamlined and toned. Sitting like that, she looked just like the Earth Mother she'd quickly become in their lives. And she seemed so much wiser than her years, even though she was three years younger than Misty.

"Why don't we put the movie on for Liberty and Vivienne," Misty said, "and maybe you can fill me in on Charlie's Cove. Sometimes I feel lost here. I mean, I grew up in Newfoundland, but you forget what it's like, really."

"Problem is, you got no real appreciation for outport living. You grew up in town, Misty. This is different, right?" She smiled warmly. "It's comfortable when you gets used to it."

"Maybe." Misty knew she sounded unsure.

"Getting used to it is the part what takes a bit of adjustment. Give it a few months and you'll be fine."

"So why are you moving to Toronto?" Misty put the movie in the DVD player. The fact it was now attached to an old TV borrowed from Duff seemed to make no difference to Liberty and Vivienne. They were content.

"I wants a change for a bit. See something different, you knows."

"So you'll be back?" Misty beckoned for Pansy to follow her into the kitchen.

"My dear, we always comes back. Look at yourself."

"But that was a mistake." Misty turned to Pansy, a hint of insistence creeping into her voice. "I didn't plan this. This, this—just happened." She took a bag of popcorn from the cupboard and dug for a pot.

"Ya thinks? Your subconscious was working overtime on this."

"Oh, give me a break." She shut the cupboard door and moved to the stove where she loaded the pot with kernels and oil, then turned on the burner.

"Suit yourself, but I'm telling you it happens."

Misty shook her head. "You're wrong this time. I'm here to get things back on track and that's about it. This time next year all you'll see are my tail feathers heading for the boat."

The kernels exploded against the pot cover like a drum roll. Misty looked at Pansy in surprise. "I'd say that's a sign I'm right."

"Or wrong," replied Pansy.

The two were quiet as the popcorn cooked. It was hard to talk over the racket. Misty thought about what Pansy had said. *There's no way my subconscious could have drawn me back to Newfoundland. Coming back here was simply a matter of coincidence. I needed a refuge and great old Uncle C provided it. That's what it is and that's all it is.*

And as far as staying here? I wonder myself sometimes. One minute I'm talking about getting a goat as if we're going to stay. But none of that's congruent with the way I've planned things. Being here is a temporary thing, kind of like putting a band-aid on a cut. Once the healing is done, it'll be time for us to leave and that's the truth of it. Unless...well, unless the band-aid is put there to cover something up. Misty didn't like where that thought was heading, so she dismissed it before it got a chance to put down some roots.

When she removed the pot a few minutes later, Misty had another question for Pansy.

"Can I ask you something? I hope you won't take offence."

"Me? Offence? Is it about who I'm sleeping with?"

"God, no!" Misty was impressed by Pansy's quick wit and hoped it was contagious. It would be handy in dealing with Phonse.

"Then you can't offend me. Fire away, duckie." She passed a bowl for the popcorn.

Misty laughed. "You're one of a kind, Pansy. Here's what's been on my mind. You're a bright girl. How come you didn't go to university or trade school? Something besides this?"

"You mean baby-sitting? Right. Looks like university material, do I?" This time Pansy laughed. "We got enough degrees in my family to pave the way to Oxford. I got cousins all over the country who specializes in depression, cutting off body parts, even picking at teeth. Not one of 'ems any happier than me. May have a bit more money but it's all relative, you know. I got more time."

Misty thought about that as she carried the popcorn into the next room and passed the bowl to Liberty. "Share with your sister. Or else," she added as an afterthought, wondering where in the heck "or else" had originated. *Or else, what? I'll strand you on an island in a decrepit old house? Oops, too late for that.*

As she left the room, she looked back at Liberty and Vivienne. They were engrossed and content. That was the word. Content. It wasn't a feeling that came easily to Misty.

What have I really gained the past eight years? Here I am in the same place as Pansy with not much to show for all my worldliness except a lot more debt and a considerable bit more sadness.

"Glass of wine?" she asked Pansy as she walked back into the kitchen.

"Beer if you got it."

Misty gathered from the look on Pansy's face that she didn't care much for wine. She had a few bottles of beer, thanks again to Duff, who had used them to entice Cedric to mow her lawn.

She took one from the fridge, twisted the top, and passed it to Pansy. "What's it like to have time, Pansy? I mean, really have time."

"C'mon. You telling me you got no idea?"

"Ask my divorce lawyer. He says he sees it every day. Women with kids, working too much. Husband feels neglected. You get the idea." Misty took a bottle of wine from the fridge, opened it and poured herself a glass.

"That's what happened, was it? He was fooling around and you caught him."

"Uh-huh. Even worse. It was with my best friend." Misty sat down opposite Pansy.

"They getting married?"

"I don't know. I hope not. That would be messy, wouldn't it? It's bad enough sharing my children with a man I don't love anymore, but her? I hate the thought of her influencing my kids." Misty took a sip of chardonnay. It was a luxury she hadn't indulged in for a while. She had picked up a bottle to celebrate her new job.

"Sorry I brought it up. I guess it's hard on the head," said Pansy.

Misty appreciated her candour. "It doesn't matter, anyway. I mean, it does, but it doesn't. I'm dealing with it." Misty heard the uncertainty in her own voice. She wasn't going to convince anyone that she was all right with what happened.

"You takes a lesson or two from Skylene, no man's gonna do that to you again."

"What's up with that anyway? Stinky and Cedric, both giving me a call? New kid in town?"

"By golly, you needs an outport education some bad." She shook her head from side to side and rolled her eyes. "The bed, Misty. The bed."

"So I bought a bed. Big deal. Most people sleep on them unless they hang from the rafters and I've met a few who'd qualify for that." She still felt a bit guilty. Buying the bed had been a decisive point for her and if she hadn't run into Steve Day at that exact moment, she might well have made a more rational choice. *I shouldn't be held accountable for a hormonal moment*, she thought. *And it isn't like I've had any opportunity to do anything about it.*

"No, Misty. You're missing the point. You arrives in town one day and the next day you goes and buys the biggest bed in Charlie's Cove. And then, if that weren't enough, you has Duff and the boys drive it through town in broad daylight. My dear, your social calendar is only warming up. Won't be one male in fifty miles of here wouldn't ask you for a date. With the exception of Fig and Wilfred, of course."

"Come on." Misty waited for Pansy to say something reassuring. She didn't.

Suddenly, what Pansy was saying started to make sense and the immensity of her actions began to sink in.

She hadn't bought any old bed. That's exactly what Tiz had told her, too.

Sweet Jesus.

She'd sent out a signal stronger than Marconi on a clear night.

She, single mom, biologically ripe, totally unattached, fresh as a newborn kipper, had bought the *bed of enticement.*

Knowing full well it was ridiculous still didn't stop her from laying blame. *Damn you, Steven Day, this is entirely your fault.* She was beginning to think that man was a figment of her imagination. Like sighting an iceberg off the coast in a blinding fog. Maybe he was never really there.

It was no wonder Misty spent a restless night when she finally went to bed. Images of Steve peppered her dreams. She awoke in a sweat several times expecting to see him in the bed with her, their limbs wrapped together like a couple of twist ties.

Finally, driven to the point of insomnia, she realized something. The bed of enticement wasn't an elixir of love; it was a giant trampoline of sexual frustration. By the time the sun cracked through her curtains, she was good and bloody tired of tossing and turning. Her body obviously had other ideas because her nipples were pushing through the sheets like a couple of stanchions.

Aye, aye, Captain Steve. Prepare to come aboard. They don't call me the first mate for nothing.

CHAPTER 8

Win-Win

Fig and Wilfred's wedding turned out to be more exhilarating than anyone anticipated.

Misty arrived early wearing the only truly conservative outfit she owned, a long-sleeved, high-necked, navy-blue dress she saved for funerals. She wasn't taking any chances on anyone getting the wrong idea about her. If the bed of enticement had established her as the most likely piece in town, the dress of un-enticement would have to get her out.

She stood in the vestibule and looked inside. The church was packed. Squatting room only at this point. So much for early.

"Some turnout, what?" a familiar voice whispered in her ear.

Hayward Hedges.

"I know these events can be overwhelming to a newcomer. I've been keeping a look-out for you. No one wants to see our newest reporter left out of the action. Follow me."

Hayward gripped her elbow like a mongoose and before she could object, she was shuffling up the middle aisle in front of him. Close enough to feel his hip bang against her bottom. And that was all she hoped she would feel.

He stopped halfway and whispered into a man's ear. Immediately, the man and his buddy vacated their spots and there were, miraculously, two available seats for her and Hayward.

They sat down. Together. Mostly because Hayward still held her arm in a formidable grip.

"What do you think you're doing?" Misty said as she wrestled her arm free.

"Helping you out," he replied.

"I'm quite capable..."

"In this crowd? Sweet pea, you wouldn't get a seat tonight if your life depended on it. Have a look." He pointed at the crowd. "Friends and family at the front. Curious in the middle, and the lynching party in the rear." He gestured to a mean-looking group of men gathered in the back pews.

"Well," she began and realized there was no point in arguing with him. "Thank you. I guess."

She took a deep breath. The air was stifling, and being pressed between Hayward and a rather large woman on the other side wasn't helping matters. She scanned the crowd and finally settled her eyes on the back of the head in front of her. It looked familiar. Dark Hair. Broad shoulders.

Could it be? Hmmm. She slid closer to the woman on her left and tried to see his profile. All she got for her efforts was a soft jab in the ribs.

"Sorry," she apologized as she slid back toward Hayward. *What are the chances?* she wondered. It might not be him, but gauging from the way those shoulders were communicating with her pelvis, there really wasn't a downside to finding out.

Before she could talk herself out of it, she leaned forward and tapped him on the shoulder.

His eyes flickered immediate recognition as he turned around. That was a relie... *Cripers. I'm mummied into the dress of un-enticement.* Her hand flew to her chest, feeling the confining fabric that battened her up like a Victorian virgin. *Too late now.*

"Well, hello," said Steve, shifting to give himself a bit of room.

Beneath her hand, her heart sped up in a staccato rhythm that defied logic. "Hi." *Brilliant.* He looked even better in person than he did in her imagination. She scrambled for something else to say. "Nice evening for a same-sex wedding." *What if he was gay?* She didn't want to consider the possibility. Not the way she was feeling. Then an even worse thought struck her. *What if he thinks I'm with Hayward? Oh.* She shifted to the left again and got a quick bob in the boob with an elbow.

"Nice to see you. Without the prevailing winds." He laughed. Deep and well, deep.

"Oh, that. I'm adapting to the sudden fluctuations in weather. You'd be impressed." *Right.* Awkwardly, she wiggled back slightly toward Hayward who was doggedly tracking her conversation. She dropped her hand from her chest and navigated it toward Steve, a reflexive move that suddenly felt foolish and unnecessary.

He tried to reach across the pew and shake it but he was jammed in as tightly as she was. His fingers brushed hers, an electric connection not quite made. "Not much breathing room here, let alone mobility."

Misty laughed in response and used her hand to brush her hair out of her eyes. She could say it was the heat, but the truth was this man made her unbelievably self-conscious about her appearance.

"I'll kill the liver-lipped little faggot," a man screamed as he stormed into the nave.

The moment was lost. She and Steve broke eye contact and, along with everyone else, turned to watch the ruckus at the front of the church. Misty felt as though fate had intervened to keep her safe. *Safe from what,* she wondered. *Another chance at love? Or at least a chance to find out that she could still open her heart to the possibility.*

"That pimply-assed little bugger and his boyfriend is gone off to St. John's," the man added as he pummelled his fist against his other hand.

There was a collective hum from the crowd.

"I'll string the little rotter from the rafters when I gets me hands on his scrawny neck." The man marched back and forth in front of the pulpit like a fundamentalist on fire.

"Who's that?" Misty asked Hayward.

"Fig's father."

A second man burst into the nave. "I just got a call from my cousin in Sin John's," he said. "The buggers was on the six o'clock news. You been suckered. The whole stupid lot of you." He was careful not to implicate himself.

That was it. The church erupted.

Misty jumped up. This was her first real assignment with *The Yarn* and she wasn't taking a chance on missing anything. She felt Hayward's hand on her backside as she pushed past him. He wasn't getting away with that, but first things first; at the moment, she had an elopement to cover.

She joined the crowd surging to the front of the church.

"That's your fault," said a rather stern-looking woman pointing her finger at Fig's father.

"You bunch of ignoramuses," yelled another man to the crowd.

"Shut your mouth," cried another as he plunged forward to the head of the mob.

The swarm had a life of its own, and when it eventually came to a stop, Misty was wedged tightly against the pulpit. She could hardly breathe.

"Watch my toes," a voice whispered into her ear.

Misty tried to turn but couldn't. She managed to swivel her head enough to see what she already knew. Pressed against her back, hands resting gently on her shoulders, was Steve.

"Seems we're destined to be thrown together," he said.

The crowd surged again and she felt several of her body parts making intimate contact with him. "I guess this is what you call full body contact. Sorry." But she didn't mean it. She wasn't sorry at all about the turn of events.

"You don't sound sincere to me," Steve murmured. "I hope you're not enjoying this."

She didn't respond because there was no need. She was enjoying it and he knew it. Her cheek pressed against the pulpit this time and Steve rested his chin on top of her head. She wished the crowd would disperse, but then there'd be no excuse for them to be locked together like a couple of magnets. Being held in his embrace was something she could get used to very easily.

"What are you doing here? Relative?"

"Reporter. I'm covering this for *The Yarn*. You?"

"Used to go out with Fig's sister. Still like the family, strange though they may be." *Translation: I'm single.*

"Funny about that. I like my ex-husband's parents, too." *Translation: I'm single too.*

"Wouldn't know about that. Never been married myself." *Translation: I like being single.* That thought brought her back to reality. Maybe he was charming with all the women in Charlie's Cove, and she was making a fool of herself thinking there was some chemistry between them. The thought she could be so naïve after all she'd been through wasn't very impressive. So a guy pressed against her in a crowd. Everyone was pressing against someone. That didn't mean anything. Except that it did.

"I need to get a picture for my story." *Translation: Oh, what the heck. There was no translation for that.* She just needed to get a damn picture.

"I can give you a boost."

Oh, my God. Did he have to put it like that? An image was already forming in her mind. She could deny all she wanted but she was turned on and there didn't seem to be an off button. *Hopeless.* She really was hopeless. "Thanks." She braced herself. *Shit.* She hadn't been to the gym in months. What if he couldn't lift her? A vision of her ass bouncing off the top of his head had her rethinking the plan, but Steve had other ideas.

"Hold on." He wormed his hands down to her waist.

Maybe she'd just like to stay right where she was. But the thought of how she would feel if he didn't get her off the ground provided her with enough incentive to grab a moulding on the front of the pulpit and hope the thing was bolted down.

With Steve's help, she was soon pulling herself upright, her feet wedged on a ledge that lined the platform. The only thing she regretted as she looked back down was that he wasn't attached to her with a bungee cord so she could pull him in later to continue with the pressing and squeezing. She watched as the crowd surged around him again. It was just as though she had never been there. And maybe that was a sign she should get her head out of the clouds and into her work.

"Thanks," she yelled down to him. "I can take it from here." He nodded. She shimmied along the ledge to a railing and scrambled over. The demure little slit at the back of her dress gave way and she instantly found she had a lot more freedom to manoeuvre. *This must be quite the view I'm providing. Most likely the best display this pulpit's ever seen.* She wondered if a lightning bolt might come down from the heavens to take care of her sinful thoughts and exposures. *Nah, I'd never be that lucky. I'm condemned to live with my destiny.*

She waved to Steve and with great effort put her mind on what she was here for. It wasn't easy, but it was better than throwing herself at a man to the point of embarrassment. Charlie's Cove was breaking loose and she was there front and centre. As she turned on her flash and looked into the camera lens, she imagined the accolades she'd get from *The Phonse* when she handed him her material.

It was uncomfortable knowing Steve was probably looking at her while her world was defined by what she could see through her lens.

"The cops is coming," someone yelled. A fight had broken out. By the time the RCMP arrived, Misty's batteries had died. Correction. Not hers, but the ones in her camera. She, personally, was wound up tighter than a trawling net, full to capacity with sexual tension and euphoria for her success in capturing the event firsthand.

When the crowd moved out of the church, Misty looked for Steve but couldn't see him anywhere. Several people were taken away and Misty tried to keep track of what was happening. It was useless.

"The party's on, b'ys," Fig's father yelled. "Stuff the little buggers. Drinks is on me and the wife's got the grub laid out anyways."

It was a sight to see. A few hundred people congregating upon the Legion all at once. Shirts torn, ties ripped off, and a racket the likes of which was rarely heard outside of hockey season. Misty put fresh batteries in her camera and raced after them, the back of her dress lifting and gaping in the breeze.

If it was chilly, she didn't notice. She was far too elated; she had her story and her wish had been granted. Good or bad, she had seen Steve again. With any luck, well, the night was far from over.

CHAPTER 9

Up She Comes

"Up she comes," Fig Hendley's father yelled. "And down she goes." He tossed back a shot of something dark and nasty looking. Misty figured it was black rum, and a sure sign the party was really getting started. Almost everyone on The Rock favoured the thick, rich taste of dark rum.

He passed her a shot glass filled to the brim.

Misty laughed. "You don't expect me to drink that?"

"You is or you isn't, missus. The Rat can sniff out a purebred. I says you can put it back. Cheers." He held a shot glass in his hand, tapped it to hers and threw back the contents.

Misty raised her glass to her lips. She was totally unprepared when Mr. Hendley grabbed her hand and poured the contents into her mouth. Dark rum dribbled over her chin onto her dress. Misty coughed and sputtered. She couldn't breathe.

"You bees one of us now," he said. "Welcome home, me duckie."

"Mr. Hendley," she said, as she recovered her voice.

"They calls me The Rat, my love."

"Okay," she conceded. "Rat. How do you feel about the elopement? On the record."

"Crafty bugger, that Fig. He suckered us all. But, b'y, we bees getting the last laugh, what? This'll be the time of the year and those two bees missing it. I thinks justice has been served."

"I can quote you on that?" This was great stuff. Lots of colour for her story.

"My dear, you do what you wants wit dat."

Misty pushed a tendril of hair behind her ear. She was a mess and smelled like a rum barrel, but the upside was she could finally get rid of the dress. Permanently. It had served its purpose; she was about as *un-enticing* as she could possibly be.

It took her completely by surprise when an arm fell across her shoulders and a familiar voice whispered in her ear.

"Some sweet time, what?"

"Hayward." She wiggled out from under his embrace and turned to face him. "Fancy running into you again. I thought you'd be in bed by now."

Hayward chuckled and licked his lips. "Funny you should say that. You must be reading my mind."

This time there was no mistaking his intention. As if she ever could. Misty looked around, hoping to spy Steve in the crowd. If he was here, she could throw herself at his feet, beg him to take her home, and flip Hayward the bird at the door. It always helped to have a backup plan going into battle.

The Legion hall had almost blackout lighting, and along with the crowd, this made it hard to see your own hand, let alone find someone.

"Heard you been shopping," Hayward continued.

Misty sighed and pressed her lips together. Time to honour that little promise she'd made to herself earlier this evening. She could still feel the imprint of Hayward's hand on her bottom.

She cleared her throat and pouted her lips, then whispered in a way she thought was a fairly good imitation of Marilyn Monroe. "Well, I bought a bed, if that's what you mean." She batted her eyes a little and followed up with a wink, just in case he didn't catch her drift.

Hayward, God bless him, licked his lips again. "You sure did. Old Tiz's been broadcasting that for days." He winked back. "Nothing like a good bed christening. Ever been to one of those?"

"Hayward! You're a surprising man." She brushed her hand lightly over his arm and gave him a little push with her pointer.

"A bed christening," he continued with growing excitement, "is second only to a deck erection party." He raised his eyebrows. Two times.

It was a display of masculine prowess that left her speechless.

"Let's slip out of here," he said.

Misty looked around before she answered. "Surely not together? I've seen the ring on your finger."

Hayward's eyes narrowed, as though he was processing something in his head. He leaned forward and whispered in her ear, "Likes a girl with brains, I do. Brains and tits. A good combination."

Better by far than no brain and a dick. "You go ahead and warm up the car," Misty whispered back. "It gets chilly around here at night."

"You won't be chilly in the Hayward-mobile. Guaranteed."

"I'll bet. Give me five minutes. What are you driving?"

"A Camaro. Black with a white stripe up the hood. Can't miss it."

"Nice." She probably could have picked his car without any help from Hayward. "Flash your lights two times when I come out," Misty said. "I'll find you. And Hayward?"

"What?"

She stood on her tippy toes, her hand on his shoulder as she placed her mouth close to his ear. She wanted to be sure he heard her clearly over the roar of the drunken crowd. "Why don't you slip your trousers off? Might be hard to do that once I get there. You look like a big boy." She deserved an Oscar.

"This is your lucky night, my lover. What I call a win-win situation." He finished his beer and placed the bottle down. "Five short minutes to ec-sta-sy." He blew her a discreet kiss as he headed for the door.

Five minutes wasn't much time to get things in order, but she'd manage.

First, she called the house to ask Pansy if she'd mind staying a bit later. Then she asked the bartender for a piece of paper. In her best block letters, she wrote a brief note. That done, she headed for a posse of local beef hanging around the dartboard.

She smiled as she walked over and picked one. "Are you...?" She paused and waited for him to fill in the blank.

"Ed?" he replied.

"Ed. It's amazing I found you in this crowd. So many new faces but I remember you. You were in the very last pew, weren't you?"

"Right on." Ed grinned and poked his buddy. "With all the real men."

"I thought so," said Misty. Ed was exactly right for what she had in mind. She passed him the note she'd written. "Hayward Hedges asked me to give this to you. He just left a few minutes ago."

Ed looked puzzled as he unfolded the paper but the shadow that passed over his face a moment later took care of any confusion he may have had.

It could have been a grunt, but Misty felt it was more like a growl. It wasn't important, anyway. It was just the sound Ed made as he crossed the room and stormed out the door looking for Hayward Hedges.

Misty cleared the building tight to Ed's heels. She had a feeling he would provide her third story for Tuesday's deadline.

And for once, she concurred with Hayward; this really was a win-win situation and, as far as she was concerned, they were all getting something out of it. Ed, a lynching; Hayward, a lesson; and herself? Why, that was easy. She was getting even.

Hayward's lights flashed twice like beacons to a ship about to run aground. Misty pulled her camera from her bag, glad she'd replaced the batteries. *Be prepared* was a motto that carried you a long way, especially at a time like this. She'd bet Hayward was a briefs type of guy. Black ones. Low and tight.

And whoo-ee, if she wasn't right.

The picture she snapped of Hayward flying through the air in his skivvies was Pulitzer material.

And Ed? For a moment Misty experienced a twinge of conscience. *Ah, he'll get over it in due time. He might even learn a thing or two about tolerance and acceptance.*

♥

"You did what?" Pansy screamed, dancing around the kitchen as Misty told her what had transpired.

"I know, I know," said Misty. "But he had it coming to him." She unceremoniously dumped her dress in the garbage and finished buttoning her shirt.

"For a lotta years. You're gonna have a fan club in Charlie's Cove when this hits the press."

"You think?"

"I knows."

"I hope you're right. Hayward looked pretty angry," she replied as she sat down. "I'd like to go over to the office and write this up, but I can't leave you and kids to fend for yourselves if he shows up here."

"Shows up here? Don't concern yourself with that. Hayward's wife will be on this so fast he won't be nothing but a blur sailing up the road in front of her." Pansy broke out in laughter again. "You never met her, I imagines."

"Mrs. Hedges? No, and I'm not sure I ever want to." Misty looked at Pansy again and tapped her fingers nervously on the tabletop. "You're sure you'll be all right?"

"I can't get any surer. Hayward's got more problems to worry about tonight than the likes of either you or me. You can rest easy, Misty. He won't be nowhere near your house this evening."

Reassured, Misty pulled on her sneakers and a warm sweater. "Then I've got a story to write. I'd love to get it done while all the details are fresh in my mind. It's not like I can sleep, anyway." *For various reasons,* she added silently, *not the least of which is a tall, dark-haired, missing-in-action male.*

It wasn't until she finished her copy at four in the morning that she finally had time to reflect on the evening. She replayed the events in her head. The last time she'd seen Steve was at the church. There were only two possibilities she could come up with. Either he was seeing someone else or he'd been arrested.

She hoped like heck it was the latter, which, while kind of unfair, made her feel a whole lot better. Her last lucid thought before she fell asleep with her head on her desk was of Steve body surfing against her in the crowd.

CHAPTER 10

Yes, B'y

Phonse's beady eyes bore into her through his glasses and Misty felt this might be what it was like to lock eyes with a bear. He was holding the picture of Hayward in his fist.

"Muldoon," he said. "Sit your boney arse down." He pointed to the chair in front of his desk.

"Yes, sir." Misty did a quick mental check of her faculties. Sight, hearing, smell, touch, taste. Especially the burning sensation in her stomach. She had a feeling The Phonse was going to roast her ass.

"You took this?"

He held the picture up, directly in front of her face. He was gripping it so tightly his fingertips were white, quite bloodless, and probably an exact match to her face.

Misty swallowed audibly. *Definitely hers.*

Hayward was suspended in mid-air, his hair jetting straight back from his forehead, providing an excellent profile of his face, which was frozen in a grimace of fear, pain, or whatever he might have been feeling at the time. Ed was in the background, shaking his fist, mouth wide open. She'd give that an X-rating.

"Well?" Phonse said.

"It's mine." Misty shifted nervously in her seat.

"He's a lawyer, Muldoon. A scum-sucking, bottom-feeding parasite."

Misty closed her eyes. She was going to be fired before her first paycheque hit the bank. *Stupid. Stupid.* She had no business satisfying her ego at the risk of her job. *Stupid, stupid, stu...*

"And he's going to sue your ass off."

Misty's eyes flew open. "My ass? What about yours? Hayward is a lecherous predator and my job put me at risk." Her temper flared and with it came the last vestige of self-preservation she had. "He was colouring outside the lines. He deserved it. If he presses charges against me, I'll levitate Mrs. Hedges with all the details of Wayward Hayward's midnight adventure. It'll be a nasty can of worms if he wants to open it."

"What kind of worms?" asked Phonse, showing the first spark of enthusiasm.

"You've lived around here all your life. You know Hayward. What kind do you think?"

Phonse narrowed his eyes and pulled a cigarette from the pack on his desk. He lit it and leaned back in his chair. "Don't get smart with me, Muldoon. I needs facts. What was Hayward doing with his pants off?"

"Waiting for me and my boney arse."

"Yes, b'y." Phonse put his elbows on the desk and leaned forward, a slight upward turn at the edge of his mouth.

"And I kind of sent Ed, instead." She kept her eyes on him as he took another draw from his cigarette and let the smoke creep up around his glasses.

"Yes, b'y."

He looked at her expectantly, so she continued. "Ed may have been under the impression that Hayward had his pants off for... for... him." Misty's voice died on the last words.

"Yes, b'y." The tip of Phonse's cigarette burned brighter as he undertook a series of short puffs.

Misty wondered if yes b'y was "yes b'y," this is good, or "yes b'y," this is bad. It was hard to judge. Phonse was still staring at her, and the only sign of movement now was his nostrils as they flared to accommodate the stream of exhaust that flowed out.

Phonse puffed until the cigarette was nothing but a stub attached to a cylinder of ash. It seemed to defy gravity, hanging as it did in the corner of his mouth.

Misty's shirt was a swath of damp fabric, clinging to her like a strip of Velcro. Her back itched like crazy and deserved a good scratch, but caught in Phonse's intense gaze, she was afraid to move. She needed this job, dammit, and if she had to put up with a bit of hooey from Phonse Penney, well, she'd put up with worse in her life. It wouldn't be the first time.

Suddenly, Phonse jumped up from his seat and darted around the newsroom. "Yes, b'y. Yes, b'y," he hollered as he slammed several of the desks and tables with his fist.

Misty followed him with her eyes, wondering what in the blazes was going on. Was he going to punch her out or just fire her?

He came to a dead stop in front of her. Her nose was about parallel with his navel. If she looked up, she would get a nasty perspective on nasal hair. If she looked down, well, she wouldn't go there. She kept her eyes on his belly and waited for him to say something.

Phonse placed his hands on her shoulders and pulled her to her feet. His breath, mingled with coffee and smoke, was enough to nullify a buffalo fart.

"I fuckin' loves it," he said. "Loves it, loves it, loves it." And he planted a big, wet kiss on her cheek and danced his way back around his desk. "Now, get the hell out of here, Muldoon. I got work to be at."

Amazing—she hadn't been sacked. "Should I call Hayward?" she asked. It was the last thing she wanted to do, but if it meant the difference between having a job and not having one, she would do it.

Phonse glared at her over his glasses. "I finds pleasure in me job, Muldoon. I'll call the weaselly parasite meself. Now, get out of here like I told you."

And thinking it was good advice, particularly under the circumstances, she did.

After her ordeal with Phonse, she needed a bath in the worst kind of way. Her shirt had nothing on her pants. They were practically glued to the soft, sweaty skin behind her knees.

It being Tuesday, Misty figured she could do just that, indulge herself in a pampering session in her own tub. She had a full seven days before her next stories were due.

She scribbled her hours on a sheet of paper and handed them to Tilly on her way out the door.

"What's that?" asked Tilly.

"My time slip."

"He didn't fire you?"

"Piece of cake," said Misty, enjoying the look of amazement on Tilly's face. "Toodle-y-do."

She beat it out the door before Tilly could ask any more questions. She wasn't sure if the smile on her face was a result of having bested Hayward or simply because she still had a job. Or maybe it was because of the way Tilly's mouth had gaped like a salmon sucking air. Misty laughed aloud. The answer was simple. Like multiple choice, it was D. All of the above.

When the sun peeked out from behind a cloud, it was like the ending to a perfect day that had barely even started.

"I'm back," she yelled as she opened the door to the house and danced across the room. "Liberty? Vivienne? Pansy?"

When no one answered, she went to the kitchen and looked out the back door. Not a sign of life. It was then she spied a note on the table written in Liberty's youthful hand.

Mommy,

We've gone berry picking with Pansy. We will pick hundreds and hundreds of berries for you.

Love,

Liberty Alexis Muldoon

That was her daughter, all right. And she'd probably count every single one of them, as well.

For the first time in several weeks, Misty was alone. With free time. Maybe this was what Pansy was talking about. For Misty, it was a foreign experience.

No one clamouring after her. No one needing her services. No one demanding her attention.

She could take a shower, or…she went to the cupboard and pulled out a mug. The aroma of freshly ground coffee beans soon filled the room. She dug through the cupboard for one of Pansy's homemade jam-jam cookies and found a fresh batch, barely touched. Pansy's cookies disappeared faster than the positive balance in her bank account these days. And that was saying something.

While she waited for her coffee to brew, she sat down at the table and looked out the window of their new home.

What prompted Charlie to name me in his will, she wondered. *I hardly knew him and my best memory of Great-uncle C was the time he took me rock hunting and showed me how to chisel quartz from a wall of rock behind our house in St. John's. He sure seemed to know a lot about rocks for a fisherman.*

Then, again, maybe that was a good skill for a fisherman to have. Rock avoidance, especially.

Good old Great-uncle C.

She tapped the tabletop with her fingernails.

So, this is what it's like to have time.

When the coffee maker beeped, she jumped up and poured a cup, thankful for something to do besides drumming her fingers.

She closed her eyes and held the cup under her nose. The smell reminded her of the days when a cup of coffee was the only nourishment she had between telephone calls, project deadlines, and meetings.

Free time.

This sure is different.

Sitting here. Quietly. By myself. With time. Yep. So, this is what it's like. To have time. Lots of it.

She yawned and checked the clock.

Five minutes had passed.

Misty picked up Liberty's note, turned it over and began to doodle. After an attempt at a self-portrait, she switched to what she did best...putting her thoughts on paper.

Dear Diary, she began. *I'm enjoying a robust cup of coffee and relaxing. Pansy says it's nice to have time to chill out, but I say it's tough to get used to. Duff says Charlie's Cove is a good place for kids, and he may be right because my kids have abandoned me. I'm all alone with just you, Dear Diary.*

Misty tapped the pencil on the table as her thoughts drifted.

She liked the feel of a pencil in her hand. Computers were so cold and impersonal. Tap, tap, tap. But a pencil, that was different. A pencil to a writer was like a paintbrush to an artist. It demanded things. Like words. Ideas. And imagination.

Misty wrote her name. She liked the way she could play with the curls on the letter M. She began writing random words that began with M. Magic. Money. Moola. Moocho moola. Magnificent. Misfortune. Mistakes.

Crap. Those last two words popped at her.

How freaking depressing. *What was it those self-help books said? "In order to grow up, you have to screw up" or something like that? Whatever, I seem to have qualified. At this rate, maturity* (another dumb M word that she added to her list) *is practically oozing out of me. How Machiavellian is that? I'm getting older and smarter without any of the benefits of wealth or security. Damn.*

She added the Mach-word to her list as well. In the past year, she'd covered just about every category of failure possible. And she'd been in response mode ever since, hardly thinking about a plan, just grabbing at every life raft that came her way.

This morning, she felt the weight of her decisions. They hunkered on her shoulders like a large, sulking gargoyle. *I make a few wrong moves and suddenly I've got a life overflowing with mistakes and...* She threw down her pencil and slapped the heels of her hands against her forehead...*I end up in my dead uncle's house on the coast of nowhere.*

She didn't need free time at all. She didn't want to think about things. It was easier to be busy and feel like maybe she was moving ahead.

Mistakes. What a stupid word, anyway. She sliced it with the tip of her pencil.

They're not mistakes. They're adventures. Well, maybe misadventures, but at least that's not as depressing. She added that word to the bottom of the list. Misadventures.

Misty's Misadventures. Now there's an apt description of my situation. A label for my life. What do they call that? A motto? A slogan? A theme? And for those of you, who have failed miserably (do all the world's shitty words begin with M?) we have some memorable...misadventures from Misty. Just perfect for people who wind up in the most dead-end place in the world.

She wrote and underlined her motto, then ran her pencil back and forth until the words sat upon a thick dark line.

Misty's Misadventures.

She could see it now. Sitting upon a hill overlooking Charlie's Cove, lit up like the Hollywood sign. Two words that described her life perfectly.

"Mom," screamed Vivienne, as she opened the back door and sent it crashing against the wall. "Libby's lost her tooth."

Misty jumped up. Coffee went everywhere as her leg hit the table and sent the mug flying. "What happened?"

By the time she reached the door, Pansy had arrived with Liberty in her arms.

"Mommy," cried her daughter, reaching out with one arm for her mother while keeping the other hand clamped over her mouth.

"Iz all right, Misty," Pansy reassured her. "Liberty just tripped with her blueberries and knocked her front teeth against a rock. She's a tough little thing. I thinks it's fine."

Misty kissed her daughter on the forehead. "Let's take a peek, Lib. Promise it won't hurt."

Liberty sniffed and lifted her hand a wee bit so Misty could see in. Her lip was bleeding and there was a wonderful mixture of tears, saliva and blood, but her teeth appeared to be in one piece.

"I feels awful," said Pansy. "And she lost all her berries to boot." Pansy looked like she was going to bawl, which was all Misty needed.

"It's not your fault," she reassured her. "Liberty gets so excited her feet can't keep up. Is there a dentist around here?"

"Doccy Snow," replied Pansy, passing Misty some paper towels for Liberty.

"I'll give him a call." She gently cradled her daughter and sat down at the table. "Any idea what the number is?"

"Pull."

"What?" said Misty, staring at Pansy like she'd lost her mind.

"7855. Pull."

Misty picked up the phone. *Pull.* Doccy Snow had some original ideas about marketing. She hoped they bore no correlation to his dentistry.

While she waited for someone to pick up, she looked at her spilled coffee and the paper containing her doodles. Misty's Misadventures had expanded and fattened where the liquid had absorbed into the paper.

The words jumped out at her. This past year had indeed been one long mishap and it didn't appear to be slowing down. She added dental coverage to the growing to-do list she carried in her head and wondered what this mini-misadventure was going to cost her.

"Doccy Snow's office. This is Mavis speaking."

Misty crumpled the paper in her hand and made a mental note to revisit Misty's Misadventures when she found some free time again, which she was sure she would have sooner or later. After all, this was Charlie's Cove, the place where free time had been invented.

"Mavis," she said. "This is Misty Misadven…I mean, Muldoon. Misty Muldoon. I have an emergency."

No kidding. Emergency didn't begin to describe it.

"Oh, my love, the doctor's not in today. He's gone to Running Tickle for a clinic. Do you s'pose it can wait 'til morning?"

Misty looked at her daughter, who had stopped crying and was sniffling against her shirt. "Maybe for her, but I'm going to be a nervous wreck. What time does the doctor get back in town?"

"That depends. He works a long day. You could drive up there."

"I have no idea where…How far is it?" Misty asked.

"Only four hours. Faster by boat, if you got one."

"No boat." Misty sighed. She missed the ease of living in the city. A little traffic, a little noise, but pages of dentists in the phone book. "Hang on." She rested the phone between her shoulder and her ear and used her hands to have a look in Liberty's mouth again. The bleeding had come from her lip and the teeth appeared to be intact. She touched them gingerly with her fingertips. No wiggling. Maybe some ice for the swelling and things might look better by morning.

She picked up the receiver again. "I'm no dentist, but I think we can wait. Nothing's broken off, but I sure would appreciate an appointment first thing in the morning."

"Nine o'clock good?"

"Uh-huh."

Misty signalled Pansy to get some ice for Lib's face while she concluded the call. As she hung up, she turned to her friend. "How do you stand it here? It's like living at the end of the earth."

"At times. But cities got their own set of problems. At least around here kids can go berry-picking right out their own back door."

"You're optimistic, aren't you? There's nothing here but a stupid old paper and some boats and a bunch of decrepit houses perched on the edge of a rock." Misty felt better having vented her frustration. The feeling didn't last.

When she looked up, Pansy was planted in front of her, hands on her hips, elbows sticking out like a couple of crows wings. Her colour had gone from white to an interesting shade of pink. "Fire me if you wants. I don't care. What happened with Libby was an accident, but what you're saying is no accident. It's just plain rude. We manages around here and we manages quite well. We don't need the likes of you telling us what we does wrong."

Liberty started to cry again. The situation was out of control. Misty knew she'd been unreasonable, but she refused to apologize. "It's going to take some adjustment for me," she said curtly as she took the ice-pack and Liberty, Vivienne trailing behind, and left Pansy simmering in the kitchen.

Correction, she thought as she climbed the stairs to her room. *It's going to take a whole lot of adjustment.*

And for the second time that day, she muttered under her breath, "*Damn.*"

CHAPTER 11

Blown Away

After a fairly restful night, under the circumstances, Misty and the girls arrived at Doccy Snow's at exactly nine o'clock. Somehow she'd managed to sleep through her alarm and getting everyone out the door had been a sight worthy of a video. At least nothing was far in Charlie's Cove, and there was no traffic to deal with, which left her feeling rather sheepish about the argument she'd had with Pansy the night before. There were some nice things about living in a small place. She just wasn't ready to admit it yet.

Mavis, the receptionist, apologized fervently that they hadn't been able to see them yesterday. She explained that every second Tuesday, the clinic offered services in some of the smaller communities up along the shore, a fairly common practice around the bay.

Mavis was making up for it in any way she could and put Liberty and Vivienne at ease from the moment they walked in the door.

"Oh my, if it isn't Snow White herself," she said, admiring Liberty's jet-black hair. "And who's this?" She looked at Vivienne, as fair as Liberty was dark. "Tinker Bell?"

The girls were captivated. Mavis was well suited to her job and very motherly. Misty rather wished she would reserve some of the pampering for her. She could use a little coddling to make her feel better.

"Have a seat, ladies and princesses. I'll let Doccy Snow know his very special guests have arrived."

When she left the room, Vivienne leaned toward her mother. "Does she really think I'm Tinker Bell, Mom?"

"Well, Vivi, I'm not sure. She seemed quite serious."

"Should we tell her, Mom?" Vivi asked.

Liberty rolled her eyes behind her sister. "Vivi," she said, "she's going to figure it out. You ain't got no wings."

"Ain't got no?" Misty repeated to Liberty.

"Oh, all right. You haven't any wings, Vivi. It's a dead giveaway."

"Yeah?" replied Vivienne, looking lightly annoyed. "Well, you ain't got no poison apple."

"I'll give you a poison apple if you both don't improve your grammar," said Misty, thinking she sounded far too much like a Cuthbertson for her own comfort.

Pushing that thought aside, she focused on what was more important; Mavis's little fantasy had diverted Liberty's attention away from her teeth. Things were already getting back to normal, except for the swollen lip. And that would heal with time.

Mavis soon returned and ushered them into a treatment room where they discussed who should sit in the chair until Doccy Snow arrived. Snow White won out because she was the actual patient. Vivienne resigned herself to sitting on Misty's knee, with a frown upon her face and a lip almost as compelling as her sister's.

"Well, lookee here," said Dr. Snow as he entered the room. He was of average height and his hair was absolutely white and thick, like sheep batting. His face was ruddy and weathered, like that of a man who had spent a great deal of time enjoying nature. "A couple of salt and pepper shakers," he added jovially as he looked at a chart. "Says this little lady is Liberty Muldoon but I would swear it was Sn...."

"Uh-uh. She ain't got...," Vivienne hesitated as she glanced at her mother. "Doesn't have a poison apple."

"I recommend apple eating," replied Doc Snow. "But not of the poison variety, certainly." He looked at Misty. "Mrs. Muldoon, welcome to the office." Dr. Snow shook her hand and his grip was firm and reassuring. "Hear one of our girls had a fall."

"Liberty," Misty replied. "We'd appreciate it if you could take a look at her front teeth." As Dr. Snow sat down to examine Liberty, a heavyset woman with short brown hair entered the room and plunked down on the dental stool across from him. "Sorry, sorry. Was caught up on the phone." She looked like a much larger version of Mavis and was just as bubbly.

"Meet Ruby, girls. She's my little jewel. Aren't you Ruby?"

Ruby had the good nature to blush at Dr. Snow's comments. "'Appy to meet you," she said. "This place is some busy today."

"Let's have a peek, Snow White."

Misty was floored when Liberty opened wide, giving Doctor Snow free range to check her mouth. He gently explored. "These are the ones you hurt?" He touched her front teeth and tried to wiggle them.

"Uh-huh." Liberty nodded her head.

"Feel a little loose but I'd say they should be all right. What do you think, Ruby? Take an X-ray for me? Maybe we can get a second opinion from my nephew. He's seen just about everything, coming from that zoo in Ontario."

"He works in a zoo?" asked Liberty.

Misty laughed as the image of a dentist working on elephant teeth popped into her head.

"Just an expression, dear. Not to worry. In our little corner of the world, any place with more than 2000 people is a zoo." He patted her arm as he left the room.

"Say cheese, pleazzze," Ruby instructed Liberty as she set up for an X-ray. "Sorry to be a nuisance," she said looking at Vivienne and Misty, "but you'll 'ave to step out for a minute, too. Now, Liberty, you stay still as a mouse and we'll all be right back."

In the hallway, Misty and Vivienne watched as Doccy Snow stepped into another room. He appeared to have a few surgeries. The office was clean but old-fashioned. Misty had a feeling he'd been practicing in Charlie's Cove for eons.

Ruby beckoned them back into the room. Misty let Vivi lead the way. Just as she was following, a movement up the hallway caught her eye.

She looked up and was surprised to see someone waving at her. She did a double take. It was Steve. Misty waved back, suddenly more self-conscious about her appearance than ever. Of all mornings to sleep in. She'd selected her outfit with her eyes glued shut with sleep. She could only imagine what she looked like. Undoubtedly, the perfect follow up to the dress of un-enticement. She glanced down at her top, wishing she'd worn her Victoria's Secret uplift.

Steve disappeared into another room. Misty followed Ruby and Liberty back into theirs. What were the chances of running into him here? There most definitely had to be a curse on her. And he looked so good, too. That was it. She was buying a new alarm clock. One that came with an electrical shock to her backside.

"I 'ears you likes it in Charlie's Cove," said Ruby. "Little miss says you lives in old Charlie's 'ouse."

"That we do," replied Misty, sitting down again and taking Vivi back onto her knees. *What was he doing here?* It was hard to maintain small talk with Ruby when she was thinking of something, no, make that *someone* else. Her senses were flooded with memories of last Saturday night.

"How many dentists work here, Ruby?"

"Oh, just Doccy Snow. Unless you counts Doccy Steve. But 'e's just new 'ere so 'e don't really count yet." She smiled.

"Doccy Steve?" Misty tried to keep her voice even.

"Doccy Snow's nephew." Ruby continued with a quick change of topic. "That was some ornery, that Charlie. We 'auled a tooth for him once and he fair punched the doctor in the mouth 'isself. After that, Charlie 'ad to go to the 'ospital and be put out. Tough old bugger, 'e was."

"That's our Charlie," Misty responded, her mind now fully engaged on Steve. *His nephew?* Her head was a kaleidoscope of thoughts.

She freed one arm and opened her purse. When her fingers closed around a familiar tube, she wondered how she was going to apply lipstick without looking conspicuous.

Ruby stood up. "I'll be right back, girls. 'Ang tight."

Misty didn't waste opportunity. All those moments on the fly had taught her one thing well; she could apply lipstick on a roller-coaster, in the dark, upside-down, and still get it right. She smacked her lips together and slipped the tube back in her purse.

In a few minutes, Ruby was back with Doccy Snow and Steve. "Looks like an excellent prognosis," Dr. Snow said to his nephew. "But you've seen more of this than I have. I'd appreciate your opinion."

Steve smiled at her. Misty smiled back and tried to hide behind Vivi. Forget the bra, her shirt was a mess of wrinkles. And how these jeans had found their way back into her closet when she had put them into a give-away basket, she had no idea.

Steve was wearing chinos and a shirt and tie. He looked so untraditional standing next to Doccy Snow, who was garbed in a white clinic jacket. She liked the way Steve looked. And several of her body parts agreed with her.

"So this is the patient," Steve said to his uncle as he sat down by Liberty for a peek and a wiggle. Liberty opened like a crocodile, in an act of cooperation that could only be attributed to the kindness of the staff.

After an examination and a look at the X-ray, he sat her up and solemnly pronounced, "Your teeth are amazing. They have roots all the way to your toes." Liberty beamed and so did Misty.

Until he turned to her. "I have good news and bad."

"You do?" Misty hated the tension in her voice, but she couldn't help it. She was anxious for her daughter and, damn it all, she was thrown off-kilter by the way this man made her feel. He had the most amazing eyes, which she tried her best to avoid, as she concentrated on what he was saying.

"First, the good news. Your daughter will recover remarkably from her fall. But," he paused just long enough to draw the interest of everyone. "There is a downside. Absolutely no more berry picking...without a helmet, face shield and chin guard."

The room erupted with laughter and Misty's heart melted.

His manner, his kindness, and humour were just so nice. But then, hadn't he been like that from their first encounter? He'd made her feel comfortable when she'd felt like a total klutz.

Since Jake had dumped her, she'd developed a healthy mistrust of good-looking men, but now with this guy she was breaking all her rules.

Steve helped Liberty from the chair and held out his hand. Misty almost placed hers in it, until she realized it was for Vivienne. She barely caught herself in time.

Vivi hopped up for her turn. It didn't take long, but it was just perfect. Her youngest daughter felt included and important and Misty just felt warm all over. If he had asked for a quick peek at her mouth...Misty imagined what it might be like to see him leaning over, looking into her eyes...

"Mrs. Muldoon?"

Misty looked up, wondering how long they'd been staring at her. The girls were standing with Ruby. Doccy Snow was gone and Steve was leaning against the counter. He appeared amused.

"Yes?" she replied, trying to cover her embarrassment.

"Do you have a moment?" asked Steve.

Misty looked at Ruby.

"You go on," Ruby said. "I'll take the little ones to the toy trunk and see you in a few minutes."

Steve waited until they had left the room. "I never did get to thank you for your close companionship the other night. It was probably a bit overwhelming since we've just met, but what can you do when you're pinned in a crowd if not enjoy it?"

"We were like a bunch of sardines," she replied with a smile that relieved some of the nervousness she felt. "I owe you thanks for the boost."

"Anytime. No, really," he insisted as she started to shake her head. "I mean that."

The silence that followed wasn't at all awkward, but it was obvious he was giving some thought to his comment. For that matter, so was she. *Does this mean what I think it means? That there might be a next time?*

"I lost track of you after," he said.

"I did, too. Of you." *Oh, my God, where had she parked her brain?* "It was crazy there, but I got some amazing pictures."

"Amazing is a pretty good word to describe it. I ended up in the middle of a fight and spent most of the night in the lock-up, until Uncle Lar came and got me around three in the morning. He wasn't too happy."

Misty laughed. "I can vouch for your innocence."

"Just what I was thinking. If it hadn't been for you, I wouldn't have been in the middle of that mess. You owe me one."

The lightness of the moment evaporated. Misty wasn't sure what to say.

Steve continued. "How about dinner?"

"All ready," said Ruby, poking her head into the room. "And look what just arrived." She was waving a copy of *The Yarn*. "Doccy Snow says anyone 'o'd catch 'ayward 'edges with his pants down deserves an award." She passed the paper to Misty. "Fresh off the press, Mrs. Muldoon. You're a local 'ero."

Misty turned what she was sure was an impressive shade of crimson. Did Ruby have to put it like that? She took the paper. There, in full colour on the front page, was Hayward Hedges in all his glory, under the headline **Hedges Gets Blown**.

And right under the picture were the words *Photo by Misty Muldoon*. It was a thrill to see it there. Her first photo credit.

But wait a minute…where was Ed? He'd been standing by the car and wasn't in the shot anymore. It was just a picture of Hayward. Phonse must have wiped Ed from the photo.

"Let's see." Steve moved closer and read aloud over her shoulder. Misty tried to focus on the article, but her thoughts drifted to the casual way Steve's arm brushed by hers as he helped her hold the paper open.

> **Hayward Hedges, prominent local attorney, was blown away following Saturday night's celebrations in honour of Fig Hendley's and Wilfred Stroud's wedding. Literally.**
>
> **Condolences go to Mr. Hedges, who is currently recovering from injuries sustained in high winds that tore his pants off and carried him into Erma Gillingham's rose garden.**
>
> **After checking with Environment Canada, *The Yarn* has learned that such freak weather patterns are not uncommon along the coast of Newfoundland, particularly if large amounts of hot air collide with cold ocean winds.**

Said Misty Muldoon, staff reporter who happened upon the scene at the time of the incident, "Mr. Hedges was ripped from his car. I've never seen anything like it."

No one was more surprised than Hedges himself. "I don't think I'll ever forget it," he said when reached for comment the day after the incident.

Hedge's pants were recovered at the scene and returned to him, along with his wallet and keys.

Said Ed Turpin, who also witnessed the event, "He's lucky to be alive."

When Steve finished, Misty put her hand over her mouth and smothered a smile.

"Some story, what?" said Ruby. "You're liable to be on the front page of *The Yarn* with this lady as a patient, Dr. Steve."

"I'll take my chances. What do you say, Misty?"

"Huh?" She was still amazed at the way Phonse had rigged the story.

"What I asked. You know."

"Oh, that."

Ruby was staring at them, trying her best to follow the cryptic conversation.

Misty hesitated. She couldn't accept a date in front of Ruby, here in Steve's office. What would the woman think of her? "I...ah...think a story on your office is a great idea. Take the fear out of first visits for young patients." *Brilliant.*

"Good, then," replied Steve, with a smile broad enough to challenge a Cheshire cat. "We'll discuss it over dinner. I'll call you this evening."

There it was. Done.

He was calling her.

This evening.

The next few minutes were a blur. Mavis refused to take any payment. The photo of Hayward was payment enough, she insisted, by orders of both Dr. Snow and Dr. Steve. Everyone was treating her like she was someone special.

"Mom." Vivienne tugged at her arm as they ran through the frigid air to their car. "Let me see."

Misty realized she was still holding the newspaper. She had walked out with the clinic's copy under her arm.

As she passed the paper to her daughter, she debated whether or not she should take it back. She finally decided against it. She was too flustered for another encounter with Ruby, who had tried her darnedest to find out more about her upcoming dinner meeting with Steve. She'd just have to apologize for her oversight the next time she was in. That was all.

Getting used to life in a small town wasn't going to be easy. It really was like living in a fishbowl. Charlie's Cove, Newfoundland, Fishbowl of the Atlantic. *What a handle and I'd better remember to take mind of it,* she thought. *More than ever, now my photo of Hayward has been published.*

She buckled the girls in and headed for home. The sound of horns honking as she passed through town was festive. Each one sounded like a rousing cheer.

When she arrived back at Charlie's, she was surprised to see Duff unloading some wood.

"Some fast with them fingers, Misty," he said. "You sure picked up the pace at *The Yawn* some."

"You think?"

"Yes b'y, and I also thinks Hayward wears his underwear too tight for reproductive purposes."

Misty laughed. This was the best she'd felt in months. The girls stared at their mother like she'd grown another head. Well, maybe her attitude had improved dramatically.

"By the way," added Duff. "There was a delivery for you a few minutes ago. I put 'er inside."

"What?" said Misty as she raced up the front steps and opened the door. On the table in the entry was the most beautiful bouquet of flowers. An assortment of colours and sizes and the scent was enrapturing.

"They're gorgeous," Misty said. "But who?" Duff watched as she searched through the blooms for a card. She finally pulled a small envelope from the maze and opened it.

"With appreciation, Agnes," Misty read aloud. "Who the heck is Agnes?" She looked at Duff.

Duff grinned from ear to ear. "Well, some cute, that."

"What?" asked Misty.

"You fell in dung and smells like roses, Misty," said Duff. "Who Agnes is, is simple. She's Mrs. Hayward Hedges."

CHAPTER 12

Tender Moments

Misty had just popped Vivienne in the old claw-foot bathtub when the phone rang. Liberty, who was finished her bath and wrapped up in a towel, answered.

"One moment, please," she said in a very grown-up way as she passed the phone to Misty.

Sloughed in bubbles to her elbows, Misty shook her hands over the tub and took the phone gingerly between two fingers. "Hello?"

"How's the local heroine this evening?"

"Up to my neck in bubbles," Misty replied truthfully. It was Steve. Ever since she'd arrived in Charlie's Cove, fate seemed to be throwing them together in the most spontaneous ways but this time it was different. Steve had chosen to call her.

She liked the sound of his voice and she was glad he'd kept his promise to call. Even though they'd just met, she needed to feel she could trust him to keep his word.

"Bubbles, eh? Sounds interesting. Could you use some company?"

Misty laughed. "Sure, and you can pour the water over Vivienne's hair and put up with the screaming."

"Oh." He sounded disappointed. "I had another image in mind."

"I'll bet. You forget I'm a working mother. My day doesn't end until nine o'clock and most likely I'd fall asleep in the bath." She wasn't painting a very enticing picture for someone she'd actually like to entice.

"How about a late-night snack, then? Fish and chips at Dot's Drive-In?"

"And the children?"

"My cousin can look after them."

"Your cousin?" *Like I'd just leave my kids with anyone.*

"Yeah, Pansy."

"Pansy's your cousin?" Misty's voice conveyed her surprise.

"On my mother's side. Mom is Pansy's father's sister. Uncle Lar is married to another one of her sisters, Delphinia."

"Is everyone related around here?"

"Not really," he laughed. "It just seems that way."

"I'd love to accommodate you, but Pansy finished up at six and this is her night for darts. I don't think there's any form of bribery that would interfere with a bull's eye. She's made the play-offs and the grand prize is a weekend in St. John's."

"That's no problem. I'll give her a weekend in St. John's."

"Go on. That's crazy. You can't do that just so I can get out."

"Dot's makes up for it."

"Must be some fish and chips."

"I was referring to the company."

This time Misty laughed. "Well, anyway, it's silly to talk like this. Pansy's already gone and I've got stories to write first thing in the morning. Can't we just do it another night?"

"Because I'm a man of the moment and I still have you in my mind from today, I'd like to see you tonight."

Misty felt a warm tingle in her stomach, one that seemed to correlate specifically to conversations with Steve. He said the kind of things she liked to hear and actually hadn't heard for a long time.

"Mommy, I'm finished." Vivienne was still covered in bubbles, but she was standing up and trying to climb over the edge of the tub.

Misty tucked the phone between her ear and her shoulder. "I've got to rinse you off first, honey," she said.

"That means I would be naked," said Steve, sounding absolutely delighted. "I was thinking dinner for the first date, but we can do it your way. Like I said, I'm a man of the moment."

Misty laughed. "Very cute, but I'm talking to my daughter, not you." *This guy should come with a warning label. Caution, deadly sense of humour. Handle with care.*

"You can't blame me for trying. I'm the kind of guy who sees the glass as half full."

Misty laughed again. "Really? I'd love to chat with you about that, but I only have two hands and have to get everyone ready for bed. Couldn't we do the fish and chip thing tomorrow night?"

"You drive a hard bargain."

"I'll be well-rested and cheerful."

"Promise?"

"Promise." *Deep breath.*

"Pick you up at seven, then. We may do take-out so wear something warm."

"This is Charlie's Cove in July. Of course I'll have thermal back-up."

"You do inspire my imagination." She could hear the amusement in his voice as he disconnected.

Misty sat back on her heels wearing what she knew had to be a sappy smile. Sure, it was probably overreacting, but his call made her feel good.

"Who was that, Mommy?"

"Just a friend, honey. We're going out for dinner tomorrow night."

"Can I come?"

"Maybe next time." *If there even is a next time.* It was ridiculous to think she could develop a relationship when surviving took all her time and then some.

She looked at her daughter as she swathed her in a towel. Her precious children were number one. Not herself and not her relationships. And she had no problem with that. It was simply that this was the first time she'd experienced any interest in a man since her divorce. And it was creating a maelstrom in her gut. Did biological clocks still tick when you already had your share of kids and relationships? She sincerely hoped not.

Misty emptied the tub and carried her daughter into her bedroom where they changed into pyjamas. She was drying Vivienne's hair when Liberty showed up with a book. A few minutes later all three of them were cuddled together on Misty's bed, the two girls under the covers on either side of Misty, who lay on top of the duvet.

"What'll it be tonight, ladies?"

"Cinderella." Liberty passed her a well-worn copy of *Grimm's Fairy Tales*.

Misty scanned the story. Twelve pages. "We might not get through all this tonight."

"That's all right, Mommy. We can finish it tomorrow."

Conflict of interest, thought Misty. *Tomorrow night I'm going to be at Dot's. Surely a little adult time doesn't mean I'm backsliding on my responsibilities, does it? Pansy is perfectly good at reading stories, too. It will all work out and, besides, I know how the tale ends anyway. Cinderella gets her man. It doesn't quite work that way in my life.*

"Once upon a time," began Misty, loving the familiarity of those words. By page six, both girls were fast asleep and she closed her own eyes, finding the cozy bed was having a sedating effect on her. *Mmmm, this is nice.*

She thought about similarities between Steve and the prince in the story. Handsome, check. Kind, check. Dashing, check. Easy to fall in love with. Double check. Fantasizing about fairy tales...what had her life come to?

Misty stirred. The book was resting gently against her chest; the lights in the room were blazing. She had fallen solidly asleep. *Go figure. Some dinner companion I'll make.* She lay quietly with her eyes closed. She knew the sounds of the house by now; the moans and creaks were becoming familiar to her. Whatever had woken her wasn't one of them...and there it was again.

This time she opened her eyes and listened carefully, hoping she would hear nothing. Strange sounds, for a woman alone in a house with two children, didn't fit her idea of comfort. She was gripping *Grimm's Fairy Tales* between her fingers. It was a sort of defensive weapon if lofted soundly against someone's head.

She looked at Liberty and Vivienne, who were lost in the soft repose of dreamland. Each girl had a bed of her own and a bedroom to go with it, but more often than not, the two of them fell asleep in her bed. There was a wholesome purpose for the bed of enticement that Tiz hadn't taken into account. Heartwarming family gatherings.

A ping against the window in her bedroom set her heart racing. Misty sat up, glad her daughters were sound sleepers and not disturbed by her movements.

It sounded like someone was throwing something. She eased off the bed and peeked out. Too late, she remembered the lights were still on. She was practically blinded to the outside but was quite certain she showed up like a bull's-eye in the brightly lit room.

She jumped back. *What if it's Hayward Hedges?*

It sounded like someone was calling her name. *This is weird.* She listened again. *It is my name.* This time she cupped her hands around her eyes and plastered her face to the window. She jumped when a pebble bounced off the pane in front of her.

Who in th...omigod, it's Steve. "What are you doing here?" she mouthed, moving her lips and hands like a mime.

He was laughing as he threw a handful of gravel at her. Misty shook her head and held up her finger. *Gimme a minute,* she pantomimed.

She grabbed a sweatshirt, turned off the light and went downstairs to the back door.

"What are you doing here?" she asked as she stepped outside.

"Bringing the mountain to Mohammed." He held up a bag from Dot's and a pulled a thermos from the pocket of his knap sack. "Care to dine by moonlight, madame?"

"I don't believe this. Do you have a shoe in there?"

"What?" Steve asked, a puzzled look on his face.

"Never mind." She laughed as she shut the door. "Inside joke." *Prince Charming can't touch this.*

"C'mon. Pull on that shirt and come sit down." She noticed he'd piled wood haphazardly in front of a bench.

"Do you always plan surprise visits? You don't give a girl much chance to do her hair. I might've worn a negligee if I'd had some advance warning...instead of these," she said as she pulled the sweatshirt over her head and pointed to her baggy pj pants.

"Talk about luck, eh?" He took her by the hand and escorted her to his makeshift campsite. He had draped a sleeping bag over the bench.

"Your chair, mistress." She sat down and he crouched to light the fire.

"You're too much," she said.

"I'm smitten."

"Really? I smote you?" She added two more check points to her list of princely qualities. Fun loving and imaginative.

She watched him as he tended the fire, feeling her heart soften as he went about the task. It was almost primeval the way she felt, and it affected her far more powerfully than if he'd wined and dined her at the best restaurant.

"You are a smiter of untold abilities," he continued as he poked at the wood until the flames jumped in response. "That, and the fact

I've never seen a woman rip the back out of her dress and handle it with such dignity. If I could have levitated vertically, I would have been right behind you."

"Well, since you put it that way, my bottom was flapping in the breeze." Misty laughed. *So, this is romance on The Rock. Not bad.* She had a strong urge to wrestle him to the ground, since he was halfway there anyhow.

Steve stood up, opened the thermos, and passed her the cover. Into it he poured a steaming cup of coffee. Then he took another cup out of a pocket in his jacket and poured one for himself.

"Cheers," he said as he tapped her cup. "This should warm you up faster than the fire."

It smelled delicious. "This isn't just coffee," she said a few seconds later, as the warm liquid passed over her tastebuds.

"It's better than that," explained Steve. "It's a secret family recipe for cleaning dentures."

"Oh, joy. What's in it?" He had the same funky marketing savvy as his uncle.

"Dark rum, sugar, a bit of Baileys."

She took another sip and then another. "A bit?"

"Okay, a lot. But it warms you up and it's kind of like having dessert first."

"My favourite way to do things." She smiled at him.

"Mine too."

They sat silently for a moment and watched the fire.

"Isn't that illegal or something?" Misty asked.

"What? Having a fire in your own backyard? I don't think so."

"Oh. It's nice then." And it was. Misty took another sip of Steve's brew. It warmed her almost as much as the fire. And almost as much as Steve, whose proximity was driving her core temperature into the triple digits. It was a beautiful evening, and the cool ocean breeze was keeping the usually ravenous mosquitoes away.

"You can see all the stars from Charlie's Cove." Steve pointed to the sky with his mug as if illustrating a class in astronomy. "See that constellation over there?"

Misty looked up. All she could see was the big dipper, the little dipper and a huge number of stars in no particular pattern or shape, but she lied anyway and said yes.

"I call that one Tender Moments. Doesn't it look like a mother holding a baby?"

Misty looked hard. She really wanted to see it. Steve placed his hand under her chin and moved her head slightly to the left.

"Over there," he said, pointing with the hand that held his mug; his other hand never left her face. She watched as he traced an outline against the sky. "It took me a long time to make it out first. It'll come to you eventually." He put his arm around her and pulled her closer to him.

Misty felt comfortable and warm. She and Steve fit together like two people who were made for each other. Her head nestled easily against his shoulder. He seemed to understand she needed time to adjust to the idea of someone in her life. He was pushing, but just the right amount.

Misty swore she heard a tinkle in the air, like a bell ringing. She listened again but this time only heard the crackling of the fire as sparks flew into the night like tiny rockets.

The moment was blissful. And tender. It was probably the nicest thing anyone had ever done to surprise her. If this was what love felt like, she never wanted the feeling to leave.

Just when she was thinking she had found Tender Moments, Steve kissed her and she lost all sight of the stars, except for the ones shooting off in her head.

The cool air, the warmth of his lips, the gentleness of his touch and the residue of sweet coffee made for a powerful aphrodisiac. Misty settled against him and closed her eyes. The moment was a mosaic, one sensation folding into the other, enveloping her in a sensual and electrically charged cocoon. Misty was content in a way she had seldom experienced and wished the moment could last forever.

Steve's cheeks, rough from the shadow of his beard, brushed against her skin. It was a nice sensation, the feel of a man's face close to hers. She parted her lips so he could explore her mouth more fully. The way his tongue traced her teeth was playful with just a hint of the intensity she sensed he was holding inside. It was the kiss of a man who wasn't in a hurry. The kind of man who understood, who would be willing to wait for her to be ready for more.

Misty sighed and wrapped her arms around him in return. She heard a bump as his cup hit the ground and tossed hers after it. What did it matter? It was her yard now and she could mess it up any way she wanted. And with anyone she wanted...but even more importantly, with someone who wanted her. What a lovely thought.

She relaxed into his arms as they snuggled together. And even though he held her tightly as he kissed her, the bench they were sharing was not designed for romance. As he shifted to hold her closer, and she slid to the edge of the bench to accommodate, the delicate balance they had orchestrated on the small seat was lost.

The bench teetered precariously on two legs, and then stalled in mid-air for a moment before tossing them to the ground and following behind. She was tangled between Steve, the sleeping bag, the bench, and the grass, and for once she didn't care about stains on her clothes.

"That was some kiss," he said.

"Incredible."

"Wonder what it would be like from this angle?"

"Lousy, I expect."

"You could be right." He leaned over and covered her lips with his. "But I prefer to find out for myself."

Misty reached up and pulled him closer. The kiss immediately got better.

When they fell apart, Steve rolled his head to the side and looked at her again. "I didn't like that at all. You?"

"Terrible."

They lay quietly for a moment gazing at the stars, their legs dangling over the bench like goosenecks. Somehow his hand had found hers and their fingers had gently entwined.

"Do you like it here?" she asked him. She didn't know where to begin the conversation. What do you say to a guy you barely know, especially when you're lying nostril to nostril in the grass, to say nothing about having kissed him in ways that would revise Merriam-Webster's definition of foreplay. Talking about Charlie's Cove seemed as good a subject as any.

"Sometimes it's a relief to be here," Steve said after giving her question some thought. "Half the time I'm beating myself out in Toronto, working six or seven days a week, some nights."

"Toronto?" An awful feeling settled in the pit of Misty's stomach. "I thought you lived here."

"Toronto's where I grew up and until I came here for a visit, it was all I knew. You get used to a city. Coming here is like a whole new world for me."

"So you live in Toronto and here?" Misty tried to conceal the anxiety in her voice. This was not at all what she wanted to hear. The whole night had been perfect, just perfect, and now he's from Toronto?

"Kind of. I go back and forth, but mostly back. I'm a partner in a practice there but I've also been helping Uncle Lar. I kind of like it in Charlie's Cove, though. It's different, you know."

"I know exactly what you mean," she replied, feeling a protective wall falling into place around her heart. And if Steve wasn't around, it would be really different. She had thought...well, hoped, really... maybe dreamed was the better way to put it...that he would be part of her life here. She couldn't explain even to herself why she was so willing to take this chance again, but she was, and that realization left her feeling so vulnerable. *Why does it have to be like this? Sweet Jesus, Toronto might as well be a million miles away.* She looked at him and tried to hide the anguish that had washed over her. It was too late now to be wishing she had kept her mouth for kissing instead of talking.

"What are you thinking?" he asked.

Misty hesitated, not sure what to say. *I'm going to miss you. Please don't leave. I need to find out if this is right.* Thoughts stampeded through her mind, but she was afraid to voice them. She desperately wanted reassurance, but since she already had her big fat mouth open, there was one other thing she might as well cover. She looked away and focused on the sky and the stars, which no longer seemed to sparkle. "Think you'll stay here?" she asked quietly. She felt as though she already knew the answer.

"That's a loaded question. I have a lot of commitments back home. It's not so easy to pick up and move anymore. I was lucky to get some time off this year and I took advantage of it. What about you?"

What about me? How could he be so nonchalant after what they'd just experienced? You don't just kiss a girl to her knees and then talk about Toronto like it's no big deal. She took a mental eraser and started rubbing out checkmarks. Prince: 10. Steve: 0. Well, maybe one for kissing, but that was all she was giving him.

"Cat got your tongue?"

Oh, give me strength. I thought you had it. She rolled to her side, slipped her hand out from his and rested her head on it. "Things aren't the best for me right now," she began hesitantly. "I've been through a lot this past year and I'm trying to get things right for once. The kids need some stability, too. Their father left me in a bad situation."

"He was a fool, then. To do that to you. I could never hurt someone I loved like that, much less my children."

Well, in case you haven't noticed, you're doing a good job of hurting me right now. Misty felt tears mounting behind her lids and forced them back. Reluctantly, she gave him another check. This time for gallantry and honesty. *Why couldn't he live here like everyone else?* When he said these things to her, she wanted to lie in his arms forever. There was no rational explanation for the way she was feeling about a man she'd only recently met, but Steve had had a profound impact on her. And if she was honest, it was more than profound; she was also half out of her mind with lust. What did she expect, rolling in the grass with him like she was a teenager? That hardly qualified for love. But then again, maybe that's the way love ought to be.

Steve took her hand again and pulled her toward him.

If he tries to kiss me again, I'm going to— Damn. She had no willpower whatsoever around this man.

This time when they came up for air, Misty felt even more confused.

"Think you can stand up?" Steve was smiling now. "I may need some help. I have a serious case of tight pants." Misty rolled her eyes, secretly pleased and hoping he would suffer for hours.

They wriggled and rolled, and finally disengaged themselves from each other and the sleeping bag and stood up. He took her into his arms again. "I guess dinner's cold." He gestured to the brown paper bag from Dot's Fish and Chips. "Dot's fare isn't too appetizing when it's not eaten right away. We can try again, you know. When I get back."

"Get back?" *Is he ever going to stop? A blow to the heart, then one to the head to finish me off?*

"My office called after we got off the phone. My partner was in an accident and I've got to fly home in the morning."

It took a minute for the information to sink in. This wasn't about her. "Was he badly hurt?"

"I'm not sure. He was on his bike when a car struck him. His arm is broken and his wrist shattered and that's bad enough. He's still in the hospital, maybe with a concussion. He most definitely won't be back to work for a while."

Life was cruel. She felt bad for Steve and his partner, but she also felt bad for herself, though she didn't like to admit it. It was rather shallow of her to be so selfish, given what Steve must be feeling. "I guess we can stay in touch."

"Misty, I haven't felt like this about someone for a long time. I know we've only just met but…"

"I hate that word," she said as she interrupted him.

"What word?"

"But. I'll miss you *but*…I'll think of you *but*…It must be the worst word in the English language. Steve, I've got two kids. I'm not ready to rush into anything, *but* I'm standing here with my heart in my throat and feel like I've lived every emotion I know in the course of an hour. Do you have any idea what that's like?"

He looked at her and she felt as though he was seeing into her very soul. This time her tears did slip past the gates. She wiped at her eyes, embarrassed that she was crying but even more horrified that she had told him the truth about how vulnerable she was feeling.

"I've made you cry. I'm sorry, Misty. I didn't mean to upset you; it's just that I really find you so beautiful—beautiful and full of life." He took her into his arms. "I know it's kind of fast and I probably shouldn't have said anything, and I wouldn't have if I didn't have to leave tomorrow. I'm sorry." He pressed his hand against the back of her neck and cradled her head against his chest.

She wasn't sure she could take much more of this. Her heart wasn't up to the task. Here was the first decent man she'd met in months, a man whose very presence left her feeling breathless, and now he was leaving. "You'll be back?" she asked, with just a touch of hopefulness in her voice.

"As soon as I can. I just don't know when right now."

"I guess that's why you came over. To deliver the news." Reality descended again like a heavy black drapery.

"I could have used the phone for that. I came over because I really wanted to see you," Steve replied. "We've gotten off to a rough start, haven't we?" He kissed her again.

"It's not your fault. We never planned to feel like this. I know I didn't and I'm not even sure I'm ready to handle it. Maybe fate is conspiring to keep us apart."

"Well, fate has met its match because I'm planning to see you again." He checked his watch. "I know this sounds rather melodramatic, but I really do have to get moving. My flight leaves St. John's at five a.m."

"See? There it is again. *But*. But you do have to go." She shook her head in frustration.

Steve laughed. "Even in the most tragic of circumstances, you are like an infusion of...of...raw energy." He grabbed her in his arms and swung her around. "I feel as though I'm being drawn in like a moth to a flame."

"Très romantic. Not that I care for the image, but I feel a bit like a moth myself. Could you please put my feet back on the ground?" *Fat chance of that, the way I'm feeling.*

He set her down and she helped him kick dirt over the dying fire, taking out some of her frustrations with it. The flames died and even though the embers continued to glow, it was as if a light went out of the evening.

Misty stopped and looked up at the sky again. "I can see it," she cried out. "There." She pointed toward a clump of stars.

"I told you. Now you've found it, the sky will never look the same again. Things have shifted."

"Yes, they have," she replied feeling that with complete certainty. Things had changed very much.

Steve took her hand again and walked her to the door. They were both quiet, the reality of their situation squeezing uncomfortably between them like an unwelcome guest.

"Shifting can be a good thing," Steve said finally.

Misty nodded in agreement.

"I'll call you," he said.

"Please do." In her heart, she wanted to hear from him more than anything else she could think of.

"I will be back, you know." He wrapped her in his arms again. "And I can still see the same stars in Toronto that you see here. Only not as well. You'll have to describe them to me. In great detail. Take all night if you want."

"You fool. I have to sleep sometimes." She was glad the mood had lightened. It was easier to say good-bye like this.

"Stock up on it now. I'm in your future, Misty, and I'm counting on being around to keep you awake. Goodnight." He gave her a gentle kiss on her cheek. "But not good-bye." He pressed his finger to her lips as she stared to object to that word. "Shhhh."

She watched as he walked away and picked up the bench and the sleeping bag and put them into the back of his SUV. He turned and blew her a kiss as he got into the vehicle and headed down the lane. She didn't go in until his taillights disappeared around the side of her house.

Saying good-bye was getting to be a way of life. She wasn't sure how much more her heart could take. What kind of luck did she have? A great guy, no apparent aversion to children, and he's from Toronto. She felt as though she had won and lost the lottery all in one evening. What were the odds? She sighed and leaned against the door.

There was an awful ache in her chest; it felt as though her heart was breaking as memories and new feelings collided inside of her. *I'm not the only one doing the smiting,* she thought. *That man could smite the heart out of the wicked witch.*

Is it possible to fall in love this fast? I've only just met this man and already I'm developing my own fairy tale. Insanity might be the best way to put it...but if this is insanity, it sure has its good points.

She closed the door and flipped the deadbolt. Even the Brothers Grimm would have a challenge putting a happy ending on this one.

CHAPTER 13

A Shot in the Plexus

Getting her head into her work after an evening with Steve wasn't easy. Every second she was breathing he was in her thoughts, which pretty much took up all her available thinking time. It was lovely and great to feel this way, but it was taking a serious toll on her ability to concentrate.

She promised herself she would put him out of her mind for the next few hours and then, only a few minutes later, caught herself pondering whether or not he might call. She was hopeless. It was going to take a miracle if she were to get her mind on her work.

Fortunately, the miracle this morning came in the form of none other than Phonse.

"Muldoon," he yelled looking up from his computer.

Misty jumped. "What?"

"I bees looking in my inbox here and mother of surprises, the jeasley thing is empty. Empty. What day is it Muldoon?"

"Thursday."

"How many days 'til Tuesday?"

"Five."

"Just checkin' to see if you knew." He snorted. "You looks like a lovesick puppy. I seen that look before. Don't be getting sloppy on me, Muldoon. You wants to get paid, then sit that boney arse down and write."

He had the nerve to smile at her then. Like he was doing her a favour. There was no way he could possibly know about Steve, was there? No one had any idea except maybe Ruby, and with Misty's luck, she and Phonse were probably related.

She felt her temper flare. That...that surly old curmudgeon. He had no business watching her like that, much less commenting on her production. Had she let him down yet? Was she going to? No, by golly, she wasn't.

With some effort, she put him out of her mind and finished up two stories faster than she would have thought possible. The first was on the paperboy scandal that had rocked the community, and another was on the fifteenth anniversary of Hatty's Restaurant. One thing she could say for Charlie's Cove— there was always news of one kind or another.

Imagine a place the size of this running a Ponzi scheme? But a couple of keen young carriers who had found the story of Charles Ponzi in a book at the library had been inspired to use his ideas as a way to supplement their paltry wages and tips.

For paying ten dollars upfront, they offered their customers an opportunity to get a full year of papers. The problem was the boys didn't have a steady stream of new customers to pull it off and they ended up stealing back the papers they'd just delivered to take them to neighbours up the road.

During the few weeks the scheme was ongoing, everyone thought they had a severe case of absentmindedness and it wasn't until Myrtle Bartlett walked out of the shower stark naked and caught young

Wince Barker in her bedroom with the paper stuffed down his pants that it all blew apart.

Good thing for Wince, too, that he had the paper down his pants.

Myrtle thought he was there to ravage her, and started whacking him in the crotch with her walking cane.

Wince called the fire department for help himself and were it not for the ill-fated paper, would have been ruined. As it was, he had a hard time walking straight for days. The story still brought tears to Misty's eyes every time she thought of it.

"Hey, Phonse," Misty called across the newsroom as she hit the send button. "What's the headline going to be for Wince Barker's story? 'Myrtle Whacks Wince'?"

"Shut up, Muldoon. I needs quiet for me creativity. However, if telling you would stog your gob, I'm thinking about, 'Myrtle Barlett Exposes It All'." Phonse grinned from ear to ear. "And stay out of headlines, Muldoon. That's my affair."

"What if you get sick one day?" Misty asked. As if he wasn't perpetually sick. In the head.

"There's not a day this pecker hasn't been working. Wanna test it?"

"Give it up, Phonse. You couldn't test a glass of water with that. Wouldn't be long enough." She was getting good at this. "Seriously, if you're sick, can I do it?"

"Like I says, Muldoon, won't happen." And he turned back to his work. A short time later he got up and went to the bathroom. How did she know this? Phonse always farted first. A form of propulsion, perhaps, but it also did wonders to curb any illusion of Phonse having even one iota of sex appeal in his genetic makeup.

Misty fumed for a few minutes about Phonse and his piggish attitude. She fantasized about bringing him a plate of brownies laced with Ex-Lax, then decided that wouldn't be the right thing to do. And it wouldn't solve her current dilemma anyway, which was far more pertinent than daydreaming about ways to derail him.

He was right about one thing—the weekend was looming and she needed another story. She'd called just about everyone and she was still flat out of ideas. Would anyone really know if she made something up? The idea struck her as ridiculously funny and she laughed out loud. This was Charlie's Cove. Everyone knew everything. Even the stuff they didn't dare put in writing.

"Misty?" Tilly called to her through the newsroom door. "You got a visitor. Send him in?"

"Who?" Misty asked. *Maybe Steve didn't leave after all.* She felt a sudden rush of energy and grabbed the lipstick she kept in her desk drawer.

"No idea." Tilly shrugged.

Tilly never asked for anyone's name or took messages for that matter. It was so frustrating. What she was doing out front was a matter for contemplation. Misty figured that branch of the family must have something good on Phonse. It had to be blackmail. She couldn't see any other reason why he would keep Tilly employed.

"Well, send him in," said Misty impatiently. She crossed her fingers. It was possible, she told herself.

Misty sighed when she saw a short wiry man enter the room. Working here was like being cast in a soap opera. You never knew what was coming up next, but you could be sure it encompassed at least one of three elements: hunting, sex, or eating. From the look of this guy, she hoped it wasn't sex.

"Whoo-eee. So you're what Phonse Penney's got tucked up his sleeve these days."

She stood up. "I don't believe I know you, Mr..."

"Sharpe. Avery Sharpe. Editor-in-chief of the *Hicky Harbour Blarney*." Sharpe looked around furtively. "Where's Penney?"

"In the bathroom."

He seemed pleased with that information and after shaking her hand, made himself comfortable in the chair in front of her desk.

"I'll get right to the point, Mrs. Muldoon. We could use a writer like you at *The Blarney*."

"I...ah..." Misty was speechless.

"I understands your surprise. I been following your stuff in *The Yarn* and I likes it. Whatever Phonse is paying you, I'll give you two dollars more. And an expense account. Bet you don't have one of those, now do you?" He leaned forward and placed his hands on her desk. "Whadda ya say?"

"I...ah..."

"And a gas allowance."

"Mr. Sharpe. This is great. But I can't make a decision like this right now. I mean, it sounds interesting and all that. Where is Hicky Harbour? Exactly, I mean." Misty had heard of it, like she'd heard of a hundred other nearby communities, but she hadn't had time to do much exploring of the coastline.

"Twenty minutes up the road."

"And you have your own paper?"

"We bees three times the size of Charlie's Cove."

Misty looked around anxiously, expecting Phonse to walk back in anytime. It was uncomfortable to be discussing alternate venues of employment in the very place she was employed. "Look, Mr. Sharpe. I don't know what to say. It's an interesting offer and I'd have to think about it, I guess. Could you leave me a card? I could get back to you."

Sharpe pulled a card out of his pocket and passed it across the desk to her. "Me personal line. Call that when you thinks about it."

He stood up. So did Misty. It was about eating, after all, she decided. Defined as a sudden and inexplicable offer to further her career and bolster her finances.

"Have a good day now and I expects to hear from you soon, Mrs. Muldoon. And I'll throw in a load of firewood, too," he added as he turned to leave. Misty watched him cross the room. He was a fast mover. In every way.

She sat back down. Well, more like dropped into her chair. Totally floored. Imagine. More money, an expense account, a gas allowance. Was she really that goo...

"Sleeveen!" Phonse Penney screeched.

Misty came out of her daze. *Oh, shit.* Sly and deceitful, Avery Sharpe might be all that, but when Phonse called someone a sleeveen it was even more insulting than the insult, if such a thing could be. There was a crash in front reception and she raced to the door. This wasn't going to go smoothly.

Phonse held Avery Sharpe in a headlock and was pummeling him with his fist. Avery was kicking Phonse in the legs. They covered the room in a tight circle.

"Oh, my," said Misty. "Stop." She ran over to the two men and grabbed Phonse's arm. "Call someone, Tilly. Hurry up."

A solid jab in the gut from Phonse knocked the wind out of her. She released his arm and dropped to the floor where she rolled over on her side, gasping for air. So intense was the ruckus between him and Avery, he didn't even seem to be aware that he had socked her in the gut.

From her vantage point on the floor she could see both men's feet. Avery seemed to be winning. He was darting at Phonse's legs like a jackhammer.

"Take your jeesley sleeveening out of my building, you skinny little maggot," Phonse yelled.

"Screw you, Penney," said Sharpe. "You keep your slimy paper outta my market." He had pulled Phonse's shirt out of his pants, leaving his gut exposed and vulnerable. Misty hoped she could block the sight from her memory.

"Screw your market," said Phonse. "They wants it, they buys it."

"Cheap bugger. I wants her."

"She's mine, you maggot."

"Two dollars more."

"Three, you little pervert."

"Expense account," wheezed Sharpe.

"Monthly allowance, you pimple."

They had moved to the door.

"Gas allowance," yelled Sharpe as they smashed into the glass.

"Tires and gas," countered Phonse.

"Wood," said Sharpe.

"An oil furnace, you little twerp."

Sharpe crashed through the door. By now Misty was back on her feet. Phonse kicked the rest of the glass out of the door over Sharpe.

"Now, get the hell off my property before I calls the cops." He raised his fist at Sharpe. "Rodent!" he yelled as a final jab.

Avery Sharpe stood up and gave Phonse the finger. As he brushed glass off most of his body parts, there wasn't a drop of blood visible anywhere.

"Shove it, Penney." He gave Phonse another finger for good measure and took his sweet time walking over to his car. He got in, backed out and drove away.

Misty was dumbfounded. She'd seen it happen. She'd heard it happen. She even had a damn sore solar plexus to prove it.

"Phonse," she said.

"Shut the fuck up, Muldoon. You works for me. And don't you forget it." He turned to Tilly, who hadn't moved at all, much less called for backup. "Get Coot Sanger on the phone. I needs another new door."

Another, thought Misty. *Another?*

It took about two days for the new office door to arrive. A bit longer for her new furnace and not much more for her True-Treads and gas card.

All in all, Avery's attempt to steal her away from Phonse resulted in a bountiful promotion, and she was almost inclined to send him a thank-you card. God knows, a sleeveen of that calibre probably didn't get many of them. In the end she decided it might be wiser to keep Avery on standby, just in case Phonse ever turned on her and she really did need another option.

Instead, with the extra money on her paycheque, she and the girls went shopping at Tizzard's for a new TV.

Twelve easy installments was, apparently, an ongoing plan and no one had to know she secretly called her new Toshiba the Avery.

CHAPTER 14

You Bees the One

Phonse's outbreak had resulted in one other piece of good fortune. In desperation for a third story, she had resurrected her idea for a column. And Phonse had gone with it.

As she glanced down at the copy of *The Yarn* on her desk, she admired the way her header looked. **Misty's Misadventures**. Phonse had even put her picture next to it. *How often,* she thought, *does desperation give birth to bold and reckless ideas?*

She scrutinized her work. It wasn't all that unusual to see her words in print. What was different this time was that it was her opinion that counted. Not some inane press release for a bio-solids facility making human fertilizer. Uh-uh. This was her own brand of fertilizer. Misty manure.

She uttered a silent prayer to the Goddess of Creative Shit with a conditional clause that she would produce the ideas if the column would take root and grow. This was her baby, after all, and to heck with ego, she couldn't resist reading it one more time...

Misty's Misadventures

By

Misty Muldoon

For those of you who don't know me, I'm Misty. I was named for a weather pattern on the east coast of Newfoundland and even though my family had a rather strange sense of humour, I've come to love my name and forgive them for their mischief.

In my first column, I'm going to open my heart about a lot of things, including my feelings about coming back to The Rock, this exotic island perched precariously on the North American shelf of the cool Atlantic Ocean.

Since moving to Charlie's Cove, the folks I've met have made me feel better about myself than I have for a long, long time. So good, in fact, I'm ashamed to admit my favourite view of Newfoundland once was the one in my rear-view mirror. That's true. I couldn't wait to grow up and leave this island.

I believe many of you will have family members under the same impression that things are better on the other side of the Cabot Strait.

After all, there has been a steady stream of people relocating to Ontario, Alberta, British Columbia, and even Maine, Massachusetts, and Florida for as long as I can remember. New York skyscrapers were built by Newfoundlanders who scaled them without fear or vertigo. Even my grandmother travelled to Boston to visit relatives way back then, and I've managed to forage some of those ties to long-forgotten branches of the family in northern Maine.

As Newfoundlanders, we are very skilled at leaving our homes and sadly, not nearly as adept in coming back. "Newfies" you'll meet on the streets of Toronto always speak fondly of home and rattle on about all that they miss. And when they get a chance, a break from the reality that is their life away, they come to visit, to pitch down and show off their riches, while secretly longing for the simplicity of the life that is and always will be Newfoundland. And then there are others like me who do come back, reluctantly so, because life hasn't been kind.

Since I'm opening my heart to you, I may as well explain. I'm a divorced single mom of two beautiful young daughters. Like anyone else, I've had some disappointments in the past and foolishly thought coming to Charlie's Cove was one of them. I arrived here with a carload of worldly possessions and an attitude that could only be described as "poor." And what did I find? A home waiting for me, albeit a fixer-upper, and oodles of people willing to give me a chance, even when I was ungrateful.

Thank you. Each and every one of you. This experience has renewed my faith in me, in the kindness of strangers, and maybe even in the strangeness of discovering people who still live simply and understand what it takes to make a community a home.

Coming back is a worthy goal and even though I've made a few mistakes since my arrival, (which I prefer to call *misadventures*), I'm willing to share my experiences with other Newfoundlanders who can't make it home this year, or next. And just maybe it will inspire them to book that ticket, plan that reunion, and make it happen.

I've seen license plates from Florida, Georgia, and many other states since my arrival and these folks are buying up homes here. Our coast is on the verge of becoming a multicultural smorgasbord that also includes Europeans craving our less-congested streets and towns, our robust wilderness, and rugged beauty. Even if we forget, they realize the value of an unlocked door and neighbours who wave good morning.

And if anyone tries to tell you there's nothing to do here, knock them upside the head for me, will you? Because even having time here, just free time... is to be cherished. I may remain a bit awkward, steeped as I am in my fast-paced ways, but hey, I'm starting to figure it out and I'm ready to share. If you're ready to be reminded, keep reading because there will be plenty more Misadventures in the weeks ahead.

Until next time,

Misty

Her column lifted her spirits. She liked it. And even better? Everyone else liked it, too. Even Phonse was whistling Dixie these days. Sales were up and he was looking at her with the kind of affection that left her feeling as though she were a stuffed partridge at Christmas dinner.

"Hey, you."

Misty looked up from her keyboard.

"Stinky Pelly called. Says to tell you he's sorry."

Misty loved these little moments with herself and couldn't hide her disappointment when Tilly interrupted as she so often did these days.

"Stinky called?"

Tilly's long dark hair was pulled back into a tight ponytail. Her face was full, with just a hint of the bone structure beneath.

"Yeah, to say he's sorry."

"Did he want to speak with me?"

"Nope. Just told me to make sure you gets the message and to tell Skylene he called if you sees her. So that's what I'm at, delivering it."

"Okay. Great. Thanks." Misty poised her hands over her keyboard. When Tilly didn't leave, she looked up expectantly. Tilly was a clash of Walmart and online shopping, even attractive when she took care with her appearance or smiled, which she wasn't doing at the moment. "Is there anything else?" Misty asked.

"I read your column this morning."

"Okay." Misty wondered where this was leading.

"You really feels that way, do you?"

If Misty had missed the animosity in Tilly's voice, one look at the way her arm fisted on her hip supplied more than enough information to make Misty uneasy. "Yeah," Misty replied carefully, "I really do feel that way." She paused before continuing. "But I'm not sure that's what you're really asking. You want to know if I'm sincere? Is that it?"

"Maybe."

"Well, yes. I'm speaking from my heart. Everyone here has been great. With a couple of exceptions. You know, like Hayward, but he's all right in his own way as long as he leaves me alone."

Tilly continued to stare at her. "I kind of thought you might be just saying those things because it's what people likes to hear. Makes 'em feel good."

Misty was surprised Tilly would think such a thing. If nothing, Misty was as good as her word. What she said counted to her and was a reflection of her feelings. She wouldn't lie about that; she'd had enough deception to last her a lifetime and then some. "If you don't mind, I've got some work to finish up."

A dark cast settled over Tilly's face. Misty pushed her chair back from her desk, instinctively moving away from an energy that felt surprisingly volatile and negative.

Tilly leaned over and planted her hands on the desk. Misty was momentarily distracted by the plunging view of her ample bosom, thinking it was much more of her co-worker than she wanted to see. She edged her chair back a little farther, sensing Tilly was about to blow.

"You comes sailing in here, like a schooner with a broken keel, and everyone's lining up to fix you. And now you can't do nothing wrong." Tilly slammed Misty with a burst of energy that felt like a miniature nuclear explosion. "All everybody's talkin' 'bout around here is *you*. Like you dropped from heaven or something. But I knows different. You don't mean none of this." She grabbed Misty's copy of *The Yarn*, tore it into two pieces and threw it on the floor. "It's a load of hooey and everyone's fallin' for it. But not me." She jabbed her chest with her finger before she turned the finger on Misty. Tilly's red-tipped forefinger was an awesome weapon, and Misty compressed her neck into her shoulders, providing the smallest target in case it went off accidentally. Fortunately, Tilly holstered it on her hip and continued. "I knows I'm right. I seen operators like you before. You cares about us as long as it's convenient to you and when you gets what you wants, you're outta here on the next tide. What a lot of shit."

Unprepared for Tilly's attack, for a moment Misty said nothing. But then her brain clicked in about the same time as her tongue, and, fortunately, before Tilly had a chance to launch at her again. "How dare you say that? You don't know the first thing about me. We've hardly had one conversation since I started here." Her response was just another opener for Tilly.

"That's right. You don't got time to be talkin' to the people who does all your clean up. You're too busy sucking up to everyone else who can help you get a career and then you're outta here."

"What gives you the impression I'm leaving? And furthermore, I don't see you working so hard." Her words lacked the impact she'd hoped for, and she felt rather let down by her pathetic attempt to redeem herself, not that Tilly was listening anyway. She'd already formed her opinion and managed to brilliantly knock Misty on her ass.

"My life was good here before you come around. Uncle Phonse never expected much from this paper and left me alone to do my job."

"You mean your nails, don't you?" Misty snapped back. "Because I've never seen much evidence of you doing your so-called job."

"A proper snot, you are. You needs to leave here and go back to Nova Scotia. You don't care about us. You might fool Uncle Phonse, but you don't fool me. *Oooo, Phonsie,*" she mimicked as she minced around in a circle. "*Do you really like it?* What a crock."

"Really?" *Shut up. Shut up. Shut up.* But, of course, she ignored her own advice and lashed out at Tilly once again. "Yeah? Well, at least the blood reaches my brain, which is more than I can say for you."

"Listen up, when you're built like me, you don't need a brain."

Misty raised her eyebrows and looked at Tilly in wonderment. "You said it, honey, not me. I'm in total agreement. You don't need one and I venture to say, don't have…"

"I got a brain all right," Tilly snapped, not losing any ground. "For your information, someone named Steve called but I didn't get a number. I was too busy taking new subscriptions for your crappy column. Screw you." She gave Misty the finger as she huffed out of the room.

"Yeah, well, screw you back," Misty yelled after her. Amazing. Totally amazing. How could she have missed it? All this time, while she was thinking she was doing such a good thing for everyone, Tilly was building a bazooka of resentment aimed directly at her.

Misty slumped in her chair as she came down from the adrenaline rush of her interchange with Tilly. She sure as hell didn't deserve this from Tilly or anyone, for that matter. Maybe there were other people feeling much like Tilly, thinking she was using her situation and them to climb out of a hole. The thought made her feel quite uncomfortable.

Blindsided by a bimbo.

Unless, of course, Tilly was right. What if she was doing exactly what Tilly accused her of? *No way.* She didn't have any plans to leave, not at the moment. And if her life turned around, she should have to feel bad about that? This was jealousy. Plain and simple. At least, that's what the left side of her cranium told her. And the right? The side that just maybe knew what lay deep in her subconscious? What if everything she did was geared to finding a way out once she recovered financially and emotionally? Would she really want to stay in Charlie's Cove? What if Steve were here? Would she feel differently then?

Steve! She had completely forgotten what Tilly had said. He had called. And she didn't have a number to call him back. Totally ludicrous and totally Tilly.

Screw Tilly, to hell with blue-eyed dentists. Her first concern ought to be survival and if that meant a few hurt feelings and.... She stopped. It wasn't Tilly's hurt feelings she was worried about. No, she was tending to her own bruises here. Bruises to her ego and her heart. And they weren't fresh ones. Tilly may have stirred things up but the bruises she was feeling had been with her since Jake left and her business failed. Was it worth it to open herself up to hurt again? Maybe she should just give up and...and...what?

There was no option. She thought of Liberty and Vivienne, her two very precious daughters. They deserved better than a mother who crumpled at the first sign of adversity. And they'd have it, too.

She'd write another column and she hoped it would give Tilly plenty to fume about. Misty grabbed the phone book and looked up

Skylene's number. If Tilly thought she could push Misty Muldoon around and intimidate her, she had a lot to learn. And so did Steve, for being dumb enough not to leave her his number in the first place. Misty felt certain she had healed at least one bruise today. And no one needed to make any judgments on her. She'd handle that all by herself. What she was doing was trying to make a life, and that really was no one's business but hers.

On her third attempt, Misty reached Skylene. Skylene's line had been busy for an hour straight, and Misty's coffee was long gone along with one of her fingernails.

"Skylene, this is…"

"I been wantin' to talk to you," Skylene interrupted.

Maybe this was a bad idea after all. Misty didn't think she could take another attack on her integrity in one day. She hesitated and a space was apparently all Skylene needed to get started. Thankfully, what Misty heard was a great deal better than she expected.

"Stinky's after askin' me to marry him and I blames you. I needs marriage like I needs a pet lobster."

Skylene could fit a lot of words into the space of two seconds. But at least she was reasonably friendly, so Misty plunged on. "I thought you and Stinky have been together for a long time. What would be wrong with marriage?"

"I never minds sleepin' with him but as far as being an opportunity for him to stop workin', not friggin' likely."

Misty was lost. "What, he can't work if you get married? What's he got? Some disease?"

"You catches on quick for a born again. We gets married, he'll get cant'zer faster than you guts a fish."

"Cancer? Stinky has cancer?" There was something vulnerable about Stinky that stirred her motherly instincts. Surely nothing was wrong with him. She certainly hoped not.

"He will if I marries him," she said. "Cant'zer the phone. Cant'zer the door. And definitely, cant'zer a job ad. I knows a situation when I sees one, Misty. Marriage. Right."

Misty stifled a laugh. Skylene was talking about that aversion to regular full-time employment so many of the island's men were known for. The one that interfered with moose hunting and rabbit snaring. Stinky was seasonal. The original playboy.

Pansy had told Misty that seasonal work was a lifestyle for many families, and the men weren't entirely to blame. They were just adapting to an environment that provided plenty of work at certain times of year and at others, pathetically little. So they filled their days with other stuff. It was just that the other stuff sometimes became entirely too enjoyable and the work ethic suffered. Either way, it didn't make for an easy life.

"But what about now?" Misty asked.

"He gets off his lazy duff and looks after hisself."

"And it works for you."

"Girlfriend, ain't no one messing wit dat."

It was strange to hear sitcom lingo peppered with Newfinese. Television was changing the world in ways it shouldn't. "Are all the boys like Stinky?" Misty asked.

"Until they grows up, and that takes varyin' amounts of time. Some never does. They goes away and works and then they comes back and redevelops cant'zer."

And then there was Stinky, she figured, who preferred to stay in Newfoundland and make do. She could understand why Skylene might be resentful. The situation wasn't inspired entirely by fiction; it was just human nature at work.

"You've cleared up a lot of things I've been wondering about."

"That's a fact. They calls me Oprah at times. Now, I needs you to do me a favour," said Skylene.

"Sure, anything," said Misty, still feeling indebted to Skylene for putting her back in tune with the way things worked around the bay.

"I wants you to go out with Stinky."

"What? No. Absolutely, no...I can't. Me and dating are not happening anytime soon." And besides, she could recognize an isosceles love triangle when it punched her in the chops.

There were two equal sides and two equal angles here. Stinky and Skylene were holding their own. Provide the third angle? Excuse me, was there an "ie" at the end of her name? No. There was a "y". Misty with an "ie" might do that sort of thing. But Misty with a "y"? Never.

She held her breath as she waited for Skylene to respond. It took a while.

"You leaves me in a difficult spot." Skylene's rattle had slowed down to a more decipherable speed.

"But, Skylene, this isn't about me." Misty struggled for something meaningful to say. "Stinky's your guy, not mine."

"And I loves the little bugger," she admitted.

"I've never been a maid of honour," said Misty. *Where did that come from?*

"You hasn't?" Skylene perked up again.

"I hasn't," Misty replied, cringing as she did so.

"I'll get back to you, what?"

"You call your man, Skylene. I bet he can get over his cant'zer."

"Ya thinks?"

"I thinks."

"Dat's it then. I wants you, Misty."

"What?"

"Yeah, I wants you. You're it. When I marries Stinky, you bees my number-one maid of honour." She hung up.

Oh, sweet dancing Jesus. Being named for a weather pattern was one thing, but creating one? Mistie with an ie jumped up from her desk. Phonse chose just that moment to walk into the room and she looked at him much as a drowning sailor seeks a life raft. "Oh, my God, do they have big weddings in the outports?"

"Big?" he said, a broad grin transforming his face. "They goes on for days."

CHAPTER 15

Getting Personal

Misty had just walked in the door. The phone was ringing and Tilly wasn't behind her desk. Maybe that wasn't by accident, but Misty really didn't care. Tilly wasn't someone she could avoid and she wasn't about to let last week's outburst make her feel unwanted. She'd manage and Tilly could figure out her own path. The phone continued to ring and Misty reached across Tilly's desk and answered it. "*The Yarn*," she said as she sat down on the edge of the desk.

"You don't sound too excited. Sorry if I caught you at a bad time."

"Steve?"

"The one and only. Did you get my messages? I never heard back from you and I was beginning to think you didn't want to hear from me."

Messages?

"Only one last week. And Tilly conveniently forgot to take down your number." Tilly's resentment was going to be a concern if she continued filtering Misty's calls. "There are some problems at the office," she explained to Steve. "Since my column took off, Tilly's questioned my ethics and she's fed up with the increased workload. Could be she's working to rule. Her own ones." Misty laughed. Just talking to Steve made her feel light-hearted and joyous. There was something about him she couldn't deny; he was exactly the type of man she imagined in her life. Only he wasn't. He was too damned far away for that.

"Up here we fire that kind of person."

"Would that I could. She's Phonse's niece. Better chance of me being fired than her."

"I wouldn't think so, but maybe nepotism is alive and well in Charlie's Cove. How are you?"

"Slightly bruised from Tilly's temperament but basically busy. You?"

"Lonely."

The breath left her body as though she had been punched in the stomach. He had said the one word that immediately put her heart in a vice. She was more caught up in this than she wanted to be and it was hopeless, really. "How can you be lonely in a city of millions?" she asked, hoping for the right answer from him.

"What do you think?"

"You miss me?"

"And the lady wins the prize. Don't you miss me?"

Steve's way of getting to the point brought a flush to her cheeks. She wasn't used to being so open with her feelings. She hesitated. "Kind of."

"You're not seeing anyone else, are you?"

Good God. "No."

"Plan to?"

"No."

"So you do miss me."

"That was sneaky. Yes, I do miss you." She was smiling, beaming really, and acting like a woman in love. But, truthfully, it wasn't so bad to admit how she felt. She couldn't protect her heart forever.

"Why don't you come up for the weekend?" he said.

"You're crazy. I can't do that."

"Why not?"

"The girls, for one thing."

"Pansy's reliable."

"Money."

"I'll pay."

"Ohhh," she sighed. "It's not that easy. I can't just up and go. I have my work."

"You can write on the plane and email it back."

"No laptop."

"I'll buy you one."

"You don't take no for an answer, do you?"

"Now you're getting to know me. How about it?"

"I'll think on it. Why don't you fly down here? It might be easier."

"I have to work."

"Well, what would be the point of me being there? I'd only distract you."

"Yes, and your point?"

"Stop it," she laughed. "You make it sound so easy."

"It can be if you just stop putting up roadblocks."

"Muldoon!" screeched Phonse. "Muldoon!"

"Who's that?" said Steve.

"Phonse."

"I know Penney can be loud, but how do you put with that?"

"I've started wearing earplugs," said Misty.

"Get your ass off my desk," said Tilly, coming out of the newsroom with a coffee in her hand. The past week had been like working in a minefield, and Tilly's manner toward her was getting worse by the day.

Tilly swaggered to her desk as though she owned the place and Misty wondered if she might be the reason behind Phonse's current outburst. "And take this with you." She passed Misty the morning edition. "Fresh off the press."

"Hold on." Misty put her hand over the receiver. "What's his problem this morning?" she said to Tilly, not really expecting an answer. "Did you…"

"Page fourteen," she replied, a self-satisfied smile on her face.

"Page fourteen? Oh, the personals. Wha…" said Misty but she was cut off when Phonse yelled again.

She put the phone back to her ear.

"Misty? Are you all right?" asked Steve.

"I'm fine. It's only page fourteen," she said by way of explanation.

"Page fourteen? You know, I'm going to need a subscription to the paper to keep up with your life."

"Phonse is a pussy, really. I can handle him but I do have to get off the phone."

"Can I call you later?"

"Tonight would be good. You still have my home number?" she asked as softly as she could, knowing Tilly was listening to every word. "I may need a sympathetic ear."

"You'd better believe I have your number. In every way. Look, think about what I said. Okay?"

"I will. Promise."

"Until then, I'll be missing you." Steve blew a kiss into the phone. It was cute. Misty blew a kiss back as she hung up.

"Who was that?" Tilly asked.

Like I'd share that with you, Misty thought. *I'd never get another call from Steve ever again if you were armed with that piece of information.* And then a delicious idea hit her. "Avery Sharpe," she replied, masking her sheer delight at Tilly's reaction.

To hell if she thought Avery was visiting her at home. Maybe Tilly'd tell Phonse and Misty would get herself another raise. The world worked in strange ways in Charlie's Cove. Anything was possible. And besides, the look on Tilly's face was well worth the risk. So what if word spread that she was having a relationship with Avery? Unless, of course, he was married. *Oh well, it was too late now.*

She stood up and headed into the newsroom. *The Yarn* office was strangely becoming a battle zone. No matter. Her heart was light and airy. Not even The Phonse could wipe the glow off her face. Maybe.

"Sit your maggoty ass down, Muldoon."

Maggoty? What happened to boney? She preferred boney. Boney meant toned, in her dictionary. Maggoty was just plain nasty.

She plunked down in front of Phonse. His beady eyes bored into her and his normally pasty cast was a mottled mix of red and purple, kind of like a splotchy beet. Still, she felt calm. It was rather entertaining watching him operate.

"I can't fuckin' believe it, Muldoon. I gives you a few simple instructions. Simple, simple, simple."

Out of his line of vision, Misty flicked the paper to page fourteen. *Why did this have to be such a big deal?*

"I gives you a few simple, simplistic instructions a jeasley simpleton could follow. Stay out of me personals. You understands that, or what?" He looked at her.

It sounded more like he was referring to certain body parts, but Misty refrained from pointing that out. She knew she wasn't expected to say anything and she didn't. Not yet. Phonse wasn't finished. Far from it.

"What..." He was frothing at the mouth by now. "Is..." Spittle landed on her pants. "This?" Phonse held up a page he had torn from the paper. She glanced at it. Holy moly. Page fourteen. With this ability, she might apply herself to lottery tickets.

Phonse stopped to breathe.

Misty figured now might be a good time to interject. "A change," she replied. "It's a change, Phonse."

"Muldoon, I makes the changes around here. I changes me underwear in the mornings, I changes me socks every couple a days, and I changes the arse-wipe when the roll is empty. This weren't no empty roll." He jabbed his finger at the personals. "No scurvy changes required." He glared at her.

"I disagree."

"You disagrees now, do you? Tilly!" he yelled out. "Muldoon disagrees with me. Tell her what happened last time someone disagreed with me."

Tilly peered into the room, a smirk on her face. "We ordered a new door, Uncle Phonse."

Misty simmered at the fact that Tilly was probably enjoying every minute of her roasting, most likely standing outside the door so as not to miss anything.

"A new door." Phonse clapped his hands together. "That's right, Muldoon. We ordered a new door. You know why we ordered a new door? Huh?"

"Settle down for a minute. I saw you in action with Avery and you're going to have a heart attack one of these days. I'm a lot stronger than I look, and you can't intimidate me with your threats." Misty with a Y met his gaze without faltering. "The personals suck and I'm sick and tired of hearing it. Whether or not you agree, they needed this."

Misty shut up and waited for Phonse to carry on. She was probably the only person in the history of *The Yarn* who had ever stood up to him.

And she might also be the last.

But it was a chance she was willing to take, because sooner or later there had to be some guidelines between herself and Phonse if she was going to be happy here. She was getting good and sick of people pushing her around.

"I'm fucking speechless, Muldoon. You got a nasty mouth for a boney-arsed woman."

She had a nasty mouth? But anyway, at least they were back to boney-arsed, which, in her opinion, was every indication that things were going reasonably well.

"Look at this." Phonse pointed to the first personal and read aloud.

"Lonely woman seeking company. Loves to knit naked and bake with only apron strings. Flexible. Box 779."

He shook the paper. "Flexible? Jesus, Muldoon. What's that mean? She locks her legs behind her ears when she kneads bread? I'm going to have every jeasley Christian on my back from here to Joe Batt's Arse."

"Arm," Misty corrected. "The name of the community is Joe Batt's Arm."

"No, Muldoon, I means arse. That's the tone we bees setting here."

Misty could see his point. Charlie's Cove and the surrounding communities were pretty conservative. For a moment she almost wavered in her conviction, but no. She'd heard it loud and clear from almost everyone. As long as no dirty words were used, personals were just that. Personal. Written by the person who was yearning for something. And if she had injected a little creative license, it was only in retaliation to the ludicrous crap Phonse was trying to pull off as personals.

"Well, maybe I pushed it a bit," she conceded. "But I'm telling you, people were good and fed up with you editing the personals."

Phonse wasn't listening. He was pointing at the next one.

"Hetero couple seeking fun-loving company for fishing excursions. Well equipped, stereo, bar, beds..." Phonse stopped. "Muldoon, only thing is missing here is the size of his..."

"Phonse!"

"Keel, Muldoon. Keel. You gets my point?"

"Oh, I gets it all right. You want this paper run by your wife. This stuff is real, Phonse, and it's entertainment, too. Our readers are tired of censorship and I'm tired of being told I work for *The Yawn*."

Misty caught her breath. She wasn't sure anyone had ever directly confronted him with that terminology. He had to know about the slur that was regularly used to describe his paper, but no one was foolish enough to say it to his face.

As Misty debated what she would say next, if anything, she found herself caught up in trying to figure out if the fact that Phonse had taken out a cigarette and lit up was a good sign or a bad one.

"Been years since Avery been sniffing around here."

Did that sound like a softening of position? Misty jumped in immediately, "I agree. But we need to keep moving and shaking, Phonse." *Avery, of course!* She felt as though she had uncovered a secret weapon. Phonse would do just about anything to out-manoeuvre his competition. She continued with renewed vigour. "Did I mention we've had several requests for extra copies of the paper in Hickey Harbour?"

Phonse put his hand over his eyes, but not before Misty caught the sly way he beaded and narrowed his gaze into a parody of Clint Eastwood. *Hot damn, she had him.*

"Jesus, Muldoon. You are a nuisance. You pisses me off at times."

"So? What's happened to readership?" She jumped to her feet and leaned over his desk.

"Up."

"And?"

"We bees making a small profit."

"So? Is it too much to modify personals?" Misty bit her bottom lip with her teeth. If she could just get a concession on this…

"Like I said, Muldoon. You pisses me off. Get out of here."

"So I can do it?" She realized her persistence was somewhat akin to goading a hibernating bear, but in her mind, she was never going to get a better opportunity than this. "Well?"

"I sees another increase in readership, you can do it."

That was as good as a yes, and probably the most she would ever get from Phonse. She stood up and held out her hand. "Deal?"

"Bugger off."

"You want me to call Lottie?"

"Like I says, I finds pleasure in me job. I can handle me wife without your help. By the way, column you did on marriage wasn't bad."

"Really?" This was her first sort of compliment from Phonse.

"Particularly the part about keeping separate rooms."

"I was kidding about that."

"Inspiring, that's what it was. Now blow off."

There was a funny smile on his face. Any smile at all was nice to see. She walked out with a smile on her face as well. Dealing with Phonse hadn't been so bad after all. Her optimism was short-lived; Tilly was smiling, too, in a way that sent an uneasy feeling up her back.

"You just had a call from the naked knitting club."

"What?"

Tilly smirked. "No, b'y. Made a mistake. It was the naked prayer club and I sent it into Uncle Phonse. Aunt Lottie didn't sound too happy either. You've been stirring up a lot of people."

"Thanks for the favour." It was hard to overlook the sarcastic tone in Misty's voice.

"Think nothing of it, Muldoon," Tilly said as she mimicked her uncle. "I takes pleasure in me job, too. You really seeing Avery Sharpe?"

If she didn't want that thorn getting back to Phonse, Misty figured she'd better come clean with Tilly. "No, actually, it was Steve."

"Steve Day, the dentist?"

Misty nodded.

"I'm surprised. I thought he was hot. Avery, I could see."

"You know, Tilly, your attitude is wearing rather thin. I'm not planning on going anywhere real soon and every day, you and me, we're going to have to see each other and just maybe it would be a good idea for us to try to get along."

"I'm not as pliable as Uncle Phonse. I still thinks you're full of shit."

Misty rolled her eyes and shook her head. "Well, honey, you can think what you like, but there's a limit to how far you can push me." Misty grabbed her coat from the tree and pulled it on. "Your uncle and I have an understanding. If push comes to shove, I'm not sure if he won't pick me over you. Keep that in mind and have a nice day." Misty opened the door and breathed in the cool, fresh air of fall. She had a full week before anything else was due, and she was taking some time for herself. "See ya later," she called over her shoulder. "Maybe."

Let Tilly stew on that for a while. Misty wasn't going to ease her resentment in one short conversation. Maybe it would never disappear, but she'd be damned if she'd allow Tilly to make her feel insecure.

"Hey, Hatty, what's going on?" Misty asked as she settled on the stool at the front counter.

"You're the one with all the news."

"Likely. What'd you think of personals this week?"

"Missy, you got this town buzzing. I'm thinking the consensus is in your favour, but there are a lot of people royally ticked off."

"As in?"

"You know, some of the local censors."

"Like Lottie."

"Un-huh." Hatty placed a cup of tea and a piece of blueberry pie on the counter in front of Misty. "I'll say one thing, you're a local celebrity. You got all the luck, lassie."

If this was luck, Misty would like to see the alternative. Nevertheless, she put up with the ribbings from the other customers as she enjoyed her snack. Seemed like everyone was reading the paper these days, and that gave her a true feeling of satisfaction. For the first time in several months, she felt her confidence returning. It was a small glimmer, but it was nice.

CHAPTER 16

Well-Heeled

The next few weeks flew by. She decided the Toronto thing, as appealing as it was, might be a bit much the way things were moving with her work and with school starting and all. Steve wasn't happy about it, but finally agreed to put it on hold for a while.

The calls didn't stop, though. They were a daily addiction. Misty would pull on a nightshirt, curl up in bed, and wait for Steve's call. Sometimes they talked for hours. It was an interesting way to get to know someone.

This relationship, if that's what you could call it, was working out fine for her at the moment. If you counted all the time she had actually spent in his company, it didn't add up to more than three hours, which was something to think about, really. What kind of person builds a relationship based on three hours?

And she was surprised the effect anticipation had on her. Steve's voice was sexy and deep, and when she talked to him, her imagination ran wild. She pictured herself wrapped in his arms lying next to him in her bed, and the images were almost as powerful as if it were really true. Distance was an intoxicating aphrodisiac. Even now she felt a sensation that could only be described as raw desire when she thought of him. And when he told her details like he was wearing nothing but a smile, it was seductive and erotic.

She was actually playing around with the idea of doing a column on long-distance romance. There must be hundreds of Newfoundlanders burning up the phone lines. Almost every family had someone working away from home. And now, with the internet widely available even in many rural areas, there were plenty of e-romances on the go, too. How was hers any different? It really wasn't.

What was different and a matter of some concern, though, was the way Skylene's wedding was heating up. She had picked Valentine's Day to tie the knot with Stinky and was chasing Misty for measurements. She had selected dresses from a store in St. John's and was getting them sent in on the bus. Her attendants, and there were several of them, were all wearing matching shawls in heart-stopping red to coordinate with the mini hearts in the fabric of the gowns. All Misty knew was that hers had a big bow in the back. It was enough.

Her social calendar had slowed down since she'd gotten the bed situation under control. And the column she'd written on moose hunting as an art form seemed to put the kibosh on any of the available men, not that she was interested anyway. Seems no one wanted anything to do with a woman who poked fun at hunting. For Misty, who was perpetually dreaming of Steve, that suited her just fine.

Her days were full. What with Duff dropping around to help with odd chores and the radical increase in circulation, she was busier than she wanted to be.

The girls were doing well in school. They'd settled into Charlie's Cove like a couple of sculpins. They took a bus in the mornings and raced out the door as though it was something really special. There were more kids calling the house and showing up to play than Misty had seen in all their years in the city.

Liberty explained it to her one day when Misty complained about answering the door. Again. "Being new's cool, Mom. Everyone wants to see Charlie's house." You know, she'd said in a conspiratorial whisper, they even had spooky stories about him? Said he was s'picious.

Misty assured her that what he really was, and only ever was, was extremely eccentric. Eccentric and generous. And that they had a lot of reasons to be grateful to old Charlie. In a way, he'd rescued them when there was nowhere else to go and hadn't Charlie's Cove turned out to be a really great place to live? Those discussions generally ended on a pretty good note for old Charlie, who was looking much more like a hero than a villain.

By the time the first snowflakes fell in late November, they brought a sense of magic and anticipation to the stark winter landscape. Christmas was just around the corner and like icing on a freshly baked cake, the fat, fluffy flakes were beautiful and decorative. And just begging to be eaten.

"Mom," cried Liberty. "Get up. It's snowing. Let's go out. C'mon."

"Yeah, Mom," said Vivienne. "I wanna catch some." To demonstrate, she stuck out her tongue like a fly-catching frog.

Misty cracked one eye open and observed the two girls standing by the bed. It was only 7:30 a.m., a forgivable sin on any other day of the week. But Saturday? This was her day to sleep in.

"C'mon, Mom," they said in chorus, as they pulled at her duvet. "Pleeeeeeeeze."

What could she say? Misty threw back the covers and shivered. The temperature in the house was cool. She never had gotten around to checking the insulation and she made a mental note to add it to the list again. "Give me five minutes and make sure you put on lots of warm clothes."

The girls ran back to their rooms to get ready.

Was insulation invented when they built these old outport homes, she wondered as she shucked her nightie and pulled some long underwear from her drawer. Certainly didn't feel like it. She added socks. Two pairs. A sweater and some jeans. By the time she was finished, she could barely move, let alone manoeuvre down an icy driveway.

The girls had beaten her downstairs and were already dressed and ready to go. The thrill of being the first to imprint a yard of fluffy, perfect snow was far too tempting. They dashed out while Misty hunted for her boots. She stuck her head in the closet and searched through the maze of footwear that had accumulated.

No snow boots. Unfortunately, that was a highly unacceptable reason to stay in, so she pulled off a pair of her socks and stuffed her feet into a pair of dress boots. If she looked ridiculous, at least it was early and no one was likely to see. She stepped out into the frosty air.

The beauty of the morning took her breath away. Tree branches were laden with fresh downy flakes, swollen to proportions as magnificent as when they bore leaves. Crystalline, life-size ornaments. She felt as though she were walking into a glass menagerie.

"Wheeeeeeeee," screamed Vivienne as she slid across the front yard and down the slope of the driveway. Her feet made deep furrows in the snow.

"Mom," yelled Liberty as she sailed after her sister. "Your turn."

Why not, thought Misty, as she chased after them. Of course, heels were never meant for ice gliding. Misty's right leg went north and her left leg went south.

"Ohhhhhhhh," she moaned as she hit the ground, one of her legs looking suspiciously out of place. When she didn't get up, Vivi and Liberty ran over.

"Mom, your leg." Vivienne started to cry.

"Let me see," said Liberty as she pushed her sister aside. Liberty reached out to touch her and Misty pushed her hand away.

"No. Don't." She could barely speak as the pain escalated. "Call Duff. And Pansy." She couldn't move. Her breath came in deep hiccups, shaking her body. Despite her effort to remain still, she began to shiver.

Vivienne continued to sob by her side and with a great effort, Misty reached out and took her hand in hers. "It's all right, honey," she whispered between vibrating teeth. "Mom's fine." But she didn't feel fine at all. She felt like hell.

It seemed like forever until Liberty returned, carefully sliding on her backside and coming to a stop beside Vivi.

"Duff's on his way, Mom. So's Pansy. They called an ambulance for you, too."

"Mom's gonna die," Vivi cried, her sobs swelling to hysterics.

Desperate to comfort her daughter, Misty pushed back the pain that was clouding her mind. "It's my leg, honey. That's all."

Misty closed her eyes. She was so busy concentrating on staying calm she found it difficult to talk. She knew her daughters were frightened. Anything that threatened Misty meant their world might change, too. It was a sobering thought and one Misty had to address. Her kids were vulnerable in ways she seldom thought about, and maybe this accident was a good thing. It would settle her down from ideas of romantic liaisons and keep her mind on the business of looking after herself and her family.

"I'm all right, girls," she whispered. "This is nothing and you two are the best nurses in Charlie's Cove. I'm so lucky." And she was. She was about as lucky as anyone could be. It just didn't look like it at the moment.

CHAPTER 17

If It Ain't Broke, Don't Fix It

Misty looked out the window of her bedroom. The whole leg incident was a blur. She remembered Duff showing up and even riding in the ambulance with her to Gander. After that, she was so hyped on pain medication, she really couldn't recall much.

She did remember his calloused hand holding hers tightly and his voice whispering in her ear. "I wants a dance on New Year's, Misty Muldoon. We're not heaving you overboard yet."

Even half-crazy with pain, it was hard to overlook Duff's strangely endearing ways. Just the thought of being heaved overboard was enough to make her a stellar patient. She was back in Charlie's Cove in less than three days.

Tucked under the covers with her leg in a cumbersome cast now elevated on pillows, she felt like a whale trapped in the shallows. There was nowhere to go, no way to move around and certainly no comfort at all. *How to keep a boney ass if all you do is lie on it?*

"Pansy," she called. "I'm dying up here."

"If you was dying, we'd have something nicer on you," Pansy yelled back. "Hang on. Be right up."

A few minutes later Pansy sat down on the side of the bed and passed Misty a cup of Earl Grey tea. "So you think this is it, do ya?"

"Dying has many definitions. I'm dying of boredom. Talk to me." She took a sip of tea. It was steaming hot and put some warmth back into her bones. *Nothing like a good drop of tea to ease away the blues. A little Grand Marnier wouldn't hurt, however.*

"Your problem is you needs a man in your life. It weren't no accident you bought this bed, and you looks pitiful in it. I knows you likes my cousin. You two bees talking up the wires like a couple'a lovesick fools. It's time you gets on with it."

"It's amazing how everything comes down to the opposite sex with you. Look at me. Do you really think your cousin is going to want me? I've got two kids, I'm just getting my bank account in the black and I'm a personal wreck." Misty scowled at Pansy but found she couldn't maintain her sour disposition and started to laugh. Pansy joined in. "Ow, ow. My leg," she whined between howls of laughter.

"Look at you. Feeling sorry for yourself." Pansy was breathing heavily now. "You don't take up but one measly eighth of this bed. If that's not a sight for sore eyes, I don't know what is."

Misty put her cup on the small table she had jammed between the bed and the wall and sighed. Their laughter faded away like the aging wallpaper in her room. "Having Duff with me the day I went to Gander was strange. Don't get me wrong. I was grateful he was there, but you know, it should have been someone else."

"Like Steve," suggested Pansy.

"Yeah. Like Steve." The words weighed heavily on Misty's mind. Her heart felt like a pancake, pressed down and flattened by the aloneness of her life. It was an entirely different thing from loneliness. Loneliness could be temporary, but aloneness was like a swell in the ocean that gave you a view of nothing but more ocean.

"Ah," said Pansy. "You'll work it out. There's a fish out there for all of us. Maybe it's Steve, maybe it's not. You're used to pulling up roots. Why not move to Toronto and find out?"

"I can't uproot us all again. The girls are just getting used to Charlie's Cove. When I broke my leg, I realized just how vulnerable they were and that makes me even more reluctant to chase after a man. I need to make a life here if that's what works, and it looks like it is." Misty paused for a moment and considered her situation. There was a question looming in her mind, but she really didn't want to know the answer unless it was the one that counted. "Think Steve would ever move here?" she asked hopefully.

"Possibility, I suppose." Pansy didn't sound convinced.

"You think I'm crazy?"

"Nah, b'y. You're just sizin' things up, is all. You'll figure this out and when you do, you'll be top shelf."

"I hope you're right."

"C'mon, Misty. You know what they says. If it ain't broke, don't fix it."

"You talking about my heart or my good leg?"

"I dunno. You tell me." She looked at Misty and smiled; a broad grin that practically oozed with anticipation. "Forget about it. Anyway, I got a bit of exciting news for you."

"Blow me away," Misty said rather flatly. The melancholy she was feeling refused to evaporate. Her heart was wide open and she was just waiting for love to rush in and fill the void, but the darn feeling of hopelessness just wouldn't leave her alone. Was she going to grow old in this outport? Old and wrinkled and still covering tea parties? The thought was unbearable.

"Phonse stopped by with a present for you." Pansy was smiling again.

"This should be good."

"No, really, it is. I got it downstairs. Wait and see." Pansy stood up and left the room. There was a bounce in her step.

"Look, see? Luh." Pansy was back and holding a laptop computer in her hands like it was a bedpan.

"Wow, where'd Phonse come up with that?"

"I asked the same thing. Says it was in the budget. Says he sold your column to some papers across the country. He wants more, and this is his way of getting them."

"Really? He sold my work? Without consulting me?" She was both amazed and pissed at the same time.

"You're gonna be famous, Misty. And I knows you, too." Pansy seemed genuinely pleased.

"I don't think Misty's Misadventures is the kind of thing that makes you famous." Still, it felt rather good to know her audience was growing.

"I dunno. I'm psychotic at times. I thinks it might."

Misty laughed. "Here give me that. I'm psychotic, too. Plug it in before I strangle myself."

They both laughed.

"I'm gone," said Pansy. "I sees you needs some time alone with the object of your affections. I'm going for groceries, but I'll be back before the girls gets home."

Misty was already absorbed in firing up the computer. "Sounds good," she said to Pansy but she really had no idea what she was agreeing with. Her mind was miles away.

Incredible. Phonse might be a geezer but he was getting better at the team thing. This little gift was the very item to take her out of her doldrums. She opened Word and looked at the flashing cursor. It beckoned to her with all the charisma of the Vegas strip and it couldn't have been any brighter if it was the North Star pointing the way safely home.

Her fingers danced over the keys as another thought jumped into her head. *A laptop makes me mobile. And my leg makes me mostly immobile.* It seemed to her that fate was yet again intervening, but this time not to bring her and Steve together but to keep them apart. If there was a message in that she preferred not to know. She exhaled audibly as she pondered what to write.

Misty's Misadventures...she looked out the window at the snowflakes drifting down. Slowly floating to earth. Hundreds of them. Millions. But each one completely alone.

Do they ever experience longing? Probably not. The party's waiting for them when they land. One big happy family of snowbanks and drifts.

What about people who are alone? When there's no big fluffy ending? Especially at Christmas. All those Newfoundlanders living away from home. Missing things like family and friends.

Won't they experience longing? With Christmas looming, feelings of aloneness are all the more intense. And if you don't have someone in your life? In a way, I know exactly what that feels like.

She looked out the window again. *That's me. Just like one of those snowflakes. Drifting. Down. To nowhere in particular.*

And what if, she pondered, *what if you're totally alone, the one snowflake that isn't going to land with the rest of them?* The prospects were pretty humbling. Her excitement at receiving the computer was beginning to morph into a full-blown session of self-pity. *Snap out of it, Misty. You've got more going for you than that. Besides, at least you're on The Rock. There are hundreds of Newfies out there who would trade places with you in a minute.*

That was the real kicker.

She decided she would write of longing and loneliness, and what would make the perfect Christmas gift. A ticket home? An unexpected knock on the door? Or love? All wrapped up in a down-filled jacket with dreamy blue eyes.

Her fingers began to tap the keys as her thoughts flowed directly from her head to her keyboard. It was as though there were angels guiding them, showing her how to say just the right thing to pull heartstrings all over the country, and maybe even inspire a few unexpected reunions.

She was glad Steve had a subscription to *The Yarn*.

What if her column inspired him to take a trip to a remote, romantic island somewhere in the North Atlantic? Now that would be a Christmas gift to remember.

CHAPTER 18

Cupid's Arrow

"Bend over."

"Like heck. I'm not bending for anyone." Misty felt as stiff as a board.

"Look, Misty. I has to check your flexibility. Now, bend over," said Nurse Fanny, with more than a little bit of irritation.

"Oh, for Pete's sake." Misty dropped her arms to the floor, letting her fingertips graze the linoleum. "How's that for flexibility?"

"Can't hear you."

She felt a hand on her rump and a sudden ping of pain shoot through her backside. Up she came like a migrating salmon. "What was that?"

"Just a shot." Nurse Fanny winked at her.

"It felt like an arrow in my butt. Do you always play these games?" Misty rubbed her backside where Fanny had stabbed her.

"Just with my difficult patients. Now pull your pants up. I've seen enough. You wears interesting step-ins, Misty."

"Thongs, Fanny. They eliminate panty lines." Misty straightened her pants. She was wearing sweats, of all things, but they were all she could comfortably fit over the cast still around her leg.

"Looks like dental floss for your bottom. Gives me a good playing field, though." Fanny laughed heartily at her last comment.

"I'll give you some for Christmas."

"No, thanks. They'd disappear on me and someone would unearth my body someday and say the cause of death was strangulation by dissection."

"Very cute. Have you ever thought about stand up? You're quite funny for a nurse."

"Not near as entertaining as you, dear. I loves reading your column, by the way. Never knows what you're going to come up with. That was a muscle relaxant I gave you. Go home and take it easy for another two weeks. We'll see you in the New Year."

Good lord. Fanny's offhand remark took her by surprise. Would it really be the New Year in a couple of weeks? Time had a funny way of creeping up on you in Charlie's Cove. One week sailed into another.

It just seemed like only yesterday she'd ordered up Christmas from Amazon, poring over images while the girls were in school. And now the holidays were only one short week away? She'd lost days, weeks even, to her darn leg without even realizing time was passing.

When she grew up, she remembered the old Sears Wish Book landing on the doorstep in September. Or maybe it was October. Now, Christmas arrived in July or August, and in her opinion, looked slightly ridiculous and embarrassed to be so out of season. It was like wearing a parka on the beach. Not that it couldn't be done in Newfoundland in July and on occasion, even was. *And your point, Misty?*

Her point? Commercialism was trashing Christmas, showing up like an uninvited guest, making everyone uncomfortable and even a little panicked.

Which, thankfully, I'm not, she reminded herself. Amazon had come through just fine. Pansy had picked up the gifts, which were now stored in the attic awaiting Christmas morning.

Just yesterday a box had arrived from the girl's father. *Yuck.* He had even signed "from Dad and Kelly, with love." Having a best friend whose name rhymed with jelly…no, make that smelly, was asking for trouble, anyway. It was a mistake she'd never repeat.

Since writing her last column, she had a new outlook on what it meant to be single. Misty's Misadventures had woven a funny and touching tapestry of life on the edge of aloneness, and it had even made her feel better about being single herself, which she wasn't. Not exactly. At least, not if you counted relationships nurtured by Bell Canada.

The Christmas column was her first to run from coast to coast, as Phonse was inclined to say when he was bragging her up at Hatty's or the Legion.

What he meant was that it appeared in a few papers in Northern BC, a handful in Alberta, one in Yellowknife, Ottawa, Toronto—actually, a number of places in Ontario—Moncton, Halifax. Geez, he was right. Misty's Misadventures was kind of coast to coast. With all that was going on, she really hadn't thought about it or taken it seriously. Her column had started on a whim and it still surprised her that people would want to read her stuff. And actually pay for it, too.

She was incredibly awkward as she navigated the steps to the parking lot where Pansy was waiting for her. No ramps for her. Just rails and stairs. She still wasn't driving, and the way Nurse Fanny's shot was making her feel, that was probably a good thing. Running down the locals is never looked upon in a friendly way.

"You looks limber," said Pansy, as she leaned across the car to open the door for Misty.

"You have no idea. Nurse Fanny just gave me a shot in the fanny. I'm floating here." She used her hands to lift her encased leg into the car. She had a worsted wool sock over her foot to keep her toes from freezing off. "I can't believe I have to keep this thing on all through Christmas. My leg is itchier than a case of hemorrhoids."

"Aren't you doing just ducky. Sure it wasn't cupid's arrow what caught you in the ass?"

"Still on that train of thought, are you? Trust me. It was Fanny's arrow and you're going to have to take me home. I was hoping to stop by the office for a few hours, but I guess they'll manage without me."

"Don't be so sure."

"They've managed for years."

"That's not what I bees talking about. Fanny Faulkner's a matchmaker. Don't think she don't pull some shenanigans."

Pansy drove like she was trying out for a Targa Rally. Misty's hand clamped the dash. "Do you mind slowing down? I know I put in for a new car for Christmas, but I was hoping it would come from Santa and not by way of an insurance claim."

"Scares ya, do I?" Pansy looked over at Misty instead of at the road, which would have made Misty far more comfortable.

"You have no idea, Pansy. Absolutely no idea. Driving with you is an experience, but telling me I've been zapped by a matchmaker? If that's not scary, I don't know what is."

"I'll tell you what is. Fanny Faulkner bees scary. She's got the gift."

"You don't seriously believe in that foolishness, do you?"

"I seen her work. Flap Mercer weren't never getting married. Mincie paid Fanny to cast a spell and look what happened. She bees bringing on number four in January."

"What?" Trying to decipher Pansy when your head was like a wad of cotton batting wasn't easy. "Flap and Mincie? Cripers, Pansy. That sounds like a breakfast menu."

"They's cooking up something all right. L-O-V-E." She jagged her eyebrows at Misty.

Misty silently rejoiced when they pulled up her driveway. "I hope you don't drive like this with the kids."

"Nah. I lets them do it."

Misty shook her head. *There were times... Whew. I'm woozy.* Pansy took her arm and helped her into the house and directly to bed where she slept soundly for a good eight hours. It was dark when she awoke.

"Pansy?" she called out. She fumbled for the bedside light and turned it on. Leaning neatly against it was a note, obviously written by the girls.

Mommy,

Pansy invited us for a sleepover. Call us when you aren't comatose.

Love,

Liberty and Vivienne

"Really? Comatose?" Misty shook her head.

On the bright side, it looked like she had the homestead to herself for the night. This was the first time she'd had an evening alone since moving into Charlie's old house. It was strange and strangely exciting, too.

She got up and pulled on a sweatshirt, but didn't bother with pants, taking the throw off her bed instead. That would keep her warmer than baggy old pants and it was also a lot easier. Dragging it behind her, she went downstairs to the kitchen. Once again, kudos to Pansy who had left her meal on the table. She put it in the oven and called the girls.

They were totally content and in the middle of makeovers. Pansy had painted their toenails bright red and green. There were many remarkable ways to celebrate the season and Pansy had nailed one of them. Misty promised to cook them all breakfast in the morning.

Fanny's relaxant had worn off, so she poured herself a glass of wine. Getting around with her leg locked from mid-thigh to the tip of her toes took a lot of effort. Wine helped. So did chocolate. And, better than either one of them was her laptop. She had even given it a name. Minerva, for the goddess of wisdom. At one point she had toyed with Aphrodite, the goddess of love, but Minerva won out. Probably a reflection of her headspace at the moment. Love had gotten her where she was. Before she entangled herself too deeply in another relationship, she'd use her grey matter. The old "think before you leap" was a good philosophy. Good and, unfortunately, often forgotten.

She settled comfortably in the front room with the television for background noise; a chocolate bar from her secret stash; her wine; and the finishing touch, Minerva, her beloved computer. Dinner was still simmering in the oven. That's what was neat about being grown up. You could have dessert first.

That thought reminded her of Steve. She wished he were here with her to indulge in their passion for eating the best part first.

She got up once more. This time to get the mobile phone. Distance had a way of making the heart grow fonder, but it also had a way of cooling things off. Just thinking of Steve made her want to hear his voice, even if it was only his message manager.

During quiet moments like this, when she had too much time to think, she seriously wondered what she was doing moping for a man who lived thousands of miles away. It was unlikely he would ever move here. Eventually, they would run out of things to talk about, but until that happened, she would try to enjoy every minute of their friendship.

She took a sip of wine and savoured the taste for a moment, then swallowed it along with her concerns and hit the phone button with his pre-programmed number.

While she waited, she opened a column she had written a couple of weeks ago when she was feeling particularly isolated and single. The one she had never given to Phonse. It was far too personal to share.

But here, by herself, she could dare to read it again and let her imagination soar. *What if I send it to Steve? Would it make any difference?*

"Hello?"

It was a woman's voice. Misty almost disconnected, but her upbringing prevailed and she politely inquired for Steve, expecting to hear she had a wrong number.

"He's in the shower. Can I take a message? Is this Pansy? He got your message to call."

"Yes, I mean no. No, it's not Pansy." *In the shower? What did that mean? Where was the part where she said this was the wrong number?* Misty could barely think.

"Oops, sorry. I never know when to shut up."

No kidding.

"Who shall I say is calling, then?"

Misty caught her breath. *This could be anything. This did not mean Steve was seeing someone else, except maybe the part about the shower. What was he doing in the shower with another woman in the house?*

She had to say something. "Tell him Misty called. You know…like the weather. Misty, rainy and all that."

"Misty. Cute name. Wait a minute. You're not the one who writes that column, are you? It's in the paper every week."

What are you doing reading Steve's paper every week? Misty grabbed her wine glass and this time took a sizable gulp before she managed to respond. "Yeah, that's me. So…you read my column, do you?" *Funny he didn't mention that you were reading it with him.*

"Read it? I love it. You're so funny. You people from Newfoundland can sure laugh at yourselves. We'd be too embarrassed to admit to the things you do."

Misty scratched her head and made a face. She wasn't warming up to Miss Chipper for a number of reasons, the least of which was her opinion of Newfoundlanders. "That's how it is around here. We know when we're doing stupid things." *Unlike some other people who shall remain nameless, but not blameless.* "Right, then. Just tell him I called, okay?" She cut the connection.

This is crazy. I'm acting like a jealous teenager. So someone else answered Steve's phone. Big deal. Don't Liberty and Vivienne answer my phone every day? It's probably some relative. Maybe even his sister. Christ, I don't even know if he has a sister. Still, I hope he calls back with an explanation. No, let me rephrase that. He'd better call back with an explanation.

Her computer screen went into sleep mode. Something not even remotely possible for her to do at the moment, she was so hyped. She ran her finger across the mouse pad and Minerva sprang to life again.

The thought that Steve could have someone else in his life gave her a renewed interest in what she had written. Maybe she should publish it. She seriously needed to look out for herself instead of pining for a man who let other women answer his phone. The more she read, the more sense the whole article made.

Misty's Misadventures

By

Misty Muldoon

True love can arrive in the most unexpected of ways.

But never when you want it, and almost never when you expect it. At least, that's been my experience.

In fact, if I'm being brutally honest here, and I most always am, I couldn't have made true love more welcome than if I'd left a dozen beer on the stoop and a bottle opener hanging from the knob. Invitation issued. So where the heck is it?

I'm tired of waiting and, quite frankly, I've had enough of leaving my key in the door. If true love

wants to find me, it's going to have its work cut out. That's right. You read me correctly. Those are brave words for someone who spends Friday nights cuddled in the arms of a La-Z-Boy, feels bad about it all day Saturday, and then turns around and hugs into the same unfeeling lover that night, too.

I'm inspired to ask, what would it be like to find your one true love? Actually, maybe I'm not inspired at all. Perhaps what I am is desperate. Desperately longing for love.

And who do I think is going to rescue me? No one, that's who. Here I am in Charlie's Cove, where the definition of an available man is anyone not at the cabin for the weekend. I mean, come on, how am I supposed to deal with that?

Oh, sure, tell me I made the choice to come home and now I have to live with the decision. I say phooey to that. I want true love and I want it to walk in the door right now.

If it's wrapped up in rubber boots and a plaid shirt, that's fine. If it's got facial hair and a beer belly, I can take that too. If it's seasonal, well, all I can say is I'm an adapter as long as the loving is year-round. Bring it on, baby.

This isn't any misadventure. Absolutely not. This is just a clear missing you in my life. Where are you, Mr. Right? I'm here in Charlie's Cove and I'm waiting.

Ring my bell, knock my knocker, email, text, or phone.

Honey-babes, I'm waiting. Tall, short, who cares?

Come on in, I'm home!

Until next time,

Misty

She took one last look at her column and closed it. Buried, along with all her good intentions in the file she had labelled "Goals for the New Year." That was a nice place for it. Maybe when the New Year rolled around, she would kick it off with a new intention by finding someone to love in her own neighbourhood.

She caught a whiff of her dinner and wondered what Pansy had left for her. It smelled interesting. She got up to find out what was cooking and was almost there when the doorbell rang.

Could this be it? True love at last?

She gathered the blanket around herself and like Quasimodo, with her leg dragging along behind, she answered the door.

"Duff!" she said. "What are you doing out this hour of the night?" It was really only nine o'clock, but she was on Misty time, which was all messed up since her accident.

"Jus' checkin' on you. Mind if I comes in for a minute?"

She stepped back to welcome him. She had a moment of panic thinking he might be here to ask her out, but he'd had ample opportunity in the past and hadn't made a move. She made a mental note to add a condition to her secret column—*no one over sixty-five.*

"What's up?"

"Was wondering if you had a tree for Christmas?"

Omigod. She had completely forgotten.

"Got one if you wants it."

"Now?" *Tree delivery unlimited.*

"Yes, b'y. It's in the truck."

Misty knew Duff didn't have a truck.

"The truck?" she asked.

"Cedric's. He bees waiting in it."

Not Cedric. No. She made another mental note. No one without his own teeth.

"That'd be great, Duff. What do you want to do with it?"

He looked at her kind of funny.

"Get some old sheets, b'y, and we'll put her up for you. That way, they catches the drippins."

"You and Cedric?"

"And Stinky."

The three musketeers. She hadn't laid eyes on Stinky since Skylene held a wedding announcement party in November. He didn't look too pleased about it at the time.

Forty-five minutes later, the four of them stood back to admire the tree.

"It's a beauty," Misty said. And it was. It stood six feet and was full and bushy.

"Now, that's a proper tree," said Duff.

She'd given each of them a beer, which only left nine if her true love actually came calling.

Duff turned to her. "The boys wants to ask you somethin'."

"Ah, sure," said Misty. She looked at the boys. When they didn't say anything, she turned back to Duff.

"They wants to sign your cast," he said.

Stupid. That's what it was. A decision not to wear pants when you've issued an invitation to the universe for love to walk in.

"That would be…nice," she said. "I have a marker in the kitchen. Let me get it." She lurched out of the room, still mummied in the blanket. She shut the door behind her, flung the blanket off, and headed straight to the laundry. There had to be something there she could put on.

In between all the kids' clothes, she finally laid her hands on a pair of boxer shorts that would fit. It took her a few minutes to navigate herself into them. She grabbed the marker and went back to the other room.

In-between the lurid remarks Phonse had printed on her cast and the autographs of most of Hatty's customers, Cedric and Stinky added their monikers.

Merry Christmas, Misty. Loves the leg. Cedric
Looks good on ya! Leave it for Santy Claus. Stinky
And, finally, Duff got in the action.
You casts a spell on we. Yes, b'y. Duff. He had drawn a little heart with an arrow at the end of his autograph.

Misty didn't know quite what to say. This was a big deal to them. The boys poked a bit of fun at each other and were finishing up their beers when the phone rang. Misty froze. It had to be Steve. She couldn't take a call from him with these boys still here. Then an inspired idea hit her.

"Cedric, could you get that for me and take a message? I'd really appreciate it. Just say I'm indisposed." She smiled and feigned exhaustion. They were like boy-men in some ways. Kind and gentle and immature and perfect for what she had in mind.

Cedric walked over to the phone and picked it up.
"Hullo?"
Misty followed the one-sided conversation.
"No, b'y. She can't come to the phone. She's exposed."
Indisposed, you idiot. There's a big difference.
"Who's callin'?"
What was I thinking? I deserve this. A total idiot, that's what I am. Misty Idiot Muldoon.
"Steve. Right on. I'll get her to give you a call." And he hung up.

Misty was relieved to finally lock the door behind them. She felt as though she were caught in the middle of a horror story that had no ending. It was bad enough she was playing games with Steve, but letting Cedric be the messenger boy was the ultimate act of stupidity. What was she going to do now?

The phone rang again. She just knew it was Steve and the caller ID confirmed it. She was surprised at the intensity of her feelings. Part of her wanted desperately to speak to him to clear up the matter of the woman who answered his phone and another part of her wanted to simply run away from what might be a painful or even deceitful situation. As the phone continued to ring, Misty debated what to do. Finally, she gave up trying to see into a non-existent crystal ball and simply pressed the button and said hello.

"So, the exposed woman decides to take a call, does she?"

Steve sounded just a bit annoyed and Misty bit back a smart retort. Her experience with her ex had left her particularly susceptible to feeling insecure and vulnerable, but she wasn't about to let those insecurities rule her mouth, any more than she wanted them to rule her heart.

"I was indisposed." She looked down at her boxers. The heart-covered shorts might have been a hit at her divorce party, but their time had passed. They looked ridiculous and too suitable a match to the way she was feeling. Further, just hearing Steve's voice set off a ripple in her pelvis that telegraphed something much sexier like thongs or crotchless, edible drive-through bloomers. Not bad at all for someone whose brain officially ceased to function when her hormones kicked in.

"I figured it out all on my own, sweetheart. What was Cedric doing at your place?"

"I might ask the same of you."

"Cedric wasn't at my place," Steve replied, with just a hint of amusement in his voice.

Misty wasn't buying. "You know what I mean. The person who answered your phone, who was she?"

"No one important."

"No one important? That's your answer. No one important. Okay, if that's the way it is. Fine." But it wasn't fine at all. She needed to know who answered his damn phone and why.

"So, what are you doing?" he asked.

Misty was incensed. That was it? He was going to drop the matter like that? "Nothing." The silence on the phone was ominous and spoke volumes. Misty realized she was behaving like a spoiled child, but nothing she could say to herself could convince her to change her tactics. She was angry at Steve, especially since he refused to explain what was going on. But if he was going to play this game with her, she wasn't going to grovel and beg for him to clarify things. She'd learned a thing or two about being elusive herself in the past year. She yawned, feigning a tiredness she didn't feel at all. Truthfully, she could have dissembled a Mac truck with only a screwdriver in about thirty minutes.

"Not much in the mood for conversation this evening?"

"No." *Big fat lie.*

"Phone sex, then?"

Her nipples responded enthusiastically to his comment, but she pressed her lips into a tight seam and lied again. "No."

"C'mon, Misty. Lighten up."

Lighten up? Have I just materialized on the planet Mars? Could a man really be this dumb? Misty took a deep breath. "Steve, I'm standing here with only my cast on. If you were close enough, I'd show you some very amazing new stretches I've mastered but honestly, since you aren't, I'm going to slip into bed by myself and read a good romance novel and hope I don't get all hot and bothered." *Take that, you idiot.*

"Shit, Misty. Don't talk like that. It makes me miss you too much."

I'm sure. The idea of exciting him was having an interesting effect on her own libido, so she decided to continue to torment him, a fitting if not slightly malicious punishment for his behavior. "If you were closer," she said seductively, "I might be inspired to show you just how much you miss me. I could run my hands over your back and soothe you, press my lips to every place my fingers touch. I'd give you a perfect and memorable massage that you'd never get anywhere else without paying a lot of money, honey." She waited to see the effect of her words.

Steve groaned. "You know what's happening, don't you?"

"Uh-huh. That's the part when my fingers and lips get mixed up."

"Oh, babe. I've got a problem now."

"Yes, you do," she said simply, and hung up.

So much for being naked. Misty's fantasy popped like a hot air balloon and she looked down at her boxers with dismay. The baggy drawers just weren't cutting it for her and never would again. They needed a new role in her life and she had just the perfect one for them. They were going to provide a way for her to work out her frustrations and her sexual fantasies. They were going on the tree.

It took her a couple of hours and the activity helped keep her mind from wandering to Steve and her insecurities. When she stood back to admire her handiwork, the tree looked positively festive. Dancing merrily on its branches were the world's cutest little stuffed ornaments.

Heart balls.

Her tree was the perfect accessory for someone longing for love. With her leg resting on the coffee table, she curled up on the couch and counted hearts. Exhausted emotionally and physically, in no time at all she was fast asleep.

"You gets up to some stuff when you're left to yourself," said Pansy.

"What?" Misty's mouth was dry. "What time izzit?" She opened her eyes and saw Pansy and the girls staring at the tree.

"Ten o'clock. Where," Pansy pointed at the tree, "did that come from?"

"Like it?" Misty asked stifling a yawn as she struggled to sit up.

"It's beautiful, Mommy," said Liberty. "Let's make some more ornaments. C'mon, Vivi." She took her sister's hand and they ran out of the room.

"Sure won't be no one else with them ornaments," said Pansy. "They looks a bit familiar." She pursed her lips. "Are they…"

"My boxers? Yep. Even thought of a name for them."

"What's that?"

"Heart Balls."

"Looks more like Fanny Balls if you asks me. But if you're crazy enough to decorate your tree from a bottom filled with hearts, you deserves to find true love sooner or later. I doubt you even needs Fanny Faulkner's help with that kind of talent."

Misty smiled. For once she agreed with Pansy, but she had more pressing matters on her mind. She got up and beckoned Pansy into the kitchen. "C'mon, I'm going to make breakfast."

"Not a chance," Pansy replied pushing Misty toward a chair. "You sit down. I'll do it. I feels guilty watching you work."

"Anything else you feel guilty about?" asked Misty, hands poised on her hips.

Pansy looked at her blankly. "Me? No. Should I?"

"Steve?" prompted Misty, raising her eyebrows.

Pansy shook her head, looking puzzled.

"Calling Toronto?" Misty prompted further.

"Oh, that. I told you I might be moving in the spring. I wants his advice on a few things."

"Such as?"

"What is this?" Pansy asked. "You makes me uncomfortable when you looks at me like that. Giving me the evil eye or something."

"A woman answered his phone last night," said Misty, pointing her finger at Pansy. "Could your guilt possibly have anything to do with that? You might know something I don't, for instance?"

Pansy smiled weakly. "I knowed this would come up sooner or later."

"Oh, my God. He's living with someone. I knew it."

"Settle down. No, he isn't. Not anymore. He was. You understands that, sure? He's easy on the eyes, b'y. Imagine he did have a few women before you. One of the reasons he came here was to give her a chance to move out."

"Well, I'm not sure she did. She answered his phone, she's reading his paper. She knows who I am, but I'll be damned if I've ever heard of her." Misty was unleashing all the frustration she'd held back last evening. "He invited me up there for a visit. Don't you think that would have been rather cozy? I can't believe you didn't tell me."

"He made me promise. I didn't like her anyway. He brought her down here one time and she was a real prima donna. An airhead. You got no worries about her."

"Pansy. It's not the woman I'm worried about. This is about Steve. He didn't tell me. That worries me. I've been through this before. Remember?"

"That's why he didn't say anything. It was over. I told him he gots to tell you. He's stunned for someone so smart."

"We've been talking on the phone for a few months now. I've been sharing my life with him and he doesn't see fit to mention he was living with someone? Do I have stupid tattooed on my forehead? Do you see it because I'm sure it's there?" Misty brushed her hair from her brow and glared at Pansy.

"That's not true. I knows he thinks the world of you. You has to talk to him. Let him explain."

"Oh, blood sure runs thick. I was talking to him and do you know what he said? Nothing, that's what. He breezed right by my concerns like he was brushing off a flake of dandruff. Do I really look like a flake of dandruff to you?"

Pansy opened her mouth to make a comment, but Misty didn't give her a chance. "You, of all people. Don't try to cover for him. After what I've been through, trust means everything to me."

"But Misty, you have to give him a chance to explain."

Misty could see the distress on Pansy's face but it was nothing compared to what she felt in her heart. All the hurt and misgivings she'd experienced with Jake came flooding back to her, as though they had never left.

She felt insecure and defensive. It was all wrong, really, but her feelings were doing the driving. She was just along for the ride; sitting in the backseat with her skirt hiked up around her ass to boot.

CHAPTER 19

When Love Comes A-Knockin'

Misty refused to take any further calls from Steve and when Monday morning rolled around, she blew out of bed and was sitting at her desk in *The Yarn* office almost as early as Phonse, which was saying something. Like a lot of outport men who had spent most of their lives rising with the sun, Phonse still preferred to be up and at it early in the day.

Misty sat at her desk and put the finishing touches on her work, then emailed two stories and a column to Phonse. Writing seemed to take the edge off her frustration with men.

When she thought about Steve, she pictured him with an erection as large as a flagpole and while the image was funny, it was also intriguing. She couldn't deny that even though she was mad at him for keeping secrets, she would have enjoyed being around to help him take care of his problem.

The way she was flipping sides created quite a paradox, and it was requiring a lot of effort on her part to keep her mind focused on work. If she stopped to think at all, she slammed into a brick wall of such emotional intensity she much preferred keeping busy. Unfortunately, ignoring her problem was like trying to overlook an elephant in the bedroom.

"Hey, Penney. Check your inbox."

"Filing early, hey? What's that? Me Christmas present?"

She watched him finagling with his mouse. "Oh, give it up." She stood up and manoeuvred around his desk and opened the file for him. "Since when did you forget how to operate a computer?"

"I wants some of what you're on this morning," said Phonse. "You bees in some hurry."

"It's like you say, Phonsie. Things has to get done. Now, since I've met my obligation for the week, any problem with you if I go finish some last-minute Christmas shopping?"

"Not a one."

"Season's greetings, then." She leaned over and gave him a peck on the head.

His mouth dropped in surprise and he grabbed her arm. "Give me some, Muldoon. I'm so sick of all the foolishness." He looked at her slyly. "How come I can't smell it on you?"

"I'm not drinking, you old fool. My heart is filled with joy," she lied. "I've just made some decisions in my life. Namely, getting on with it."

On her way out of the newsroom she almost collided with Bram Healy from the courier service.

"Morning, Misty. Got some load of stuff in the van, most of it's for you."

Because he put it that way, Misty felt obligated to help him by holding the door. He wasn't kidding. There were three parcels and a large bouquet of flowers carefully wrapped to protect them from the cold.

"Someone's got it bad," said Tilly, walking in the door behind Bram, ignoring the fact Misty was pinned behind it. "Those for me?"

Misty frowned and let go of the door, rather wishing it had whacked Tilly in the head.

"Nope," said Bram. "All this stuff's for Misty."

There was a certain satisfaction in wiping the smile off Tilly's face. "All for little old me," said Misty. She glanced at the tag on the flowers. Steve had obviously been up early, too, but she wasn't about to let him buy his way back into her heart.

He had some explaining to do. She valued honesty a great deal more than presents. She was tempted to give the flowers to Tilly but knew, since Tilly was still holding a big grudge, they'd probably end up in the trash. Better to accept them graciously and move on to the next stage of this reconciliation, if there was to be one at all.

Once Bram left, she called Pansy for a ride. Since the incident with her leg, Pansy was providing childcare *and* chauffeur services. Misty hoped she would change her mind about moving. Pansy was such a part of their lives, and now Misty needed her more than ever.

Christmas shopping took so much longer with her leg in a cast so by the time they had finished, Misty had rehashed the whole Steve episode and made some decisions.

She realized her behaviour had been vindictive and that she still had a long way to go to shake the legacy of mistrust Jake had bequeathed to her. And as much as she understood that one bad apple did not the whole bunch spoil, her first reaction was still to toss the whole bag. Hardly the actions of someone ready for another relationship.

The only part that didn't support her theory was her body, which was so attuned to Steve she practically radiated sex goddess in every lopsided sway of her backside. Torn between these conflicting feelings, she was glad to finally sit down and call him.

"Dr. Day will be right with you," the receptionist said as she put Misty on hold. Misty used the time to admire the flowers Steve had sent. She'd put them in her living room. They weren't going to win her over, if that's what he thought, but she wasn't going to lie. They were stunning and their scent put her in a better mood.

Steve came on the line a couple of minutes later. "Misty, it's about time." He sounded like a young boy with his feelings badly hurt.

Before she had the chance to be seduced by the sound of his voice, she wanted to say a few things but when she opened her mouth to speak, she wasn't quite sure what it was she needed to say. Steve decided to speak at the same time so the first few minutes were spent over-stepping each other without accomplishing much.

Finally, Misty found her composure and took control of the conversation. "Why didn't you mention you were living with someone?" she asked.

"I realize that was a mistake," he said. "I just didn't think it was a big deal."

"She answered your phone. That leaves a lot of room for interpretation, Steve. What am I supposed to think? You're running up Bell Canada on my account and giving me the impression there's no one else in your life."

"There isn't." There was an uncomfortable silence as though he wanted to offer more explanation but decided against it.

"What about in your apartment?" Misty prodded. "Is there someone else there?"

"Sandra just dropped by to get a few things. She had no business answering the phone. Habit, I guess."

"And you always take a shower when old girlfriends drop by?"

"That's not fair. I'd just gotten back from the gym. Be reasonable, Misty. You sound like you don't trust me."

"I haven't had the greatest experience in trusting men. You're right about that much." She tried to cover the resentment in her voice but failed miserably.

"I understand how you feel. Look, I have a patient waiting. Can we talk later? You're really blowing this out of proportion. It's not at all what you think. C'mon. I was a bit of an ass on Saturday night. I don't like having someone checking up on me."

"Is that what you call it? I was calling because I missed you."

"Please? I'm sorry. I really mean it."

Misty felt her heart soften. Maybe she had over-reacted. But if he was lying to her, she would never, ever forgive him. She saw herself standing on the edge of a precipice looking down. If she went over the edge, the landing might not be soft. On the other hand, building a nest where she was at the moment was just as risky. She took a deep breath. "The flowers are nice," she said in a conciliatory manner.

"You li…"

She cut him off. "But they don't make up for everything."

"Well, leaving me in the condition you did wasn't very nice either."

"I hope it was painful."

"Hmmmm," said Steve. "We seem to have survived our first fight."

"Don't make light of this. I need some backstory filled in."

"You'll get it. Every sordid detail."

And she did. Later that evening, she and Steve talked for several hours. Sandra had been a part of his life for a year and a half, but she just wasn't the one for him. When he finally told her, he was surprised to discover she had come to the same conclusion.

The whole explanation was rather anti-climactic and Misty was embarrassed she had handled things so poorly.

"You know," she said to Steve, lying back with her head on the pillow. "This whole thing has made me realize I'm probably not ready for anything serious in my life. There's still a lot of hurt from my relationship with Jake. I don't know if I can ever trust someone again the way I trusted him."

"Give me a chance, at least. Things seem to be stacked against us at the moment, but it has to get better. Looks like Frank is coming back to work after Christmas. I've managed to hold things together and I'm due some time off."

"We could be friends," she suggested.

"I am your friend. But I definitely want to be much more than that. What you make me feel isn't simply friendship. We're at a whole other level and don't you ever think we aren't. I can just close my eyes and picture you and I'm like a fourteen-year-old who can't control himself."

Misty smiled indulgently. She felt that familiar tingling in her lower belly, followed by a sudden urge to roll on top of Steve. "I hate you being so far away. I'm in a constant state of agitation. My God, if someone touches me by accident, my temperature goes up and I think of you."

"Shut up, Misty. This is hard enough."

"Really? How hard?" She laughed deviously. "It's contagious, see? I'm acting like a fourteen-year-old, too."

"It works for me so don't ever stop. Promise me one thing. Don't make any rash decisions. Give it a few weeks and then see how you're feeling. Now promise."

"Promise," she replied softly. *With what's left of my heart.*

"Good. Besides," he added before he signed off, "I've put quite a lot of thought into your Christmas present."

CHAPTER 20

Ho, Ho, Ho

Christmas Day broke on the heels of a fresh fall of snow. Charlie's Cove looked as if it had been whitewashed by Debbie Travis.

The whole experience of passing the day in a small rural outport was far different than being in a city. Kids stopped by. Pansy dropped in. Duff showed up with a Christmas cake. Misty truly felt as though she and her daughters were part of a community. December 25 of the first year on her own was a day, she decided, she would carry in her heart forever. With it came the most joy and contentment she had felt in a long, long time.

When the phone rang, Misty expected it to be Jake and Smelly. When she heard Steve's voice, it was magical. It had been almost five months since she'd seen him.

"Merry Christmas, Misty. Still miss me?"

"Like Santa misses Rudolph," she laughed.

She heard a pause as Steve thought about what she had said. "Santa and Rudolph are always together. How can they miss each other?"

"Exactly. Maybe we should make some decisions in the New Year," she replied, not believing what was coming out of her mouth. One minute she was glad for the separation and then next, she was hoping he might do something radical like move to Charlie's Cove.

"You think you're ready to move forward with this friendship?"

"Are you?" Misty wasn't going to be the first to say it.

"You'd move here?" Steve asked.

"Or you'd move here?" she countered. "Your uncle has to retire sometime."

"It's more complicated than that," said Steve, a hint of sadness creeping into his voice. "I just can't walk away from what I've got here. Not for a few years, anyway."

The lighthearted moment she had hoped to create with her question had landed with all the buoyancy of a water balloon. Why did life have to be so difficult? They were both quiet for a moment. Finally, Steve broke the silence and changed the topic. "Did you get my present?"

"I'm wearing it," she said. "Under my big flannel nightie," she added, in case he thought she was prancing around the house in only *that*. "It fits great." She sounded more lighthearted than she felt. In reality, her mind was racing.

Why should I be the one to give up everything? And what is everything, anyway? When did Charlie's Cove suddenly come to mean that much to me? She closed her eyes as if that simple act would make the problems disappear.

"What about you?" she asked suggestively. "You wearing yours?" Just like Fanny Faulkner, she'd been trying to create some magic of her own, only hers was with a different type of needle. During her convalescence Misty had taken up knitting. She'd made a sweater for Steve, hoping it might make him homesick for The Rock.

Steve ignored her question and continued on his train of thought. "Tell me what you look like. Describe it to me."

"Don't you think it's a bit early in the day for this type of conversation?"

"It's never too early for what I have in mind." He laughed. His voice was deep and sensual. She pictured him lying on his bed with the covers rumpled around him, maybe wearing her sweater but definitely not wearing anything else.

Steve's gift was from some ridiculously expensive lingerie boutique.

"Will you wear it all day under your clothes? Just for me?"

How did you cool off a relationship that seemed to be endlessly hot? The man drove her crazy.

"And you still haven't told me what it looks like," he continued.

Against her better judgement, Misty played along. "Kind of naughty," she said softly with just a hint of huskiness.

Steve didn't stop. "What does it feel like?"

"Soft and smooth against my skin."

"And how does it make you feel?"

"Excited...and..." She took her time, drawing it out. "...very, very sexy." She heard him moan in response. Misty closed her eyes and pictured him again, only this time she was lying next to him and he had absolutely nothing on.

"Who you talking to, Mom?"

Misty nearly dropped the phone. Her eyes flew open. How much had Liberty heard? Oh, my God. This could be all over town in a matter of hours. Misty looked at her daughter and wondered what to say. Finally, she figured the truth was the best option and she crossed her fingers and hoped like heck that Liberty hadn't overheard anything. "A friend," she said.

"A boyfriend?" Liberty asked.

"No, dear. Just a boy who is a friend."

Liberty's eyes narrowed and Misty held her breath. "I'm not sure about that," she said to her mother. "You look pretty gooey to me."

Misty felt her cheeks burning with embarrassment. "I always look gooey at sentimental times like Christmas."

Liberty looked like she was evaluating what her mother had said. "Yeah, you're right, Mom. You are gooey." And she gave Misty a kiss and headed back to the living room to join her sister.

"Steve?" Misty asked, wondering how much he had overheard. "I told you we shouldn't be talking like that. Liberty walked in on the conversation," she scolded.

"Like this was all my fault. You have to take some responsibility for being so damn seductive and leading me on. Woman, you have me so rattled I can hardly think straight. Do you know how much of my day is lost fantasizing about you?"

"Are you sure you want to be involved with a woman who has kids?" she asked him.

"I like package deals and I like you. I always wanted a woman who could knit."

"So you like the sweater?" Her heart was filled with a warm, nurturing feeling. She really cared that he would like it. Hell, that he would like her and appreciate what she had given to him, something made by her own hands with a bit of her in each clumsy stitch. It had been years since she had knit anything, much less a sweater for her lover. She liked the way that word sounded. It slipped into her mind like a forbidden delicacy.

"It feels soft against my skin," he said.

"Will you stop it?" Misty tried unsuccessfully to stifle a laugh.

They chatted for another half hour and kept to subjects that were much less likely to raise either suspicions on the part of eavesdroppers or parts of the anatomy, for that matter. Misty regretted when the time came to say good-bye, but she really had to start dinner and she also wanted to watch a movie with the girls.

She wore the negligee all that day and night but didn't get a chance to tell Steve. Liberty came down with stomach flu, and Misty did double duty in the bathroom most of the night. When she finally fell into bed, the dial on her clock read three a.m. Steve hadn't called her back as he had promised. She knew he was having dinner with friends and her imagination played with that thought. She couldn't shake the idea that there were hundreds of women in Toronto who would be ready, willing, and able to comfort a man like Steve. Once her old insecurities surfaced she spent a restless few hours until daylight, tossing and turning as though she were cast adrift in a sea of emotions.

Boxing Day was quiet and relaxing, and soon the magic of Christmas Day was only a memory. A warm, fuzzy memory, mind you, and one that left her feeling something special had happened in their lives.

Duff had given her a hint to expect visitors on Boxing Day. She had lots of food on hand and a good selection of spirits, but the day passed without anyone knocking on her door. She felt a little disappointed and finally gave in to putting on a comfortable pair of sweatpants and a t-shirt. But underneath, she was still wearing Steve's negligee.

By nine o'clock the girls were tucked in bed. Misty was about to shut off the lights and go to bed herself when a loud knock sounded on the door. Geez, a bit late for visiting if you weren't invited. She cracked the door and looked out.

A group of oddly dressed people stood on her veranda garbed in old, tattered clothing, their faces covered by cloths and fabric.

Her first instinct was to slam and bolt the door but when they called her name, she took a second look and realized that this was what Duff had been talking about.

"Is there any mummers 'lowed in?" they chorused in strange indrawn voices.

How could she be so dumb? Mummers. Of course!

"Well, now," she replied artfully. "I'm a poor, single woman living all alone in this big house with only my two little children. Will I be all right if I let you in?"

"Missus, the only damages we does is to your liquor cabinet and the floors. Waddaya say? In we comes?"

Misty stepped back. "In you comes," she agreed and let them traipse into the house, wet boots and all.

Things took off rapidly and she was glad the girls were sound sleepers.

She had no idea who the people in the group were. There were men dressed as women and women dressed as men. Some wore pillowcases over their heads and others just used pieces of cloth attached to ball hats and toques. A few had used pillows to change their shapes and sizes, and between them all they had a guitar, an accordion, an ugly stick and three or four sets of spoons.

She hadn't ever seen anything like this in her life. Pansy wasn't wrong when she said Misty had forgotten all about outport living.

"You knows me." One of the men approached and gave her a big hug.

"I do?" Misty had no sweet idea who it could be.

"And you knows me." Another man came up behind her and gave her a pat on the bottom.

She jumped. "Whoa-ho. You're a frisky one." Just to be safe, she backed up to the counter where her hindquarters were protected from sudden, unexpected attacks. Her encased leg looked gargantuan in the sweatpants. A full-blown case of thunder thigh.

"We wants a swally," they chorused, banging their fists on whatever surface they could find.

"If I give you a drink, what'll you do for me?" asked Misty.

The man with the guitar strummed a few chords. "We plays for our cups, missus."

With that they broke into a rather off-key rendition of "We'll rant and we'll roar like true Newfoundlanders…"

"Okay, I'll get you something. Based on your ability to harmonize, you can use it." Misty offered beer, wine, and dark rum. Pretty soon, she joined in the singing whenever she could remember the lyrics of the old island songs.

She had a few ideas as to who was in her kitchen but unless she could guess, the masks stayed in place. She made a few feeble and hilarious attempts. No one seemed to mind as the masks didn't appear to provide any impediment to sipping a beer or swigging a glass of rum, and so the guessing game continued.

When the crowd showed no sign of dissipating, Misty slipped into the pantry to dig for potato chips and cheezies, something to absorb the alcohol and keep the party at a manageable level. She knew the mummers would be on their way soon enough and maybe a bit of food would help them stay on their feet.

The munchies were on the top shelf. Pansy was usually around to help out but, of course, Murphy's Law had to come into play sooner or later. How in the heck was she to get at them? Climbing a stool with a cast was a recipe for disaster.

"Hey, I need some help in here," she called from the pantry. No one was paying her any attention. "A bunch of drunken sods," she said as she looked up at the shelf. It wasn't that high. If she held on to another shelf with her free hand, it should be possible.

Misty pushed the stool up against the lower cupboard and took a step up. Then another. Excellent. About more four inches and she'd have it. She spied a set of tongs. Ideal.

This time when she reached, she was able to get a grip on the munchies and, with a sweeping motion, pull them off the shelf. They tumbled down over her, bouncing off her head as one of the bags split open. She was instantly adorned with salty chips.

Just perfect. It was bad enough she was dressed like a sloth but serving herself up with a little dill pickle dip? Totally unacceptable.

She dropped the tongs and wiped her face. There were grains of salt all over her lashes, on her lips, in her hair.

"There you are."

At the sound of a man's voice, she turned, losing her balance in the process. Her arms flailed and reached out for anything, something to hold on to. They cut through empty space. She was going down and to someone with a leg in a cast, going down was akin to leaping off the edge of the Grand Canyon.

This was bad.

"Oh, nooooooooo."

Omph! A set of arms wrapped around her tightly and lifted her into the air.

"Mmmmmmmm, look what I caught. You look good enough to eat."

"I am good enough to eat," said Misty, referring to the potato chips in her hair, then suddenly realizing that voice was very familiar.

"Steve?" she asked feeling her heart beginning to pound. "Is that you?"

"Just in time, I'd say."

He set her down on the counter and picked a chip from her head. He slipped his hand under the pillowcase he was wearing and ate it.

"Delicious," he said.

Ordinarily that type of manoeuvre would turn her off, but knowing who was doing it made everything perfectly all right.

"I can't believe it. How...what...when..." She gave up, not knowing where to begin, and it didn't matter anyway. All that counted was that he was here.

"It's a good thing you don't make your living on the radio."

Misty tried to lift the pillowcase, but he grabbed her hands and wouldn't let her.

"Who's this Steve you're talking about? I'm the Kissing Pirate. And I'm here to collect some booty."

"Why didn't you tell me you were coming? I'm a mess."

"That depends, really. Kissing Pirates tend to prefer their women seasoned with salt and vinegar."

"Steve," she said drawing out his name. "Will you stop?"

"Why? This is fun. And besides, next to you salt and vinegar chips are my worst addiction. This can't get any better."

"Take off that cover."

"Un-unh. Don't you like a little mystery, Misty? Maybe I'm not Steve."

Steve's attempts to engage her in the game made her feel shy and awkward and more than a little nervous. She felt as though she were a teenager again. It had been months since she had seen him but the effect of his presence upon her flooded her senses much as one might feel if they were drowning in champagne. It was, she decided, a totally delicious sensation.

She looked into his eyes. They were an even softer blue than she remembered. *Such nice eyes, she thought.*

"Let's see," he said as he wedged himself between her legs and selected another chip from her hair and slipped it under the pillowcase into his mouth.

"Well?" she asked, meaning a lot of things. Mostly, why he surprised her like this.

"I'm not sure we'd be having this moment if these had been barbecue."

So, this was going to be a game. "Is that right?" She looked down at him pressing against her thighs. If there were ever a moment she should close her legs, it was long past. The heat of his pelvis and the many months of telephone foreplay pumped through her, reminding her of just how powerful Steve's presence was, especially like this when their bodies were so connected, so intimate.

His eyes penetrated hers and Misty felt a connection that stirred her deepest soul. This man's effect on her was unsettling. No wonder she hadn't been able to reach him by telephone. He'd been on his way here. To her. She wondered if this was the part of her Christmas present that had garnered the most thought. Because if it was, he had made an excellent call. She loved surprises. Especially the kind that came in faded blue jeans with soft cotton shirts with no instructions for self-preservation.

She took a chip from his fingers and ate it. "I've never been able to stop at one or two, either," she said.

He selected another from the front of her t-shirt. "Right to the bottom of the bag?"

Oh boy, she thought. He missed his calling. He should have been an actor, in those old swashbucklers where breasts heaved and pants swelled.

"And then, do you chase that last little bit of salt? Kind of like this," he continued. To make his point, he used his tongue to lift a granule of salt from her lower lip.

She reached out to pull the pillowcase fully from his head and he stopped her, grasping her wrists with his hands. A wave of excitement raced through her and she hoped he would seek another taste, this time of her. She was raging with desire for him and the more he played, the worse it got. She tried to settle her mind, to think, to meet him halfway in the spirit of this game.

"You certainly don't sound like you're from here, Mr. Kissing Pirate." She wiggled her hands, attempting without really wanting to break free of his grip. When he tightened his hold on her, heat flared instantly and raced through her veins. She was afraid for a moment of how deeply she craved him.

"I'm not quite ready to let you go. Just yet." He leaned over and the warmth of his body so close to hers reminded her of hot summer days, when the city streets simmered with radiant waves so intense she could see them.

"Have you missed me?" he asked.

"Yes," she replied. "I've missed you very much."

"Tonight is our time. I've come a long way to be with you, Misty."

She felt he was referring to far more than the distance he had travelled. "And I've come a long way to be with you," she replied, knowing somewhere deep inside there remained, still, a tremor of fear and uncertainty.

When he released her arms, she slipped them gently around his neck. "I can't believe it's you," she said.

"I've just been away for a while," he replied.

"Me, too," she said. "Way too long." Misty almost began to cry. She felt a confusing mix of emotions. On one hand, she was enjoying the way he was playing with her. It was fun and light and easy. But on a far deeper level, she longed for an unbridled and passionate reunion, one that unleashed all the sensuality building inside her.

After all these months, he was really back and not only back, standing in front of her, resting between her legs, pressuring her body to respond.

A blast from an accordion intruded into the pantry. She had almost forgotten about the guests in the kitchen. Apparently, they had completely forgotten about her.

"Why didn't you tell me you were coming?" she asked, still looking into his eyes which had turned a deeper blue, kind of like the ocean in late fall.

A deep and sexy laugh floated up from his chest. He placed his hands on her waist and looked deeply into her eyes. "Because it was part of my gift. I wanted to surprise you."

"It worked." Her voice wasn't much more than a whisper.

"Uh-huh."

He was holding her more tightly than before, but she knew without a doubt, he was holding himself back, taking his time. In his eyes there was magnetism so primitive her womb responded in kind.

"How long are you staying?"

"A few days. I have to be back in the office on Monday."

"A few days? How?" Her mind went blank. "I don't understand. I thought you were tied down."

"Nice choice of words…" he paused, then continued. "Fact is, I quit. I was fed up and no good to anyone. I figured if I didn't see you, I'd become the dentist from hell. I'm rehired Monday but until then, I'm yours."

"Will you take off that stupid pillowcase and kiss me?"

"First you have to make a promise."

"What?"

"That I can spend the night with you."

"What about..."

"Pansy. It's already arranged. We're staying here. They're going there."

"But they're already in bed."

"All the easier. They'll sleep all the way."

"You really are impossible."

His fingers played gently with the soft cotton of her shirt. "I'm really a rogue, you know. I come from a long line of pirates."

She was tempted to tell him to do what pirates always do. *Take me now. Here. On the countertop.* What came out was far more rational. "What are you going to do?" she asked.

"Plunder."

Oh, my. She might be rational but he wasn't stopping the game. He lifted the pillowcase again. There was a shadow of a beard and it looked different... dangerous, even. She waited for him to remove the cover completely, but he didn't. He stopped when it reached the top of his lips.

"Do you know what else?" he asked. His voice was soft and sensuous. She watched as his lips formed each word.

"No," she replied, secretly hoping he might ravage her. She wanted this man like nothing else on earth.

"I'm going to kiss you." And he placed his lips upon hers and slowly tasted her with his tongue. A gentle kiss that graduated into a deep and sensual tour of her mouth. When he released her, she was breathless. *About the plundering part, he was absolutely right.*

Once again she tried to take hold of the pillow case and pull it off but his free hand clasped hers and held it at bay.

"That wouldn't be fair, sweet miss. You haven't given me your word. Am I to stay the night?"

"Oh," she whispered. "Ple..."

"Misty, what the heck are you doing in the pantry?" Hatty Pond stuck her head around the doorjamb. "Oh, I see." She laughed. "Think I'll leave you two alone. It's too hot in here for me."

The moment was broken. *Damn Hatty and her timing.*

Steve lowered the pillowcase. "Guess we'll have to continue this later."

"You're not going to leave me like this?" Misty asked.

"Not at all. What do you take me for?" He lifted her from the counter and set her down on the floor. "Better?"

That wasn't what she meant at all and he knew it.

"Is there a back door out of here?"

"No!" The word was out of her mouth before she realized what she was saying. "Well, I mean, yes, there is. But you can't leave."

"Honey, I've got no choice." He looked down at his pants. "Unless you want to explain this to a room full of drunkards."

Misty blushed. "They won't notice. Like you said, they're drunk. I'll stand in front of you."

"I don't think that would help. Standing close to you is what got me in this situation in the first place."

"Well then, stay here. I'll get rid of them."

He lifted the pillowcase again, just enough to brush his lips with hers. "Hurry up."

If this had been the time when real pirates had coursed the shores of Newfoundland, thought Misty, she would have been in serious trouble. She could never say no to those eyes. It wouldn't have mattered who was in the next room.

She took a few seconds to compose herself, the chips and salt in her hair completely forgotten. When she emerged from the pantry, Hatty grabbed her arm.

"And where do you think you're going?"

"To bed," said Misty.

"Don't doubt that," Hatty replied. "Question is when."

"As soon as I can get the guests to move on." Misty said. "I have a terrific headache."

"Really? Must have developed very quickly. You didn't look like someone with a headache from what I saw." She laughed and her heavy stomach shook. "Wants I get these fools out of here?"

"Please." Misty was relieved. All she could think of was Steve in her pantry.

"I'll give you a piece of pie tomorrow. On the house." And she slapped Misty on the backside and gently pushed her toward the living room. "Sweet dreams."

No kidding. Misty floated into the other room where she spied a note from Pansy on the front table.

Merry Christmas, Misty. Remember what I told you. Fanny Faulkner is behind all this. Don't worry about the girls. We'll have a great time and call me in the morning when you gets up. Pansy

She had drawn a big happy face at the bottom of the note. *Cute.* Misty sat down and waited for Hatty to clear the revellers. The Fanny Balls on her tree appeared to be dancing. *Holy Toledo. Maybe there was something to Fanny Faulkner after all.*

CHAPTER 21

Shiver Me Timbers

As soon as Hatty hollered good-bye, Misty got up from the couch and went into the kitchen. Steve was leaning against the countertop waiting for her. The pillowcase lay in a heap next to him.

He looked every bit as good as she remembered and then some. She viewed him with full appreciation, taking her time to survey his body from head to toe. He had a lean, muscular build that looked extremely attractive in his faded jeans and t-shirt. His chiselled arms were folded over his chest and he took a long, slow drink from his beer as he surveyed her in turn.

Now that they were totally alone, she felt a little nervous and she wasn't nearly as confident as she wanted to be. Her heart and stomach were doing nothing to help. They were busy playing some game of their own that left her feeling lightheaded and breathless.

Flirting in the pantry had been an intoxicating game but now, in the silence of her home with all the revellers gone, it was time to make good on all those promises. Steve was aroused and desiring her. She felt the same way toward him. But she was also very edgy and her head was awash with so many conflicting thoughts. She and Steve had really been seducing each other for the past five months; a slow striptease of words and emotions.

Misty couldn't resist dropping her gaze to where his pants pulled taut across his hips, knowing that even as she did so Steve was watching her. He was aroused in a powerful way, and she was suddenly self-conscious of how she looked and what she was wearing. She ran her hand through her hair and wished she looked more exotic than she did. Her cast felt like an anchor and she was embarrassed to be caught in sweatpants and a t-shirt.

The silence between them was odd. It was as though they had stepped through a portal into another world. Everything and everyone had disappeared but the two of them. And now, after all these months, all those evenings of longing and frustration and friendship, they were finally standing here, with no barriers of time or distance.

"No one is going to miss you?" she finally asked to break the silence.

"That bunch? They wouldn't miss their heads at this point."

"I guess you're right." She smiled shyly, veiling her insecurity. She hadn't been with another man for more than eleven years. Thankfully, she had looked after herself. That wasn't the part she was worried about. What scared her was whether or not she could go through with this. She was about to enter a whole new phase of her life.

"Come here." Steve seemed to understand she was caught somewhere between desire and timidity.

When she didn't move, he put the beer down and came to her and took her hands in his. "I know what you're thinking," he said. "But we can't stop what's inside of us. There were things I didn't say to you these past months, but you have to know you're very special to me." He took her into his arms, a warm, engulfing hug that felt so right. "I've missed you," he whispered gently against her face.

She rested her head against his chest. "I feel like I've known you forever." Her words seemed inadequate to describe what she was feeling. She wanted to be possessed by this man, filled with his essence and soothed by his touch.

"I feel the same way about you. I know you love your children. I know you're brave and courageous. I know your eyes are amber, that you're funny and spontaneous. And I know you've missed me." He released her and placed her hands upon his chest. "Can't you feel every part of me is calling to you?"

Misty closed her eyes and felt the rhythm of his body beneath her hands, the gentle rise and fall of his chest, the soft beating of his heart. When Steve pulled her into his arms this time, there was no resistance on her part. She felt as though she belonged to him.

"I don't know what we're afraid of," he murmured, his lips pressing into her hair. "We can't change how we feel and I know you feel the same way I do."

"That's true, but in my case there's more than just me to think about."

"I would never do anything to separate you from your children or to bring stress into your lives."

Misty buried her face against his shoulder. She craved him as she breathed in his scent. He smelled like spice and fresh air and virility. He was everything she had dreamed of and more. Funny, kind, and caring. Compassionate and honest.

"Sometimes we're the last to see. It's not easy to find the right person, Misty. And we both know in our hearts we should be together. It just feels so right." His hand slipped under her t-shirt and he caressed her back.

Misty moaned. Every feathering touch sent charges of desire through her. Such sweet words. Such tenderness and understanding.

As he kissed her she slipped her arms around his waist and traced the muscles of his back with her fingertips. His skin was smooth and firm and his muscles undulated as he began to move in an easy rhythm to a song he was humming.

It took her a few minutes to place the song. It was "White Christmas." He stopped singing but kept directing her as though the music continued.

"May I have this dance?" he asked, cradling her head in his hand as she leaned against his chest. He began to hum the tune again and then drifted into the words of the song.

It was easy to lose herself in his arms. To let her body move in syncopation with his as though they had been doing this for years and years, and not just this one time.

Steve had a clear, melodic voice. Misty closed her eyes and let him guide her. Theirs was a waltz with a funny, awkward gait.

He gently supported her as they slowly circled her kitchen. They could have been anywhere, so lost was she in her thoughts and feelings for this man. She was surprised when she joined her voice with his and they sang together. It was so unlike her to do that. They sang the song again as they continued their dance. When they stopped, they were by the door to the front room.

Misty opened her eyes and saw Steve looking at her Christmas tree. The Fanny Balls danced gaily in the branches.

"That is one of the most unique Christmas displays I've ever seen. Your handiwork?"

"Uh-huh. Fanny Balls. Named for Fanny Faulkner."

"She must be someone important to have decorations named in her honour."

"She works at the hospital."

"She's saved many lives?"

"In a way," said Misty and smiled. "You could say that."

"I'll have to meet her someday."

"I'm sure you will," replied Misty. "I'd count on it."

Steve looked at her with a funny expression on his face. "Is there something I don't know?"

"Oh, Steve. Fanny's a matchmaker. She zapped me a couple of weeks ago."

"Right."

"You don't believe me?"

"I'm in no position to argue. Why did she zap you?"

"For love. Which sounds ridiculous, I know, and I really didn't believe it myself but then Mincie had her fourth child and Fanny zapped Flap, which was what got it all started."

"Hold on." Steve put his finger over her lips. "Misty, shut up. You've lost me. I have absolutely no idea what you're talking about and you know what? I don't care. Fanny can zap whomever she wants; it isn't going to make any difference to the way I feel. I'm in love with you."

"You're what?" Misty was afraid to believe what she had heard.

"I love you. Every crazy part of you. You're like a drug. I can't get you out of my mind day or night. Do you know the only time I'm not thinking of you is when I'm asleep and even then I dream about you? There's no relief for me."

Misty took a deep breath and hugged him. Then she did something totally out of character. Leg cast and all, she jumped into his arms. In retrospect, it was a pretty silly thing to do because Steve lost his balance and the two of them tumbled to the floor.

Steve cushioned the fall with his body and Misty lay on top of him. She looked into his eyes, tantalized by the way they changed colour with his moods. Under the tree lights they had turned a bold, intense blue. She felt the evidence of his desire pressing into her belly and also an urgent need to have him inside of her.

"I love you, too," said Misty. "I can't believe I've met you. How could all of this happen in Charlie's Cove? This was supposed to be a dead end for me."

"What we have going is not a dead end. Christ, Misty, I'd walk to hell and back to be with you." His slid his hands down her back and stopped when he could squeeze her bottom. He used just a little extra pressure to hold her against him. "If I don't get out from under you, I can't be responsible for my actions. I've thought about you in just about every way you could possibly imagine and some I'm sure you couldn't."

Misty pushed her pelvis against him. "I have a better imagination than you might think, honey."

"Maybe you do. Slide up a little more and kiss me."

Misty did just that and as her lips touched Steve's a Fanny Ball fell from the tree and bounced off her head and onto his brow.

"What the..." he said in surprise as his eyes flew open.

"Don't worry," laughed Misty. "It was just Fanny having the last word."

"No, this is the last word." Despite the awkwardness of her cast, he rolled over and pinned her beneath him. A single cry escaped her throat.

"It's never been like this before," she said. She was trembling, sizzling as her hands found their way to his hips. "I have a perfectly good bed upstairs. It's never been used for anything other than sleeping." Despite the heat she was feeling, she giggled.

"Misty, I need twenty-four hours and a padlock for your door. I don't need any bed."

"But I do."

Steve gently rolled off her body and before she could say a word, he had hoisted her over his shoulder in a fireman's hold. Misty had never seen her tree from this angle. *It still looks nice,* she thought as she bobbed up the stairs, her hands bracing Steve's backside for balance. *Kind of upside-down, but nice.* In fact, she was suddenly feeling that way about her whole world.

She blew a kiss to her Fanny Balls as Steve reached the top steps. There was, without a doubt, more than just the magic of Christmas in the air.

CHAPTER 22

Yo-Ho-Ho and a Bottle of Rum

"So, you're not admitting to it either?" Misty used her fork to stab another piece of Hatty's excellent partridge berry pie and pop it in her mouth. "This is unbelievable," she said referring to both Hatty's denial and the pie. Normally, Hatty couldn't keep a secret for ten minutes.

"I didn't know it was Steve until I saw you two glued together in the pantry like a couple of jam-jams. He just showed up and joined us. Kind of like the old days when mummering really happened by chance." She patted Misty on the head.

It was almost New Year's and Misty was lovesick. Steve had left early on the 28th. Their night of bliss had been just that. Blissful, romantic, and funny. Making love with a cast on your leg required almost as much creativity as writing a column for Misty's Misadventures. They'd tried a few things that worked and a few that hadn't but even then, being held in Steve's arms and having the chance to talk and see him at the same time had been unique enough. No matter what Ma Bell said, there were things the telephone just couldn't replace.

Now that he was gone again, she was back to a ten-digit romance but this time there was a discernable difference. Something between them had gelled in those two days and it felt real and good. Steve was in her thoughts day and night, especially night when it was quiet and she could let her imagination run wild. At those times, Steve wasn't very far away at all. She felt very connected to him. It was hard to explain, but those feelings were real and magical.

Misty looked up to find Hatty staring at her.

"That's some case of the lovesicks you got. You been tuned out for about five minutes. Let me guess, you was thinking of him, weren't you?"

Misty's face immediately felt like Hatty's red-hot grill. "More often than not," she confessed before pleading with her confidant for more information. "C'mon, Hatty, I know you're holding out on me. People around here always know everyone's business, but when I want some information, they can't recall anything. Don't you find that peculiar?"

Hatty cracked a smile. "We been told for so many years we don't know nothing that it don't mean much to us anymore. We know what we knows. That's what counts."

"But you didn't know Steve was coming home."

"Apparently not."

Hatty's grin looked suspiciously like that of a Cheshire cat. *These people are not to be trusted regardless of how much food and hospitality they force upon you. They have their own ideas and their own ways of doing things, and nothing I say will ever change that.* Even though she might not admit it at the moment, she found the way Newfoundlanders cared for their own a very endearing quality. And they all loved a bit of fun—maybe even a bit too much when it was at her expense.

Having rationalized her way through the piece of pie and coffee, Misty gathered her things and placed a generous tip for Hatty on the counter. "I'll see you later, then," she said as she lurched across the restaurant to the door.

Next Tuesday couldn't come too soon. She was scheduled for a visit with Fanny and Dr. Roberts. There was a good chance her cast was coming off. And if they didn't remove it, she had a deal cooked up with Duff to take a chainsaw to it. Either way, her leg was hatching.

Things were busy at *The Yarn* and she wasn't surprised to smell Phonse when she walked in the door. The residue of cigarette smoke was a tell-tale sign he was working overtime. Thanks to increased readership, which Misty attributed this time to the improvements in the personals, advertising was at an all-time high. Boxing Day sales abounded and they had even received ads from several of the surrounding communities.

"Didn't they pass legislation about smoking in public places?" she asked as she placed her briefcase on top of a pile of papers on her desk.

"Shut up, Muldoon. Who says this is a public place? I feels it's me personal and private domain."

"You act like it, too. Who put all this stuff on my desk?"

"Santy Clause, b'y. While you been running around acting like Farley's billy goat, he been working."

Word spread in Charlie's Cove like a good dose of the flu. Steve had spent one night in her house and it was almost front-page news. Still, there was nothing to be gained by locking horns with Phonse, so she put on her most cheerful expression and changed the subject. "What puts you in such a joyous mood this morning?"

"In case you hasn't noticed, Muldoon, the clock is passing twelve. We bees in the afternoon now and I'm up to my snout in work. Nice o'you to drop by."

"You gave me the time off. Why didn't you call if you needed help?"

"You reads minds on everything else," said Phonse as he glowered at her over his glasses. "I just figured you'd show up sooner or later. Now, quit your griping and take a look at this."

Griping? Me? Boy, did he have a dose of kettle and pot disease. Misty sat down in front of his desk as he passed her a copy of *The Blarney*. There, on the front page, was a picture of *The Yarn's* office.

"What's up with this?" she asked.

"They says we's poaching, moving into their market and taking their readers. Poaching? By thundering, I'd like to poach and pickle Avery Sharpe's privates. They bees asking their customers to boycott *The Yarn*. He's not getting away with this, the sneaky, cowardly, snivelling, little ferret."

Misty stifled a smile. "What do you think we should do?" she asked, even though it looked as if the battle lines had already been drawn.

"We needs something to knock them on their arses," replied Phonse with certainty. "I wants a story everyone feels compelled to read. He thinks he's got problems now, when our next issue hits the stands, he'll be wishing he'd kept his measly trap shut." Phonse locked eyes with her and licked his lips. "And I wants you to write it, Muldoon."

Of course. Why not? "Where am I going to get a story like that this time of year?" she asked. The very idea was ridiculous; setting up a feud with *The Blarney*.

"Make it up, for all I cares. Just deliver it by next Tuesday."

"Phonse, that's only the day after New Year's."

"Yes, b'y. And now you got a goal already. That's luck, Muldoon. You bees starting the year like all the other fools who makes resolutions."

Misty stood up as forcefully as she could. "I'll give you a goal, Phonse Penney. Try getting along with Avery this year. Folks are going to do what they damn well please. Avery can't boycott *The Yarn*."

"That's what you thinks. I seen him at work before. You don't know squat. He's bees a pasty-faced sewer rat who'd bite his own mother if she weren't wearing army boots. We're going to make good and sure he don't get one up on us. I wishes you luck, Muldoon. I wants a doozie."

A doozie? Misty returned to her desk and sat down. She looked in despair at the mess deposited there. Flyers, letters, advertising copy. It took her about two hours to clear enough space for her laptop and as she cleaned she thought about many things, including ways she could outsmart Phonse. He seemed to have a bottomless bag of discrediting remarks when speaking of Avery. *Wonder what he'd say about me if I fail to land a freaking doozie?* The very idea was disturbing. The man was going to drive her crazy. She paused a moment to utter a short prayer. *Dear, sweet Goddess of Creative Shit, anoint me with material. A crisis, a fire, a hurricane. Anything. And deliver it in five days, please*, she added as a codicil.

Thursday passed. So did Friday and Saturday with absolutely no visits from the Goddess. Misty was suffering her first full-blown case of writer's block. Her only relief was her preoccupation with Steve. And when Pansy invited her to a New Year's Eve party at her father's house, she was very tempted to beg off and wallow in her misery. Pansy, however, wouldn't hear of it. So, on New Year's Eve Misty dutifully packed up Viv and Liberty as well as her underactive imagination, and all four of them headed out just after nine o'clock.

"Will they have fireworks, Mom?" asked Liberty.

"I don't know. I forgot to ask. Maybe."

"Duff told me everyone gets drunk," said Vivi.

"Oh, he did, did he? I'm sure he was mistaken." *Maybe I need to monitor these conversations with my kids.*

"Duff said they do," insisted Vivienne. "And I believe him." She giggled.

"I believe Duff, too," added Liberty as she launched into a song. "Ninety-nine bottles of beer on the wall, ninety-nine bottles of beer. Hic."

"Where did you learn that?" asked Misty. "And please don't say Duff."

All she heard from the backseat was more giggling. Misty was happy enough to let the subject drop for the time being. But while they followed the winding road to the other side of the harbour, she decided that it might be time to go over a few guidelines again with both Duff and Pansy. "Ninety-nine Bottles of Beer" was not the song of choice for her children. Whatever happened to *Sesame Street* and *The Count*? Maybe she was spending too much time working these days, but no wonder. Phonse had put her under pressure and she still hadn't come up with a story idea.

He was entitled to his feud with Avery, but it wasn't fair to involve her. You couldn't just manufacture news on a whim. It took something worthwhile happening. This was Christmas. Just what did he expect her to do?

"Pansy!" Vivienne and Liberty ran through the door and into Pansy's arms. She picked them up and gave them a ferocious hug. Both girls were chattering excitedly.

Pansy set them back on the ground. "Now, get on in there and say hello to everyone. They's waiting for you." Liberty and Vivienne ran into the kitchen, leaving their bags at Pansy's feet.

"By the way, do you have anything to do with a counting song called 'Ninety-nine Bottles of Beer?'" Misty looked at Pansy who blushed under her scrutiny.

"Ah, that's no big deal, Misty. It's all for fun." She picked up Vivi's and Liberty's bags and placed them in the corner.

"Right."

"You seems some uptight."

"Who wouldn't with someone teaching her kids songs about drinking beer?"

"I'm sorry. I'll come up with something else. There's always coolers." When Misty opened her mouth to vent, Pansy began to laugh. "Gotcha." She leaned over and gave Misty a peck on the cheek. "That's better. You needs to lighten up and I guarantees you will. Wait 'til midnight when they comes at you with their lips puckered up like tommy cods. Even Scrap Nichols bees here tonight."

"Scrap Nichols?"

"Only the most available piece of work in Charlie's Cove. You might like him, Misty. He's single, he's got his own business, and he don't disappear into the night like Zorro. I kind of fancies him myself."

"Not interested," said Misty. Ever since Pansy had found out about Steve's surprise visit, she'd taken to calling him Zorro. Misty wondered sometimes just how much Pansy knew about Steve's life and if she might be trying to warn her off.

"Is there some reason you think I shouldn't be involved with Steve?" she asked abruptly. "Because if there is, I want to hear about it straight up. I'm not interested in any guessing games."

Her friend and helpmate blushed. "It's nothing like that," said Pansy apologetically. "It's just I seen him come and go the past few years. A few of the local girls fell hard for Steve, but he never let it slow him down. It's probably different with you, Misty. At least, I hopes it is, because I don't want to see him hurt you."

"You think I haven't thought about that? I have, I really have and there are times I'm scared out of my mind. I'm not sure I'm ready for another commitment, but what can I do?" She lowered her voice. "It seems I've gone and fallen in love with him. It feels like the real thing, Pansy. It really does. But I'll be damned if I can figure out how it's going to work. That's the part that worries me."

"I don't think he'd ever hurt you on purpose. But things happens so just keep an open mind. That's all I'm saying and if someone here wants to take you out, it might be a good idea to give it a chance. If there's no ring on your finger..." she said as she grabbed Misty's hand. "And I don't see one, then don't put all your faith in one guy. You knows what they says."

"I rather doubt it," replied Misty, referring to her inability to figure out the thinking in Charlie's Cove.

"Why buy the cow if the milk's free."

"Oh, for God's sake, Pansy, I'm not into games. You want me to play hard to get? I'd say I'm doing a pretty fair job of that without even trying. I'm not moving, I've got two kids and I'm beginning to enjoy the company of Phonse Penney. Don't you think that pretty much takes the shine off of little ole me?"

"Just make sure it's what you wants. That's all. I'm only looking out for your best interests."

Misty realized Pansy was being sincere but it was hard to appreciate her advice when every nerve in her body was vibrating for Steve. "What kind of work does Scrap do?" she asked just to be polite.

"You can't be serious? He's got the scrap yard just outside town. You knows the one. He advertises in *The Yarn*, sure." Pansy seemed buoyed by the fact Misty was showing a little interest in Scrap.

"He does?"

"'We buys wrecks.' You seen that?"

Misty couldn't say she had but maybe she should get a bit more interested in advertising. Not because of Scrap, but because Phonse was so territorial about it. It might be a small and annoying way to get back at him.

"Anyway, never mind Scrap," continued Pansy. "C'mon into the kitchen. That's where the action bees."

Misty wasn't quite prepared for *the action*. The White's kitchen was filled with people. All sizes. All ages. A heavyset man was playing an accordion with a zeal that seemed to defy the rather intricate balancing act of resting the instrument against his protruding stomach and reaching the keys. Another fellow, tall and lean, was working a fiddle like it was an extension of his arm and a tiny but wiry woman wearing a long, cotton dress with an embroidered collar, was beating a set of spoons between her leg and the palm of her hand. For a makeshift orchestra, the music was upbeat and surprisingly good.

Misty wasn't even inside the room when a man grabbed her arm and pulled her onto the dance floor, if you could call a cleared area in the centre of the room a dance floor.

"Slow down," she cried out. "I'm not stable on my feet." She had worn a silk blouse and a short black skirt, giving her plenty of mobility with her cast. The worsted sock that covered her toes was slippery on the canvas flooring and she felt like Hop-A-Long Sid.

"I'll hold you up. Not a problem," said the man who held her hand. She had never seen him before. He was tall with dark, wavy hair. Not bad looking, in a rugged, unbridled way.

"Okay," Misty managed to say before he locked his arms around her and lifted her off the floor, swinging her like she weighed nothing at all. She could see Pansy looking at her and mouthing *Scrap Nichols*.

So, this was what Scrap looked like. About two hundred pounds of sinew and muscle, levelling off at six-foot-two or three. Misty wrapped her arms around his neck and hung on, hoping "The Squid Jiggin' Grounds" would soon be over.

When it was, Scrap set her down and helped her to the side of the room where it was safer and much less congested. Leaning against a countertop with a man hulking over her had a familiar feeling but there were none of the bells and whistles going off this time. Just the slightly uneasy sensation of someone being in her space, too close for comfort.

"I reads your stuff in the paper," said Scrap. "Likes it, too. 'Specially that story on Hedges. Might get one of them tonight if the action keeps up."

Misty shuffled to the right where she could talk to Scrap without getting a cramp in her neck. "Actually, that would be great. I need a story for Tuesday. And thanks for reading my stuff." Scrap seemed like a nice guy and maybe if Steve hadn't come to visit, she might have been more willing to give him a chance. As it was right now, there was only one man she was yearning for.

"Give her a break, Scrap. She only just got in the door."

"Shove off, Pansy. I just joined the Welcome Wagon committee and I'm setting her up for a big, fat, wet one at midnight."

Pansy punched Scrap in the arm. "I knows Welcome Wagon needs the likes of you. Give it up, b'y. Here, Misty." Pansy passed her a beer. "Finest home brew on the island. It's got a bite that'll take a piece of your tail with it. Careful."

"Where are Vivi and Liberty?" Misty asked as she took the bottle from Pansy. She wasn't sure her kids could distinguish between a social drink and someone getting drunk. She certainly didn't want them coming to any conclusions about their mother based on Duff's stories.

"They're upstairs with my sister's kids. We got some movies for them and popcorn and all the goodies. Bride Powell's up there with them. If they isn't safe with Bride, they isn't safe with no one. Bride's good with kids. Wants some herself, what, Scrap?" She nudged him in the ribs. "You likes full bodied women, don't you?"

"Prefers them smaller, Pansy. You knows that. Like your friend here."

Scrap looked at Misty like a hungry man eyeing a four-inch sirloin and she suddenly felt very uncomfortable. She took a swig of beer, hoping to break the magic moment developing in his eyes. When the beer hit her taste buds, she started to cough, which sent it into her nostrils. It burned and tickled at the same time, a sensation she didn't want to experience again any time soon. Pansy gave her a sharp slap between the shoulder blades.

"Told you this was powerful hooch, Misty. They calls it Iggy's Pop and don't no one swig Dad's beer but Dad and maybe Phonse Penney. You learns a lesson some fast, though." She was laughing and so was Scrap. "Watch for the sediment on the bottom, too. You tips it easy, like this." Pansy demonstrated for Misty.

When she could actually breathe again, Misty joined in the laughter. Was there anything she could do right on the first try these days? "How's this?" She demonstrated her new technique at swilling beer. "I'm beginning to think living in Charlie's Cove should come with an instruction manual."

That set off another round of laughter, which ended with Scrap pulling Pansy onto the dance floor. Misty was glad to have a few minutes to take in the action. She was especially pleased for Pansy, who was beaming with Scrap's attention. Even if Misty had been attracted to him, she would never interfere with what might be Charlie's Cove's next big romance.

So, she thought, this is a real outport time. In all her years of growing up in Newfoundland, she had never been to one before. Maybe there would be a good story here and she decided to work the room as best she could and talk to as many people as possible. An hour later, she put down her bottle, empty almost to the dregs. Her head was floating with ideas. Too bad she'd left her computer at home. Otherwise, she'd escape to the second floor with the girls and get to work. Maybe she'd check on them anyway.

"Whoa, where are you going?" It was Scrap. He had a grip on her hand like a gaff. "I wants another dance with you." Before she could object, he picked her up in his arms and carried her back to the dance floor. Once again, he acted as though she weighed nothing.

Soon he was gyrating to accordion music with Misty draped over his chest. She didn't know the song but it kept a good pace and Scrap was no slouch. He hefted her like she was a sack of potatoes and folks moved out of the way to avoid being clipped by a few pounds of plaster.

It wasn't long before everyone had cleared the floor, hooting and hollering from the sidelines as Scrap and Misty took over the space like a double-bodied whirling dervish.

Someone whistled. "Way to go, Scrap."

"Give 'er, Scrappy. Give 'er," yelled another man raising his glass in the air.

And then Misty heard the words that turned her blood to ice. "My turn bees next, Scrap. Pass 'er over." And that's how the next hour flew by. Misty was passed from man to man, each of them taking a turn swinging her around the floor. Maybe it was some kind of initiation rite but whatever it was there was no turning it off. In between partners, she caught sight of Phonse Penney who seemed thoroughly entertained watching her being thrown about like a rag doll.

When they finally set her down, Phonse was the first to move in. "Hey, Muldoon, you sure has loosened up some. Don't mind showing your panties to a crowd now, do ya?"

"For your information, Phonse, I'm wearing shorts and for future reference I'd prefer you weren't looking up my skirt."

Phonse took a slug of the drink he was holding and slapped her on the back before he shuffled on his way. "If I was interested in looking under your skirt, Muldoon, I wouldn't have waited all these months." His comment was punctuated with a roar of laughter.

Right, thought Misty, *and if I lit a match by your face, you'd probably combust, laden as you are with dark rum.* "I'm surprised there's a rational thought in his head tonight," she said to Pansy as she pushed her hair from her forehead and fanned her face. "It's hotter than hell in here."

"You needs another beer," said Pansy as she pushed Misty toward a chair just vacated by one of the revellers.

"Or a tankard of water," Misty suggested as she sat down. Of course, the beer was easier to find, and this time she had the good sense to take a sip and work up to a gulp.

"Time flies when you're having fun, what?" Pansy pointed to a table laden with food. "We got a scoff on, too. Fish and brewis, cod tongues, and some britches." When she saw the look on Misty's face she patted her on the shoulder. "Don't worry, there's moose burgers for the uninitiated."

Misty hadn't yet developed a taste for many of the local dishes. Fish with softened hard bread wasn't too bad but cod's tongues? Ugh. And fish ovaries called britches? *Not a chance.* "Is it always like this?"

"No, sometimes we gets in fights. No sign of that yet, but the night's still young."

Prophetically, at Pansy's comment, the back door to the kitchen opened and Avery Sharpe walked in with a couple of men who looked as though they might be on leave from the World Wrestling Federation.

"Or maybe I spoke too soon," Pansy said.

The music slowed and conversation dwindled as people sensed a change.

"Nuttin' like a good party crash," said Avery slurring his words, obviously having had a few himself. "We'se just bringing greetings from Hickey Harbour, what?" He nodded to the men with him who produced a couple of flats of beer. "The more the merrier, we says."

An electric charge radiated from Avery, and his attitude bespoke trouble but the fortifications proved too much for the crowd to ignore. A couple of men moved forward to take the beer and welcome the late additions into the room. The music began again, and the party picked up where it had left off. To someone as sober as Misty, the charge in the air was ominous.

"Did your father invite both Avery and Phonse?" Misty whispered to Pansy. "Doesn't he know what's going on between those two?"

"Avery's a distant cousin of the Snows. I don't think Dad would have invited him, but the way family is, no one's gonna kick him out either."

"Except Phonse," said Misty. "Where is he, anyway?" She scanned the room but could see no sign of her hot-headed employer. "You've got to help me find him. The last time he and Avery were in the same place it was an all-out fight."

"Last I saw he was heading to the john," said Pansy.

Misty no longer felt tired. With a rush of adrenaline, she came to her feet. "Can you bar the door from the outside?" she asked Pansy.

"Sure we can. With a chair. But you're not going to do that, are you?"

"I certainly am. I don't care what kind of entertainment it would provide, I'm not letting those two drunken fools get into a fight. Get me a chair and fast." Misty crossed the room to the bathroom door and tried it with her hand. It was locked. That meant Phonse was still in there. Pansy pulled a chair over and together the two of them jammed it beneath the handle of the door.

"You think it will hold?" asked Misty. "I've never done anything like this."

"If it doesn't we're in deep trouble. Phonse will be just as pissed at us as he will be at Avery."

"It's a chance I'm willing to take." For a moment, Misty almost smiled. Phonse Penney locked in the john. She was going to pay for this next week, if they made it that far into the future.

Misty checked her watch. It was five to midnight.

"Fireworks outside," someone yelled.

"Pansy," she said as she grabbed her friend's arm. "He's trying to get out." Her heart began to beat rapidly as she watched the knob jiggle slightly. *Hold,* she whispered to herself. *Hold.* Other than referring to Steve, she had never used those words with quite so much passion.

"Hang on. I'll clear the room and be back with Scrap," said Pansy. "That way if he gets wind of Avery, Scrap can keep him under control."

"Don't leave me here like this. Hurry up."

"Everyone outside for the countdown," Pansy called to the crowd. She began ushering the guests toward the back door making sure Avery Sharpe was amongst them. "C'mon, or you're going to miss it."

By now, Phonse was banging at the barred door with his fist and Misty could hear him cursing. She kept her eyes on the knob, bracing to confront him if he dismantled their makeshift lock. Feeling vulnerable with her bum leg, she looked around for something, anything, she could use to threaten him. If he got out he was going to be ripping mad and she would be the first person he set eyes on. She spied an empty bottle of Old Sam Rum on a nearby table and edged toward it, all the while keeping her eyes on the door.

As her hand wrapped around the bottle, Phonse began kicking. She watched as the old door began to pull away from its hinges.

"Timing is everything," she said under her breath. "Where the hell is Scrap Nichols...I wouldn't mind if he wanted to show off now." She tore her eyes away from the door to see if there was any sign of Pansy and Scrap. Nada. She wondered what she should do; hope Phonse wouldn't see her or try to out-run him. She had a fifty/fifty chance given the odds of his drunkenness against her leg. Her decision was made when the door and the chair holding it both crashed to the floor followed by Phonse cursing and swearing like a demon from Hades itself.

For a moment he appeared dazed, but as he regained his focus his eyes settled on Misty. She would have to face him and try to explain about Avery.

"Muldoon," he screeched. "I mightta knowed you was behind this. Where'iz ever'one? I been waitin' all year to wet these lips with Mary Keefe's big ole smackers. If I misses me chance..." He rolled over to his knees and began an unsteady attempt to stand up. "...I'm gonna kick your scrawny ass into next year." Phonse was slurring his words and if Misty hadn't been so accustomed to listening to him, she might actually have had a hard time understanding him.

"This is next year," she yelled back at him. "And I'm trying to save you from embarrassing yourself and landing in jail."

Phonse gave up on the effort to stand and simply reached out to grab Misty's legs in a tackle. "I wanz a kiss, Muldoon. If it ain't Mary, iz gonna be you."

"You drunken sod," she said as tried to dodge him and keep her balance.

Phonse leaned hard on her leg, anchoring her like a concrete block. She was running out of options and the thought that Phonse could hurt her leg and set her back a few months escalated her need for self-preservation.

"The only thing interested in kissing you might be a land-locked seal and I imagine Mary Keefe will thank me for this." She slammed the bottle she was still clutching across the back of his skull.

Phonse wavered for a moment, then collapsed to the floor as his eyes rolled back in his head. Misty stood over him shaking with frustration and rage, the remnants of the bottle in her hand.

"Misty," Pansy said as she ran back into the kitchen. "Oh. My. God." She stopped as she stared at Phonse lying prone on the floor. "Are you all right?"

"That...that...man..." said Misty between clenched teeth. "...is such an idiot."

"What happened? Tell me you didn't kill him."

"Someone had to stop him before he killed himself or...or me or, given a bit of time, Avery Sharpe. Oh, what the hell..." She shook her head in disbelief at what she'd done. "I...I whacked him on the head with this." She held the broken bottle up like it was a trophy.

Pansy's mouth opened in shock. Her eyes widened as if she couldn't take in what she was seeing. "Is he alive?"

"I hope so. I just hit him. It's not like I'm Hercules or anything. He dropped like a dead man." She smiled weakly. "That was a poor choice of words. Forget what I said." The bottle slipped from her hand and when it shattered on the floor, Phonse didn't flinch. She looked at Pansy with concern. "He's either dead or dead drunk.

Should we check his pulse?" She was beginning to wonder if she had committed murder.

"I guess so," said Pansy as she stepped closer.

"Wait." Misty held up her hand. "I think I saw him breathing."

They both stared intently at Phonse. "I'm not sure," Pansy replied her voice filled with tension.

Misty hesitantly leaned over and reached for his hand. The thought of touching him repulsed her but she moved her fingers over the inside of his wrist until she located his pulse. A few seconds later she looked up. "The old bastard's still alive."

"That's a relief."

Both women exhaled simultaneously, not even aware they hadn't been breathing. Pansy made a feeble attempt to lighten the situation. "We hasn't ever had a fatality at one of our New Year's parties. He'll sleep it off and probably won't remember anything in the morning."

"That would be nice but somehow I think he will. I'm relieved to find out he's still alive, though, and I never thought I'd ever say something like that." She shook her head and wiped at her eyes with the back of her hand.

"What is we going to do with him?" asked Pansy.

Misty looked around. "All we need now is for this to be on the front page of *The Blarney*. Let's get him into the front room before the crowd comes back."

"Then get someone to take him home, I guess."

"Call Lottie. With any luck, she'll finish the job I didn't do."

"Feet or arms?" Pansy asked.

Misty winced. "Neither is very appealing." She paused and sized him up. "Feet."

Pansy moved to Phonse's head and Misty placed her hands around his ankles. "Ready?" she said. "This isn't going to be easy with my cast. Let's just drag him."

After quite a bit of trouble, due mostly to Misty's inflexibility rather than Phonse's dead weight, she and Pansy managed to get him into the next room.

"Do you have any tape?" Misty asked.

"You're not serious?"

"I'm not taking any chances on him waking up and getting hold of me or you. Until he's out of here, he's a dangerous weapon as far as I'm concerned."

Phonse moaned.

"The tape?" said Misty, looking at Pansy nervously.

"I'll be right back. You bees okay?"

"Just go." She kept a wary eye on Phonse, who had now started snoring deeply. He looked amazingly harmless and innocent for someone so volatile.

All this because of a ridiculous feud. She felt both angry and exhausted. Angry at herself for getting involved in the first place and exhausted by the whole drunken affair. It was a very strange emotional brew. She was trying to account for everyone else's shortcomings when it wasn't her mess to manage in the first place. Duff was right about one thing.

Everyone does get good and drunk.

Pansy returned with some tape and she and Misty bound Phonse's hands and feet.

"This may be overkill but I feel a lot better knowing he can't do any more damage. Where's Avery, anyway?" asked Misty.

"I'm not sure, but I called Lottie. She's tearing up the pavement as we speak. You should've heard her on the phone."

The door behind them opened and Misty jumped, realizing how shaken and nervous she really was. When Scrap walked into the room, she was visibly relieved. "Thank God, it's only you."

"Hey, that's not what I likes to hear from the ladies." He stopped and stared at Phonse. "Lard Jesus, what has you two been doing? I'm not walking in on some sex thing, am I?"

"Oh, give it up," said Pansy as she whacked him in the arm. "I been looking for you. Phonse is after kicking out the bathroom door and attacking Misty."

"He don't look too dangerous now, b'y."

"Don't fool yourself. It's Phonse Penney, driven by demons, possessed by the devil," replied Misty.

"More likely possessed by Old Sam rum," said Scrap. "Not much damn difference between the two. They says it's like a drug for some people. Drives 'em mad."

Misty jumped again as a knock sounded on the front door.

"That'd be his ride," said Pansy, heading for the entry.

"I guess this is where I comes in. Come on, Phonsie. Time to go home," said Scrap as he heaved Penney over his shoulder in a fireman's hold. "Not sure how Lottie's gonna handle him on the other end."

"You ain't never seen Lottie in action," snickered Pansy, seeming glad for a bit of comic relief. "Phonse is likely to walk over hot coals tonight."

Misty watched as Scrap manoeuvred his way through the door and down the front steps. When Phonse was sprawled over the backseat and Lottie behind the wheel, she turned to Pansy. "Now, if you'll excuse me, I'm getting my kids and we're going home. It's not every New Year's I attempt to commit murder."

"C'mon, Misty. It weren't that bad," said Pansy.

"You didn't have Phonse bearing down on you. Who in their right mind would turn on someone trying to keep them out of trouble?"

"That's just it; he wasn't in his right mind. He didn't know about Avery and he didn't understand you were trying to help him." Pansy's face was a mix of emotions. "You're not writing about this, are you?" Even as she asked the question, she was shaking her head from side to side saying no.

Misty hadn't even thought about writing since the whole incident unfurled but now Pansy had broached the subject, she felt with certainty at least part of her experience would make it into her column.

"Misty, you can't," said Pansy. "Phonse will kill you."

Misty looked at her friend in amazement. "Or kill my column. The crafty devil gets the last word on everything."

"Assuming you still has a job, right?"

"There is that."

It didn't take long to collect the girls and put them in the car. They were tired but animated. Misty was thankful they had no idea what their mother had been through.

As they drove home, she looked at the Christmas lights shining brightly on the eaves of the houses and on the large evergreen trees that dotted the yards. It was hard to believe such a peaceful, postcard-perfect town could have spawned such an evening. The air was calm without a draft of wind and the moon hovered above the water like a huge luminescent bubble.

It had been a night she'd never forget for many reasons. She'd experienced the warmth of Newfoundland in a special and memorable way, but she'd also seen another side...happy go lucky, drunken sods and drunken, dangerous fools.

If she could just explain it in the right words, she felt sure her next column would be powerful and it would definitely have a message. Now whether or not Phonse Penney would have his doozie was another matter. She had an inclination he wouldn't want a starring role in any tale she would tell.

CHAPTER 23

Tidal Wave of Love

Misty pulled her hat from her head and fluffed her hair with her free hand. She had spent New Year's Day working on her *doozie* and it had taken eight drafts for her to be satisfied she had achieved a balance of truth without offending anyone.

One look at Phonse Penny and his swagger this morning and she wasn't so sure what she had written was suitable at all. And it really had nothing to do with her writing and all to do with his behaviour at the party, his apparent lack of contrition and his mind-numbing ability to act as if nothing had even happened.

"Got that copy done yet? I needs to see it, Muldoon."

Misty glared at him as she conducted a one-sided conversation with her conscience. *This man is either the dumbest sod on the face of the earth or the cagiest old geezer I've ever dealt with. He deserves a public roasting. Maybe. Unless he really doesn't get it. Could he be that dense or, simply, conniving?*

She finally decided if he could act like nothing at all had gone down, she could, too. At least temporarily.

"Happy New Year to you, too," she said as she forced a smile that barely reached her nose, let alone her eyes. "Gimme a kiss, Phonsie. You thought that was a pretty good idea the other night."

"Kiss me arse, Muldoon."

A drunken fool sober, only just slightly less obnoxious than a drunken fool drunk, thought Misty as Phonse stormed past her and into the newsroom where she felt certain he would sit at his desk, light a cigarette, and lean back in his chair straining the springs to full capacity. At least she knew where he was until she was ready for him.

She turned to Tilly next. If Phonse was a closet sociopath, what might Tilly be this morning? "Happy New Year, Til. Make any resolutions you can't keep?" She brushed the light dusting of snow from her briefcase.

Tilly turned her head and Misty felt as though she were gazing into the eyes of a coiled cobra. "A few and I'll be keeping them."

"Filled with mystery this year, are you?" Working at *The Yarn* was beginning to feel like a rollercoaster ride with a blindfold.

"It's no mystery. I'm looking for another job. Something I can stomach. According to my horoscope, it's time to make a change."

Misty sighed. Apparently Tilly was not bitten with the same memory lapse as Phonse. Her anger seemed as deep rooted as ever. "I hope this isn't because of me. We don't have to be best friends to work together."

Tilly squeezed her top lip between her thumb and forefinger as she shook her head slowly from side to side. "Newsflash. Not everything is about you."

"Well, good luck with it, then." To Misty, Tilly's statement rang false. No matter what she said, this all came down to personal resentment. Toward her.

Damn it all to hell. I'm not taking on any responsibility for Tilly's attitude. That isn't my problem. Unless…unless, of course, she senses my uncertainty about staying in Charlie's Cove. There was an element of guilt in that admission and it was darn uncomfortable. *If I truly believe I'm not taking advantage of anyone, why do I let her make me feel uncomfortable? All I'm doing is my job; doing it quite fine and surviving. No one is suffering on my account. Well, possibly one person and he'll know soon enough.*

"Muldoon!" From the tone of voice, Phonse had run out of patience.

"Coming," called Misty and she turned and headed into the newsroom.

"Where's the goods?" Phonse was leaning forward in his seat and stubbing his cigarette in the overflow of butts in the ashtray on the corner of his desk.

She really wanted to reprimand him for his behaviour on New Year's Eve. So much so, it was hard to keep her mouth shut. But with a magnificent effort she did and then forced herself to stay on topic with him. "Relax, I've got your story and you'll have it for this afternoon's deadline. Worry *pas.*"

"Worry pas. Don't be using any French on me this morning; telling me not to worry in your hoity toity lingo. I knows French, too. Shit, for instance, is merde. And I hates all the merde that goes with the New Year, Muldoon. So don't be dropping cheer on me unless it's dark and requires Coke."

"Now that you bring it up," she replied, "you might want to consider giving *that* up."

"Your story better not be about New Year's resolutions," he said, blowing her comment off without any reaction. "I'se sick and tired of 'em. Give up this. Give up that." He pulled out another cigarette. "I'm not giving up nothing. I'm increasing, that's what." He stared at her as if really only seeing her for the first time this morning. "You looks like you choked on a jeasly canary, Muldoon. C'mon, give us a look. I needs to gnaw a canary meself."

Finding the good side of Phonse was beginning to remind her of finding the sweet chocolate centre in a hard peppermint candy. It took time and a whole lot of sucking to get there.

Misty took a deep breath. "Look, I know you want Avery by the short and curlies, but you're going to need a bit of faith and patience." She could lie with the best of them when backed into a corner. "I've got a bit of polishing to do. You'll get your canary later today, in plenty of time for your deadline." *Like when I'm gone.*

Phonse checked his watch. "I wants her by two o'clock. I needs time to plan me headlines. We're taking *The Blarney*, Muldoon. I been dreaming about that snivelling weasel for days. You an' me, we're goin' in and we're goin' in deep." Having gotten that off his chest, Phonse dismissed her with a shake of his head and settled down to work. It wasn't long before he headed out for his customary visitation to the john.

Misty used his absence as an opportunity to read her story again. She had agonized over how to express herself. She felt she had unpeeled a very unsavoury side of the good natured, hard-drinking men who populated the small coastal communities. It wasn't easy to say what she had to say without offending them. She felt nervous as she read her copy.

It was solid writing but it was also questioning just how good the good times were and it took a large slice out of the myth that had become the larger-than-life Newfoundlander. That part left her with a queasy feeling in her stomach. Her story was too dark for what he wanted and like the proverbial acorn, also a bit too close to the tree. What was she saying? Clearly, if this were a court case, Phonse himself would be exhibit A and she knew handing him this story would have repercussions not unlike nuclear fallout.

She opened her writing folder and scanned through the list of her previous work. The Hayward Hedges story. That's the type of thing Phonse was hoping for. *Well, I just can't manufacture stories like that on a whim. I have to go with what life presents to me. That's what's been working for me and for The Yarn.*

She continued down the list until her eyes landed on the column she had written several weeks ago; the one that would never make it past *Goals for the New Year*.

She opened it and read it again. This time it made her chuckle. How pathetic was she? Ring my bell? Knock my knocker? Email, text or phone? She was looking for love, all right. *Gawd, Misty. You sound so desperate. It's time to get a life or at least entice a pirate back to Newfoundland.*

"Misty!" Tilly poked her head around the doorjamb. "Are you going deaf? I been yelling out to you for an hour. You got a call on line two."

The image of a blue-eyed rogue evaporated into the lingering haze of cigarette smoke. "Sorry. I was thinking about a story." Tilly looked at her accusingly, like she was caught at something she had no business doing.

Misty shrugged and took line two.

"Misty, it's Fanny at Dr. Roberts's office. About your appointment this afternoon, the doc's got a baby coming sometime today. We needs you like ten minutes ago or we can reschedule your cast removal for Thursday."

Thursday? Two itchy, cast-lugging days away? Not likely. "Fanny, there's nothing coming between me and my Calvins today. Just give me five minutes and I'm yours."

Fanny laughed. "Make it quick. Mincie Mercer can drop a bairn faster than an anchor."

"Not Mincie? Hold the door, I'm on my way." Misty jumped to her feet as she placed the receiver back into its cradle. She was now quite adept at dealing with the cast while doing other things, like putting on her jacket and hobbling out the door.

"I'll be back shortly," she called to Tilly who was filing her nails. "This boat's coming off." Tilly gave no indication she was hearing anything, but Misty continued to fire instructions at her anyway, hoping some of them would sink in. "Tell Phonse I'll be back within the hour. Keep him away from my computer. Take messages. I'll return calls this afternoon."

Tilly finally looked up as Misty finished buttoning her jacket. "Phonse's in the john. You wants I walks in and tells him or you prefers to do it?" She dropped her nail file and picked up a clothespin, which she dangled between her thumb and pointer.

"Stuff it, Tilly. If I don't go now I'll have to live with this cast for two more days. And, believe me, you don't want that to happen."

The wind snapped at the door and took her breath away. It was the kind of cold that penetrated to the lower surfaces and turned her cast into an icy block of plaster in seconds.

With as much grace as she could muster, she got into her car. At Phonse's suggestion, Scrap Nichol's had embellished her driver side door with a huge *Yarn* logo. Press privileges, he told her, and as long as he was paying the gas, he wanted it on.

Misty was in no position to debate. She needed the supplement to her income but as far as the logo making a bit of difference to her status at community events? Unless you counted the time she was egged driving through Hickey's Harbour, it didn't help one bit.

And the hideous logo also didn't make a hoot of difference at Dr. Roberts's office either. His parking lot was blocked. She solved the problem by parking in the handicapped zone, which was her privilege to do for another sixty minutes.

Enduring a second blast of frigid air, she clambered into the building and announced her arrival to Fanny.

So much for timing.

Mincie managed a feat never before heard of in Charlie's Cove. A delivery so rapid Dr. Roberts needed a catcher's mitt, or so the story went. Misty ended up following him to the hospital, which was actually a small rural clinic with some provision for emergencies. She covered the birth story while she was waiting. Twins, if you could believe it.

By early afternoon, she was restless and hungry and still wearing her cast.

"Do you think Dr. Roberts will be available shortly?" she asked Melvina Fancy, the receptionist.

"Running out of patience or what, Misty? You got the luck. Scrap Nichols just come in. Dropped a rear axle on his foot. Some sight, too. Big as what Scrap is, he bees some baby." Melvina laughed.

"You mean I have to wait again?" Ever since she knew her cast was coming off, her leg had been itching like she had her own personal poison ivy patch growing under there.

"Unless you wants to tell Scrap he got to wait."

"Ohh…" Misty sighed and sat back down. She had figured on being back at *The Yarn* office eons ago. She weighed the pros and cons of calling in or just driving over. She'd prefer not to delegate anything to Tilly, but what if she missed her one opportunity with Dr. Roberts? No, she wasn't taking any chances.

The phone rang ten times before Tilly picked up.

"*The Yarn* where we knows news. This bees Tilly Penney. I can help, ya wants." Tilly's voice conveyed the enthusiasm of a death-row inmate.

"When did Phonse come up with that? I seriously hope he doesn't expect me to use it."

"You'll use it, all right, if you wants your job."

"You're leaving anyway, why bother?"

"I needs a reference, Einstein. Where are you? He's got me drove, just drove, and he's swearing about your copy, too. When'r you going to get here?"

"No idea. I've been chasing Dr. Roberts all day."

"Phonse is gonna roast your butt. Not that I cares." She sounded delighted about it.

"Do me a favour. Please. One favour, that's all I'll ever ask of you. Please?"

Misty waited for a response, which was a long time coming.

"And if?"

Give me patience. Misty struggled to think of something which might entice Tilly. "I'll...I'll...clean your desk."

"No good."

"C'mon, Tilly. Don't do this. I left the story on my computer. Just forward it to him. Please?" Misty stressed the please part, hoping Tilly might feel some compassion. "Bring you coffee in the morning. Double cream, two sugar and a six-pack of Hatty's muffins." *C'mon, you little shit.*

"Cloudberry muffins?"

Misty made a fist and punched the air. "Is there any other kind? So, you'll do it?" Misty bit her lower lip. *Do it, do it.*

"All right but I wants them fresh and no later than 8:45."

If she personally had to pay Hatty to fire up the oven, Tilly would have her morning muffins. "Thank you so much." She was both surprised and grateful for Tilly's cooperation. "I really mean it." Melvina was waving to her. "I've got to go. I think I just won the lucky draw. Don't forget." Tilly's laugh as she hung up the phone gave her pause. What had she just done? Only given her enemy carte blanche access to her files. What was wrong with that? Plenty, but at the moment her options were limited.

She dismissed the negative vibe and racked it up to nerves. As bad as she was, Tilly wouldn't mess with Phonse. Especially not when she'd soon need a reference. She crossed the room and followed Melvina. It was a time of celebration. This was the first day of the rest of her life without a cast. Nothing could ever top that. Nothing.

"You wants this as a souvenir, Misty?" Dr. Roberts asked.

The sound of the saw left Misty in a sweat and she kept her eyes on the ceiling. "What? Ah, no, that's all right. I've got memories to carry with me."

"You sure? Lots of nice messages here," said Fanny who was assisting in the removal. "Like this one from Clayton Poole, '*Loves the look, loves the stump. You wears a skirt, I sees your rump.*'"

"It don't get much better than that," Dr. Roberts agreed. "Might want to use it in an article on memorable breakages. Most people keeps their casts, you know."

His comment got her thinking that maybe it would be a good idea to keep it. At least for a few weeks. You could never be sure when ideas might dry up and she could always use it as a defensive weapon with Phonse. "Do you have gift bags?"

Dr. Roberts and Fanny laughed heartily and Misty endured another ten minutes of torture until she felt the cast loosen.

"It's coming off. Let us know if there's any discomfort," Fanny said.

Did it really matter? Discomfort or not, Misty was prepared to endure anything.

"Like a butterfly from the cocoon. She's all in one piece, Misty," said Dr. Roberts as he examined her leg, running his hands gently over the bones.

"I should hope so after six weeks," said Misty.

"I was referring to the cast, me duckie. She's all in one piece. We'll wrap it in a couple of garbage bags."

Misty was enjoying the sensation of lightness in her leg and barely heard him.

"Beautiful. Absolutely lovely work. Let's try standing. You can expect the muscles to be weak and a bit tight." He offered her his arm to sit up and swing her legs over the table.

Misty looked down and almost fainted. Her normally shapely appendage looked like something that should be attached to Phonse. It was shrivelled and white and the hair...oh, my God, the hair.

"What happened? Look at it!" She pointed to her newly hatched leg.

"It's normal to lose some muscle tone, my love," said Fanny in a motherly way.

"But the hair?"

"I guess we should have warned you about that." She chuckled. "Hair sprouts like seaweed under a cast. Looks funny, huh?"

"Funny? It's shocking. I need a wax job. Now."

Dr. Roberts laughed this time. "No, you needs to stand up. If the leg works, then you can get the wax job." He placed a walker in front of the table. "Use this to support your weight. See how it feels."

Misty carefully edged herself off the examining table, grasped the walker and placed her feet on the floor, careful not to put too much weight on her leg. She took one tentative step and braced herself for the worst. Her leg felt like a piece of fully cooked spaghetti and had about as much stamina.

"You have any topical Viagra?" she asked. "Look at this thing. It's soft and flabby."

Fanny gave her a swift, little pat on the backside.

"Yeow," she said as she stood erect. "What was that for?"

"To take your mind off things. Look. You're actually standing upright."

"That's what I wanted the Viagra for."

"You'll be fine," said Dr. Roberts. "My, oh, my but you're even funnier in person than you are in your column. Think she'll give us a mention, Fanny?"

"Think you'd want it?" Misty replied with just a hint of seriousness beneath her laughter. "It's been known to change lives."

"That's interesting. Any examples?"

"Mine, for instance. That column has turned things around for me. All in a good way."

"And it hasn't been so bad for Phonse either, I imagine. Maybe we'll forego the opportunity, on second thought, but I'd still like to see you next week. Gimme a quick Watusi and I'll let you loose."

Misty rolled her eyes. "I'll take a raincheck on that if you don't mind." She hobbled back to the table and leaned against it. "But I would settle for a little help getting dressed."

"And we thought you were going to be dancing out of here," Fanny said as she helped Misty back onto the table.

"No funny stuff, either," Misty said to Fanny when Dr. Roberts had left the room.

"What do you mean, funny stuff?" Fanny asked innocently as she helped Misty into her pants.

"You know. Matchmaking and that kind of thing. Pansy warned me about you and I'm beginning to believe her." Misty slipped her feet into her sneakers, marvelling at the sight of two clad feet instead of one.

"Oh, she did, did she? Look into me eyes, then, and tell me what you sees there." Fanny stood in front of her with her hands placed squarely on her hips.

"I see a practical jokester. That's what I see," replied Misty a little uncertainly as Fanny's intense green eyes met hers head on.

"And I sees love," Fanny continued as she took Misty's hand. "Not in your eyes but in your hand here. You got some coming, honey, whether or not you wants it." Fanny gently traced a line in Misty's palm with her thumb. "But I wouldn't worry, were I you. It's all good what I sees."

By the time Misty arrived home, she had dissected her conversation with Fanny a thousand different ways. Pansy took one look at her and shooed the girls, who were fascinated by Misty's cast, back into the kitchen to finish their supper. Then she ordered up a hot bath and ran down to the supermarket for supplies.

When Pansy returned, Misty was sitting in her robe on the edge of the tub looking like a lost soul. She shrugged her shoulders at Pansy. "It's hopeless. I'm tighter than a banjo string."

Pansy held up a jumbo-sized pack of razor blades. "Let me do the honours, Misty. This leg is going to take a bit of work. My aunt Maude never shaved a hair in her life and her legs looked better than yours any day."

"Thanks for that comforting thought. I'd prefer this was our little secret."

"You knows me better than that. I'll be selling this to *The Blarney* for a trip south. Where's me camera when I needs it?" She lathered up the shaving gel and selected a razor from the package. "You don't mind me saying but you looks like you seen a ghost."

"Or a witch. I was Fannied."

"She got you, eh? What happened?"

Misty gave Pansy a hard look. "She grabbed my hand and made some disturbing predictions."

"Right on. What did she say?"

"She sees love in my future."

"All good. Did she have a name?"

"No, I got out of there as fast as I could. Her eyes are mesmerizing."

"You should do a story on her."

"Please don't mention work to me. Phonse is probably putting a bounty on my head," Misty said, changing the topic abruptly.

"You didn't write about the party, did you? You couldn't take my advice, could you?"

Misty watched as Pansy ran the razor under water and lined up for another pass. Instinctively, she reached out and placed her hand over Pansy's. "Easy with that. All those years of waxing had a purpose."

Pansy shrugged. "Perhaps you should take over," she said sourly.

"Will you give it up? You know I had to make some sort of comment. I can't help myself."

"Neither can I and I thinks you made some mistake writing about the likes of Phonse." She continued her work with the razor, somewhat more gently than before.

"But I didn't say anything specific. No names. No places. Just some thoughts about this island. In some ways, it reminds me of Neverland, a place where people are content to play and never really grow up. Even when things go wrong, there's something about it all: a resilience that never seems to tarnish, an innocence that no one can change. Honestly, Pansy, most people will think I'm spinning a fairy tale. Those who've experienced it will understand, and those who haven't, it'll be like looking through a Coke bottle with all the distortions that go with it. Trust me, you've got nothing to worry about."

Pansy seemed to settle down again with Misty's explanation. "I sure hope not," she said quietly.

"A normal, rational person won't mind what I wrote. Sure, there's a message in it for Phonse, and given that he's neither normal nor rational at times, I'm not sure how he'll react." Even though she felt less than confident, she nodded reassuringly at Pansy. "And I'll handle it whatever happens."

Pansy blew out a long breath through her nostrils. "There's times you reminds me of Phonse with your stubbornness."

"And charm." Misty was smiling again. "You know me by now, Pansy. I've got a strong instinct for self-preservation. And survival. Speaking of which, I saw Scrap at the hospital."

From the look of panic that washed over Pansy's face, Misty knew she'd been remiss in forgetting to tell her. "He's all right," she quickly added. "He just dropped a car part on his foot. He may need some help, though. You've got experience with casts. Why not give him a call?"

Pansy turned a soft shade of pink, the telltale sign of infatuation, or love in Misty's opinion. "A girl's got to take advantage of opportunity," she continued. "You want love to walk in, you've got to invite it."

"Right. Like you would."

"It's not me we're talking about. Call him."

"I suppose I could."

"Look at it this way, what's the downside? Everyone wants a bit of romance. A little loving when you're down and out could go a long way." Pansy had stopped shaving her leg altogether and Misty gave her a nudge.

"I'll do it then," Pansy said and she finished up with Misty's leg in only a matter of minutes.

Misty sat up and crossed her legs thinking how nice it was to be able to do that again. "That's my girl. I wouldn't mind a little New Year's romance myself." She still couldn't shake the idea of how nice it would be if Steve moved to Charlie's Cove. Thinking of him brought an unexpected rush of desire. There was something about him that left her body and her heart racing as though they were in competition for a prize and only one of them would get it.

"Check your horoscope, yet?" Pansy threw a towel at Misty. "You're going to have to exfoliate."

"You believe in that stuff?" asked Misty.

"It's good for skin. Everyone knows that."

Misty was perplexed until she realized Pansy was still talking about exfoliation. "I meant the horoscopes."

"They bees good for skin, too," she snickered, "especially when the moon is in the right place." She gave Misty a poke. "Listen, wait while I gets me guide. That'll open your eyes some."

Misty dried her leg and thought some more about Steve while Pansy hunted around the house for her book.

"What's your sign?" Pansy asked as she strolled back in.

"Aries."

"Ah, the feisty ram. Here it is." Pansy's eyes raced over the page. "Hmmmmmmmm. Not bad."

"What? What's not bad?" Misty asked with more interest than she intended.

"Says here there's a tidal wave of love headed your way. You'll have many choices but the path to your heart will be clear when the right one shows up." She raised her eyes and nodded knowingly at Misty.

"First, I've got Fanny Faulkner making prophecies and now you're getting carried away. Give me a break. This is Charlie's Cove. There's not a possibility that a tidal wave of love could hit me here. There aren't that many available men on the whole peninsula."

"Suit yourself," said Pansy as she closed the book. "But I finds this stuff pretty accurate. Buys the same book every year."

"What's it say for you then?" asked Misty.

"Someone tall, dark, and handsome is going to walk into my life."

"That's pretty general."

"And he's going to need tender loving care."

"Oh, brother. You must be crazy to believe this stuff."

"Wouldn't worry about me. I'd be more concerned about the tidal wave." Pansy passed her the book. "Read it for yourself."

Misty started singing as she took the book from Pansy. "Lookin' for love in all the wrong places…"

"Well, don't say I didn't warn you," Pansy said raising her voice over Misty's ditty. "Just leave the mess after you finishes. I'm going to tuck the girls in and head home. I'll clean up in the morning. Cheerio, you man-magnet you." She blew Misty an exaggerated kiss.

After she left, Misty flicked through the book. She had forgotten how superstitious folks could be at times. If she'd based her hopes on the horrorscope, as she liked to call it, right now she'd be ridiculously lucky and living on an exotic island. *How stupid is that?*

"Imagine. A tidal wave of love," she said with just a touch of insolence, "Right." She tossed the book into the garbage knowing Pansy would retrieve it later.

The steam from the bathtub clouded the bathroom mirror. Misty drew a huge tidal wave with a pirate ship on its crest. Around it she added a big heart. "Coming right at me," she chuckled as she shucked her robe and wormed into the tub, sliding all the way up to her neck. This was the kind of luck she related to. Great old Uncle C had the best tub in the world. A cast-iron relic made for indulgence and relaxation…and dreaming.

CHAPTER 24

Smack-Dab

Wednesdays were days to be cherished.

Phonse was tied up with the press shop and left her alone. With her stories turned in, the pressure was off and she could relax and avoid the office altogether. With this in mind, Misty stretched like a cat and enjoyed the sensation of the sheet against her leg. It was wonderful to be cast-free.

A few months ago, if someone had told her life would improve moving to a small outport on the coast of Newfoundland, she would have gagged at the idea. *Now?* She felt very differently about things. Coming to Charlie's Cove had been good for all of them.

Duff, Pansy, and, she reluctantly admitted, even Phonse were all part of their lives now and she was glad to have them in it. For the first time, she was beginning to understand why families came home. It was as though the Island had taken her in a warm embrace and set her right again. This must be the experience of other displaced

Newfoundlanders, as well, and one of the reasons they came home. Even temporarily.

Maybe they'd stay. Maybe they wouldn't. She looked at her empty bed. And maybe they couldn't. She'd never thought her future might be tied to this place.

Since Phonse had sold her column to several papers across the country even her financial situation had improved considerably. Another few months and she'd have some extra money in the bank again. Maybe then would be the right time to make some decisions about the future.

More immediately, she could focus on her exercise program and getting her leg back into shape. And there was also Skylene's wedding coming up, and that alone ought to keep her occupied. Skylene had just presented her with a five-page list of things she needed done. Who in their right mind would want numbers on the bottom of the reception chairs for a kissing game? She hated to think what her big mouth had gotten her into.

She slid across the mattress and placed her feet on the floor. Chilly, even with the socks she had worn to bed. Bracing herself with her hands, she slowly raised her right leg and held it parallel to the floor. There was just enough room to do it without hitting the wall.

Well, those are the consequences when you buy the bed of enticement. She smiled to herself. *Fat lot of good it's done me, anyway. Except for that one time.*

She thought about her Christmas surprise as she repeated the exercise sequence Fanny had given her and was amazed at the way it took her mind off her leg. She could picture Steve as clearly as if he were here in the room with her. Especially the way his eyes did that funny thing when he…

"Mom." Vivienne yelled. Actually, it was more like a whine.

"What?" *Why*, she wondered, *when you had a moment of bliss did kids always seem to interrupt? It was as though they had some built-in radar system that went off when adults were thinking of sex. Just thinking of it, not even doing it.*

"Liberty's wearing my panties." There was some scuffling and crying, followed by a loud order. "Give them to me." Then more scuffling and crying.

"For the love of Pete, girls. There'd better be a good reason for this." Misty was inclined to storm into the next room, but her leg had other ideas. By the time she reached the landing and the door to Vivi's room, the action was over.

Liberty was stark naked and wiping tears from her eyes. "They're not hers, they're mine," she said between sniffles. "I'm never wearing panties again."

"Liar." Vivi had on a pair of pink boy briefs with hot-pink banding. They were hanging on her hips and obviously too large for her small frame.

This, thought Misty, *must be the definition of insanity.* "What makes you think these panties are yours, Vivienne?"

"Kelly bought them for me. Liberty's are purple."

"Liberty?"

"I hate purple. The pink ones are mine."

"Are not."

"Are too."

"Okay, this isn't helping. Where are the purple panties?"

"I gave them to Emberlee," said Liberty.

Misty rubbed her hand over her eyes and pinched the bridge of her nose. She could handle Tilly. She could even handle Phonse. But there were times when she could not handle her own girls. "Well then, no one's going to wear the pink ones today. Hand them over, Vivienne. I'm the official panty patrol." Misty said it with an air of authority.

The girls looked at her in surprise. Then Vivi took the panties off and threw them at Liberty. It was a form of following the order,

Misty felt, although she would have preferred a little less personal resentment. Now they were both stark naked. This was progress.

"As the official leader of the Panty Patrol, I have decided we are going to have a panty raffle." Even as she said it, Misty wondered why her mouth was always one step ahead of her brain.

"A panty raffle?" the girls said in unison.

"That's right." Misty picked up the panties from the floor. "But first, you both have to get dressed and meet me in the kitchen."

From the way they responded to her idea, Misty knew Liberty and Vivienne were intrigued. They quickly got down to the business of getting ready.

Now she was up and about, Misty decided to make a pot of coffee and a plan for Charlie's Cove's first official panty raffle. Was there anything as stimulating as freshly brewed coffee and a challenge first thing in the morning? She didn't think so.

Misty put the infamous pink panties on the table, set the brew cycle on her new coffee maker and sat down and waited for inspiration to hit. She was churning through ideas that ranged from a treasure hunt to an auction, when the phone rang. After literally jumping in the chair, it took her a second or two to come back to earth before she picked up.

"Hey, Misty. How're ya doing?" It was Jake. She felt her stress level rising.

"Excellent," she replied. "We're all great. Absolutely great. Hang on a minute, I'll get the girls." The phone was like a hot potato in her hands. *Coward*, her inner voice shouted.

"Wait a minute. I want to talk to you."

Me? Whatever happened to that perfect Wednesday? Talking to Jake still made her feel awkward and self-conscious. The confident woman behind Misty's Misadventures up and deserted her at the sound of his voice. On top of that, it seemed like everything she intended to say just came out wrong somehow.

"Isn't it a bit early for you, anyway?" *See? That wasn't what she'd intended to say. What she meant was, sure, talking to you doesn't bother me one bit. I'm over things. Smile.*

"Whoo-eee, you're fired up this morning."

She heard Jake sip his coffee. Something they had once enjoyed together and apparently still did. Only not together. Just separately. Well, not him. He had Kelly. She was the one doing it by herself. "I'm not fired up. I'm busy and the kids are getting ready for school." *Why*, she wondered, *do I always sound so defensive?*

"Whatever you say."

Jake had that way of dismissing her that still filled her with anger. She pressed her lips together and breathed deeply, then waited for him to continue.

"Look, I want to see the girls for a weekend and maybe a few extra days. Think we can work something out?"

She wanted to be cooperative. After all, he was their father and she'd vowed she'd never be vindictive. But she also knew Jake's requests were usually orchestrated to suit some project he had in mind.

"What's going on?" *Damn, it really is none of my business.*

"Kelly and I are getting married and I kind of wanted to break the news in person. You know, give them a chance to get used to the idea of another mom and a new baby sister...or brother."

Whoa. If she hadn't been on her fanny, she most certainly would have landed there. Jake's mouthful of information covered just about every nightmare on her list. *Another mom? A new sister or brother?* Misty felt as though she'd been hit by a tidal wave, all right, and it had no association with love whatsoever.

"Misty? You still there?"

"Yeah, ah..." She scrambled to get her thoughts together. "When?" Her voice was dispirited.

"Probably Valentine's Day. Kelly's starting to show. Don't want to put it off too long, you know?" There was a pause.

An image of him rubbing his hand over Kelly's perfect little belly popped into her head. Kelly would probably have one of those ideal pregnancies, but Misty secretly hoped she would have every miserable symptom of a long, drawn-out nine months complete with water retention and lingering weight gain. If she couldn't see her feet ever again, that would be all right, too.

"When do you want to see the kids?" Misty asked, feeling a headache coming on.

"How about next weekend?"

"Well, I mean, I'll have to check with the girls but I guess."

"Great. Let me talk to them, will you? I'll tell them myself."

"What?"

"Misty, you sound buzzed. I just want to tell them they're coming to visit. Is that all right?" She could hardly miss the sarcasm in his voice.

"Of course. Hang on. Congratulations, by the way." *By the way?* The words popped out sounding about as phoney as she felt. *My newly released husband. My former best friend. Not a problem.* The truth was it still hurt but worse, she felt embarrassed, like the whole world had known what she'd been the last to find out.

"Thanks. I told Kelly you'd be happy for us."

Will I ever be, she asked herself as she put the phone down and called to Vivi and Liberty. *You're assuming a lot, Jake.* Her daughters ran into the kitchen, all smiles, expecting an update on the panty raffle.

"It's Daddy." Seeing their faces light up with excitement was the way it should be.

She tried her best not to eavesdrop on the conversation but the excitement in the girls' voices was magnetic and part of her wanted to know what was being said. Whether she liked it or not, these changes were going to be part of her life, too. The sooner she accepted them and stopped feeling sorry for herself, the better it would be. She understood that part, so why did it still have to be so difficult?

"What's up with you?" Pansy was standing in the porch brushing snow off her boots. "I been standing here for ages and you can't even say hello?"

"Oh, I'm sorry. Didn't even hear you come in."

"Thinking of your tidal wave?" Pansy laughed.

"Hardly." There was no mistaking the bitterness in her voice.

"What's the matter?" Pansy looked at her.

"It's Jake," she whispered. "I'll tell you about it later."

"Old love dies hard, Misty." She walked over to the coffee pot. Seeing the empty mug, she poured a coffee for Misty and took another one from the cupboard and poured a cup for herself. "Here." She passed Misty hers. "This always helps." Her eyes landed on the panties on the table. "Trying a new style?"

"That's another story. We had a panty dispute this morning. I'm working on some ideas."

"Cute stuff, I bet." Pansy started preparing breakfast.

Misty watched Pansy as she waited for the girls to finish their call. Since Misty's accident, Pansy had become a fixture in their lives. Now Misty was fully mobile again, she wondered if the budget would enable her to keep Pansy employed fulltime. She sure hoped they could work something out. Having help was certainly not a luxury to her as a single parent. It was more like a necessity.

When the conversation didn't end, Misty gave up and went to her room where she selected her perfect Wednesday outfit, a casual combination of jeans and a cozy turtleneck sweater. She had a few errands to run and she loved the feeling of comfort clothes, and being able to wear a pair of her pants again was a thrill in itself. By the time she got back downstairs, Liberty and Vivienne were heading out the door to catch their bus.

"See ya, Mommy," said Liberty as she gave Misty a kiss. "Guess what? Daddy wants us to fly to Halifax."

"We're going on a plane," added Vivi.

"Wow, that's great, girls. I wasn't on a plane until I was in high school. You sure are lucky." *So much for my panty raffle. As usual, Jake took the starring role with his big, flashy ideas.*

"Love you, Mommy." Vivienne blew Misty a kiss and followed her sister out the door.

Misty watched as they walked down the driveway to the edge of the road where they waited for the bus. When she saw it in the distance, she closed the door and went to the window to continue her motherly vigil.

"So," said Pansy, coming to stand beside her. "You don't sound convinced about the lucky part."

"Jake and Kelly are getting married. She's expecting." There. She'd said it and hadn't even choked over the words.

"He bees one busy boy," said Pansy. "How's that make you feel?"

"Like a stupid, lonely failure. Oh, Pansy, I feel awful. Why can't I just be happy for them?"

"You're only human, maid. You gives it a bit of time and it won't matter a'tall."

"It shouldn't matter now. It's over and done with. I made my choices when I didn't put Jake at the centre of my universe. I was working my heart out for us and that wasn't what he wanted at all. How could I have been so stupid? And now what do I have?" She shrugged her shoulders. "I've got work. And you know what else? It's just work and it sure doesn't keep me company at night. And when I can't sleep, it's not because someone's lying next to me. It's because I'm thinking about work again."

Pansy shook her head and pushed Misty toward the kitchen. "I can't believe I'm hearing Misty Muldoon say that. Misty, you bees one of the smartest people I knows. From where I sits, you got it all together. Look at what you done. You blows into town, finds yourself a job when most of us can't even get a day's work, and then you turns into a local celebrity."

Misty looked at her helper and friend. Was that really the way she saw it? That people looked at her like she was a success? Misty shook her head at the idea that someone could think of her in that manner. "I'm jealous, Pansy. Jake and Kelly stole what I wanted, what I thought I had. And now I've got nothing."

"Well, aren't you a pathetic creature this morning. It don't take much to toss your little ship into a squall. I read you your horoscope for good reason. You got it coming at you and for all you knows, it could be right around the corner. Now stop feeling sorry for yourself."

"I don't want to."

"Well, you should. You got two beautiful kids, a comfortable house, and you got a brain, which is the most important part of that equation. You needs to get a handle on being grateful, that's what."

Pansy is right. What she says makes perfect sense. Wallowing in self-pity isn't going to help me at all. Why, then, am I so inclined to do it? She gnawed on her thumb as she thought about how she was feeling, knowing another chewed fingernail was not going to make her feel any better. "I know you're right. I'm crazy, okay? I just need a bit of time and I'll pull myself together. Promise." *I'm not convincing anyone, especially me.*

Pansy wasted no time in telling her, either. "What a crock. What you needs is a good kick in the pants and if you're not careful I just might deliver it. Now, this bees your favourite day of the week, right?"

Misty nodded.

"Then get going. Out the door. Do something with that new leg of yours. And stay out of my way."

"Bugger off, you."

"There's my little Phonsie. Go on. Get." Pansy chased her through the living room and right into the front porch where she handed Misty her coat.

Misty put it on and added a hat, scarf, and gloves and, finally, her boots. The ones without the heels.

The rest of the day, she spent as enjoyably as possible. She ran her errands, dropped by Hatty's, and even came up with some stories for later in the week. And finally, when she ran out of things to do, she took a drive. All by herself to the end of the road by the picnic park where she could look out at the ocean.

Despite the cold and biting wind she got out and huddled against the side of her car where there was a little protection from the elements. She wouldn't have dared to traverse the path, which looked treacherously icy.

It was a brilliant day. The ocean was blue, the sky was clear. Everything was in sharp detail. A few gulls floated over the water, oblivious to the cold. Shivering slightly and watching her breath condense in the air, Misty let the solitude wash over her—let it move from the tip of her toes to the top of her head.

She wanted to banish the feeling of emptiness forever. Everything was all right and, despite her self-doubts, she was going somewhere with her life. She was strong enough to create her own dreams. She didn't need Jake or Steve or anyone else. Things happened for a reason and even if she couldn't understand why at this moment, someday she would.

At last, a small measure of gratefulness crept into her heart, pushing aside the ache of lost love. And the little smidgeon of approval that came with it was strong enough to stir her hopes, leaving her with a feeling of warmth and peace and something that almost felt like contentment.

By the time she got back into the car and warmed herself in front of the blasting heat, her teardrops were gone, banished like icicles in springtime. She felt a whole lot better and a whole lot more prepared to deal with Jake and the kids and whatever else life might throw at her. Whether her relationship with Steve worked out or whether it didn't, she was going to be all right. Feeling sorry for herself never had worked. She disliked that trait in others so she could hardly condone it in herself.

Her experience in sorting out her feelings in the isolation of this small picnic park really was remarkable. She felt small and large both at the same time. The wind and ice had been daunting but she had found a foothold and withstood them. And it was significant in many ways.

She felt readers in other parts of the country would understand exactly what she was talking about. There was something comforting about the austerity of the land, the bare, glacial rock upon which people built homes and forged lives. She felt as though the land, the new found land that once was an uncharted island, had seen sadness and understood. And its resiliency against the elements brought to it a strength that it willingly shared with those foolhardy enough to live there.

As she pulled out and headed home, she thought a brief prayer of gratitude to the Goddess of Creative Shit might once again be in order. After all, if it hadn't been for her Goddess-like intervention, where might she be today? *I really have a lot to be thankful for.*

On the winding drive around the harbour, she smiled as she passed Hatty's and Tizzard's, *The Yarn* office, and the rest of the houses and buildings that lined the shore. Lights shone in the late afternoon twilight, and she knew these were the benchmarks of life. In this isolated little town, families struggled with their own problems that were probably far greater than hers.

The windows shone brightly at the top of the hill where Great-uncle C's house perched. She couldn't think of it as her home yet, but there was a flicker of pride as she opened the front door and announced her arrival to everyone. "I'm back," she called as she pulled off her hat and scarf and stamped her feet. *Back indeed, and I mean it in more ways than one.*

Pansy wasn't long coming out of the kitchen. She passed Misty a stack of messages. "You picks some time to disappear. This phone's been ringing like a banshee. And Tilly called, too. She wants you in early tomorrow or she's walking."

"What are you talking about? Who could possibly be looking for me?" Misty scanned the list of messages. Most of the names she didn't even know. Radio stations, newspapers. "What does *The Evening Telegram* want me for?"

"I has no idea. But they called twice. I told them you was missing in action."

Misty was stupefied. She wandered into the kitchen and picked up the phone. It was still early enough to catch Tilly at *The Yarn*. "Tilly," she began and that was as far as she got. Tilly spewed off without taking a breath. "But I don't understand," Misty finally said. "Why is everyone looking for me?"

"It's that stupid article you wrote," said Tilly.

"So, what was so wrong with that? It may have been a bit controversial, but it was nothing earth-shattering." When she spied Pansy staring at her as she discussed the article, she panicked. *Could Pansy have been right? Should I have left well enough alone?*

"That's what you thinks. You got men coming outta the woodwork."

Misty was confused. "Over that? All I said was that they like to drink and sometimes it gets them more trouble than it's worth. I didn't accuse anyone of anything."

"Misty, what are you talking about? You told everyone you wanted a man."

"Huh?" Misty felt uneasy.

"Where are you, Mr. Right? Ring my bell. Knock my knocker. Email, text, or phone. How stunned are you? I got every available man from here to Cox's Cove calling. Phonse is dancing around the office like he's three parts cut."

"What article? What are you talking about?" Her face felt hot, her body clammy. "What damned article?"

"The one you gave Phonse. "Desperately longing for love." You bees desperate, all right. Most times I wouldn't want to be you, but this isn't one of them. Stud Molloy called. Stud Molloy. Gees, Misty. He bees the hottest piece of work on the island."

"Oh, my God. Tilly, what article did you send to Phonse?"

"Oh, no, you're not blaming this on me. I didn't do nothing other than what you told me to do. And I wants my coffee and muffins like you promised."

Misty placed the phone on the table. "Pansy, do we have a copy of the paper yet?"

"I thinks it just come." She went to check.

Misty could hear Tilly in the background. "Misty! I'm hanging up if you don't say something. Misty!"

Pansy walked back into the kitchen holding up the front page, a big smile on her face. "Now you believes me, don't you?"

Misty read the headline.

Smack-dab in the Middle:
Desperate divorcee looking for love: Apply within.

Right under the headline Phonse had placed the email, phone, and text numbers for the paper. All in bold.

Misty could still hear Tilly in the background. It didn't matter anymore. Misty was finished. Humiliated. Scandalized. Publicly skewered. This couldn't be happening to her. But it was and there was nothing she could do about it. She hung up the phone, her eyes locked on the paper in disbelief. She wanted to disintegrate into a million bits of flotsam and disappear on the next high tide.

Pansy danced around the kitchen. "I told you so. I told you. And you didn't believe me. The horoscope bees right. They always is." With that, she threw the paper up in the air. "This bees it, Misty. This bees it! Your personal tidal wave of love just landed."

CHAPTER 25

One Big Mistake

Duff was on Misty's doorstep first thing in the morning with a copy of the paper in his hand as well as a bouquet of flowers carefully wrapped in paper and a plastic grocery bag. At least she assumed it was a bouquet from the way he was holding it. Misty was surprised and then concerned to see him. She hoped it didn't mean what she thought it might mean.

"You're going to need some help," he said as she let him in.

"You mean the story?"

"What was you thinkin', Misty?" Duff scratched his head and looked at her as though she had lost her mind.

"It was one big mistake. I was stuck at the hospital getting my cast off and Tilly sent Phonse the wrong story. Can you imagine? I told her what to do and what does she do? Exactly what I don't want her to do."

"Sounds like most women, if you asks me. And since things seems to have taken a turn for the worse, I wants to apply for a job as your bodyguard. Cedric and Stinky's interested in the swing shifts. Here, these is for you." He passed her the flowers.

Misty blushed. "Thanks."

"Don't be thankin' me. They're not mine. They was stuck in the snowbank along with this note." He pulled an envelope from his pocket and passed it to her.

Her name was neatly printed in red marker but there was nothing indicating who it was from. She tucked the flowers under her arm and opened it.

> I wishes to submit my application for the position as your lover. I am a fully functioning man with no personal ties at the moment. I bees interested in a long-term relationship, with the understanding that there's no complaints about moose season and occasional fishing trips with the boys. Sounds as though you is prepared to accommodate these things under the circumstances of being lonely anyway. While I likes the idea of beer on the stoop, I prefers it in the fridge and since we bees on the topic, I drinks Black Horse. I hope you likes the flowers and I looks forward to your happy acceptance. I feels desperate at times myself. Year-round loving sounds good to me. I'll come by later when I gets the tranny in the car.
>
> With well-intended affection,
>
> Heber Philpott

"Oh, dear. This is going to be worse than I thought." She looked at Duff and shook her head despondently.

"Let's see that." Duff took the letter out of her hand and started reading. "Heber Philpott? That couldn't satisfy a goat, let alone a woman. Like I told you, you needs a bodyguard. Possibly two.

Where's the phone?" Misty pointed to the kitchen and he took off his boots and headed in that direction.

What was she going to do? This Philpott fellow sounded serious. She locked the door and headed after Duff. He was just hanging up the phone when she got there.

"Things bees falling into place, Misty. You're some lucky the seal hunt hasn't got on the go yet. Stinky's available to hold down the house. I'm going with you to the office and Cedric's going to manage the traffic outside *The Yarn*."

"You're serious, aren't you?"

"Missus, you got no sense or what? Talk to her, Pansy." Duff shrugged and sat down at the table. The phone rang and he looked at her for permission and then picked it up.

"Residence of Miz Misty Muldoon. Dufferon Murphy bees me."

Dufferon? He sounded very formal and un-Dufflike. Misty was inclined to laugh. This whole scenario was like a dream. She slapped her forehead with the heel of her hand and turned to Pansy. "Tell me you think he's over-reacting. Surely this will blow over in a day or so. I'll be printing a retraction next week."

Pansy merely smiled at her and handed Duff a pad of paper she'd been using for messages. "Misty, I took three calls already this morning. If you thinks this is going to blow over, I got news for you. This is the biggest thing to hit the Cove since Wilfred and Fig. Possibly bigger." She held Misty in her steely gaze. "I may as well tell you, VOCM wants an answer on whether or not you'll do an open-line show tomorrow morning. I'd do it if I were you. Might be a good way to get your message out. I gotta tell you though, folks has a way of hearing what they wants to hear." She boosted herself up onto the counter and folded her arms across her chest.

"I can't pay all these people to be bodyguards. This is ridiculous and blown way out of proportion. I don't need anyone looking out for me."

"I don't imagine they's going to want any pay," said Pansy looking at Duff. "That one there, sure look at him. He's in his glory. I'm 'spects these boys will work for the pleasure of being close to you. And that's not saying anything about the status it will give 'em. Working for you will be like working for Jennifer Aniston." She wagged her eyebrows at Misty. "Better lock your bedroom door, too. You never knows who could get in here."

Pansy's comments set off an internal alarm system in Misty's stomach. She felt a little queasy and lightheaded. "I can't believe this is really happening."

"You really got no idea, has you? Better get used to it, Misty. This bees only warming up."

Duff hung up the phone and it rang again immediately. He picked it up and used the same salutation as before.

"What am I going to do?" Misty looked at Pansy in desperation.

"For starters, I'd get some make-up on. You needs to look good. Chessie Snow called and offered to do your hair if you wants. I booked an appointment for ten o'clock. That gives you about thirty minutes to get dressed and over there."

"How can you be so nonchalant?"

"Stuff happens, Misty. You gotta go with it. As a matter of fact, if you stops and thinks about it, it could even be an opportunity. If you can't find yourself a man now, there's something wrong."

I've got a man, she wanted to scream. *Or had one. What is Steve going to think when he sees the paper?*

Misty's day was a blur. Cedric showed up and he and Duff escorted her to Chessie's salon. Chessie wanted her picture taken with Misty and her husband had set up a tripod so he could be in the photo, too. Misty insisted her hair be finished before any pictures. She kept an eye on Chessie's husband, who was walking back and forth like he was going to try something anyway. By the time she got out of there, she may have looked better but she was feeling considerably worse. And that was only the beginning.

Cedric parked his truck crossways in *The Yarn* parking lot, taking up most of the available spaces. Duff left him outside and followed Misty into the office.

"I told you Misty's not in yet," Tilly was explaining to someone. She pressed her palm over the phone speaker. "About time you got here," she said. "Those are yours." She pointed a bright-red nail at the stack of messages perched on the edge of her desk.

Misty groaned, grabbed the stack and headed into the newsroom. As she rounded the door, she crashed into Phonse. Messages sailed in every direction.

"You!" She steeled her eyes on him. "How could you print that article? And 'smack-dab'? Smack-dab? How could you even use a word like that in anything associated with me and my writing?"

"Hey, hey. I writes the headlines and smack-dab seemed perfect to me. You are just that. You're stuck smack-dab in the middle, hot pants, and don't I love it."

Misty closed in on him, her finger digging into his chest with each word. "You know I wouldn't want that article printed. You could have called me. You might have suspected something was wrong."

"I asses you for a zinger. Seems to me like you delivered one. What's your problem?"

"What's my problem? What's my problem?" Misty paced back and forth in the small space in front of her desk, pressing her heels into the floorboards and punctuating each sentence by swinging her arms wildly. "You label me a desperate divorcee in your headline. And suggest that readers 'apply within.' Within what? My panties? Who the hell knit you, Phonse Penney? You are the most insensitive, sneaky, drunken fool ever I've met. You haven't even addressed New Year's Eve. You're acting like nothing even happened." Misty stopped in front of her desk, barely visible beneath vases brimming with flowers of all varieties and colours. She pointed at them as she walked over. "You've got every Tom, Dick and …well…dick from here to Nipper's Bite sending me their love resume. How could you do this to me? Don't you have any feelings at all? I'm just a convenient piece of female real estate for you. Misty Muldoon is a person, you lunk-head, not a promotional gizmo, not a free giveaway and no one's piece of ass."

"Yes, you are. You're on my payroll and I can promote you however I damn well pleases. And I loves it, Muldoon. We sold outta papers ten o'clock this morning. Sold out. You realize that's never happened in the history of *The Yarn*? Avery Sharpe can kiss my arse." Phonse grabbed her in a bear hug and swung her around before setting her back on her feet. "You're like winning the lottery, you little boney-arsed bombshell. You're my ticket to retirement. Now outta my way. I'm running a second printing. We're shipping papers right across the province. Even the premier's office wants a bunch. You could be the answer to the cod quotas." With that off his chest, he headed into the print shop without as much as a backward glance.

"Ah, Misty?"

"What?" She spun around.

It was Wince Newhook. Wince covered sports and funerals. He was holding a camera and wearing a grin that spread across his face like a lighthouse beacon. "That's perfect. Give us a smile."

The flash went off like a series of electrical shorts. Misty was momentarily blinded, a damn good thing for Wince. Had she been able to get an exact sighting, she might have seized his prized new digital camera.

Exasperated, she walked to her desk and surveyed the mess of papers and envelopes. She gnawed at her lip, a terrible habit that seemed to surface whenever she was under stress. Not just any old stress but *Stress* with a capital *S*. She had a feeling she was about to increase her consumption of lipstick at an exponential rate.

Truthfully, she didn't know where to begin with the mess that lay before her. She picked up an envelope and looked at it. Her name was scrawled across the front. *This is only just beginning*, she thought. *What happens when the mail comes tomorrow?*

"Misty! You got a call on line one." Tilly was smiling, which gave Misty an uneasy feeling. She was familiar enough with Tilly by now to know that she never, ever smiled at her unless it was bad news.

"Misty Muldoon," she said nervously, as she picked up the line.

"Are you trying to give me a message?"

"Steve." Her heart began to beat rapidly and she felt her face stain with colour. *How did he find out about this mess so quickly?* "You read *The Yarn*, didn't you?"

"No, actually. The *Toronto Star*. It carried your advertisement this morning."

"The *Star*? Oh, my God, you can't be serious." *My advertisement?* His comment hurt. *How could he say that? I'm not advertising for anything,* she wanted to scream. *Only you. I've been sending out ads to you for months now and you haven't even realized. Things don't last forever and a day. Someone eventually makes a deal.*

"Misty, what's this all about?"

She could tell from his tone he was very upset. She wasn't sure how to begin. "You know what a zoo this place can be. I've told you at times I feel like I'm the only sane person working here. I mean... oh, how do I explain this?"

"You could try, for a start."

Misty took a deep breath and began her first version of the story she knew would be played over and over all day long. "So that's it," she finished up, grateful he hadn't interrupted her. "It was one big mistake and now no one in Charlie's Cove wants to let go of it. My God, when I think of the scale of this thing, it's going to go on forever."

"I didn't move fast enough for you? Is that what this is about?"

"Oh, Steve, how can you say that? Well," she hesitated, deciding how honest she should be. "Maybe, but I didn't plan for this to happen. It's a terrible mess and I can't believe all you can think about is what this means to you. This isn't about you. It's about me. Me and the rest of the available male population of Newfoundland."

"Not Newfoundland, Misty," Steve corrected. "Try the rest of the country. And it is about me, too. I thought things were good with us." Steve sounded like a petulant young boy. He seemed to have forgotten completely about how she might be feeling.

"That depends on your definition of good." With that statement, all of her insecurities settled around her like a heavy cloak. She felt Steve was being insensitive and selfish. Maybe she would live to regret the next few moments, but she decided she would say whatever was on her mind and live with the consequences. "What we have is nice," she began, "but it isn't going anywhere. You're in Toronto. I'm in Charlie's Cove. You live almost half a country away from me and until last week, I hadn't seen you for months. I know when we're together it's incredible. It's the time that we're apart that's hard and honestly, at times I just can't see how it will work. Maybe you think telling me you're in love is enough, but when you think about it, we haven't really answered any of the important questions."

"Well, here's one. When did you write that column?"

"That isn't the kind of question I'm talking about."

"Well, it's the one I want to ask. Hell, Misty. You hide a lot of things."

"Oh, stop navel gazing. What does it matter *when* I wrote that column? The fact is I did and now it's published. It was a stupid, stupid moment when I was feeling sorry for myself. I hardly knew you at the time. It didn't mean anything." *Misty knew that was a lie. Her feelings in that column meant a lot. A whole lot.*

"Right. I thought we had a good thing going but apparently you have other ideas. What was wrong with the way things were? I thought I made my feelings clear. But according to this little article, it didn't mean all that much to you. I hope you find what you're looking for, Misty."

"Steve, this isn't my fault. We do have a good thing going. Don't do this." She was suddenly desperate to make him listen, to understand.

He was making assumptions that were entirely untrue. *Listen to me*, she wanted to scream at him. *Just understand, this wasn't planned.*

"It's a bit late, don't you think? What am I going to do now? Put in my application?"

"You could try." Misty said, hoping an attempt at humour might lighten the mood.

"No thanks." Steve hung up.

Misty collapsed in her chair, staring at the receiver in her hand. Finally, the bleeping of the lost connection drew her back and she slammed the receiver down so hard it bounced off again and dangled over the side of her desk. She picked it up and put it back on the base. *I knew it. Sooner or later every man turns into a jerk. I'm dealing with a mess that's getting bigger and bigger by the minute and all he can focus on is his damaged ego.*

What about my ego? Practically everyone in the country must be laughing at my pathetic attempt to find love this morning. Including my ex-husband. Oh, sweet Jesus. How humiliating.

"Misty?"

"What," she snapped as she looked up.

"A camera crew from the CBC is comin' here."

"I'm not doing it." Her eyes flared at Tilly.

"Yes, you are," replied Tilly rudely. "You are so doing it. If you thinks I'm putting up with all this and you're going to walk away with your tail between your legs, you got something coming to you."

"Not you, too."

"Not me, too, what?"

"Everyone is griping at me today. There's a limit to what I can take."

Tilly chuckled and gave a careless toss of her head. She had such a self-satisfied look on her face that Misty barely refrained from throwing one of the vases at her.

"You're getting what you deserves," said Tilly. "You spends all your time writing about us. How does it feel to be the one we're laughing at? Not very nice, I imagines, but the punishment fits the crime, missus. Now, get yourself moving. Do you want to do the interview inside or out?"

"I don't care." She was so angry at herself and at Tilly, she could barely speak.

"Do it in your office, then. There's a wind blowing a gale that would take the skin off a moose. Besides," she suggested with a smirk, "The flowers adds a nice touch."

"I hate the flowers." *Almost as much as I hate the petulance in my voice.*

"Five minutes, Misty. That's all you got. When they gets here, I'm sending them in." For the first time in days, Misty saw a small bit of compassion in Tilly's eyes. "Honestly," Tilly continued, "I wish I could say I deliberately sent the wrong story to Phonse but I didn't—it was an accident. You, on the other hand…you think I really screwed things up when most of us would say it turned out perfect. You can deny it if you wants to, but I really can't see a down side to this." She threw up her arms and spun out of the room like a star in a music video, but not before imparting one final word of advice. "Lighten up, Misty. It's raining men."

"Oh," Misty moaned, covering her face with her hands. "I only ever wanted one."

CHAPTER 26

Chemistry Lesson

Three days flew by like five minutes. Misty thought about calling Steve. In fact, she rehearsed the scenario in her head giving herself all the best lines even while knowing she would never ever pull it off quite like that. Nothing she said ever came out like a movie script, so in the end she gave up and hoped he would do the calling.

It was difficult to accept that Steve could be so unsympathetic to her situation. His comments played over and over in her mind like an anti-motivational talk that reinforced her personal fuck-up factor. And if she had to take credit for messing things up, well, she could do the stiff upper lip thing. What she couldn't do was carry the heartache. *That* she wanted to shuck like an oyster, if only it were that easy.

She was angry with herself and on top of that, since she'd slept with him, she felt used and discarded. It wasn't a feeling she liked very much and it reminded her of the residue Jake had left her with. Could she indeed be dancing with the same devil in different pants?

Misty Muldoon, Loser at Love. Twice smitten, twice bitten, legs chained shut on any future commitments. Yeah, that about summed up her anguish and frustration.

Oddly enough, juxtaposed to her personal turmoil was the phenomenal success of her column right across the country. It had a counter-balancing effect and brought with it a perverse sense of fulfilment that actually nudged at her self-confidence. Her column wasn't just relegated to the smaller community newspapers anymore. Phonse had received calls from several of the larger papers interested in picking up Misty's Misadventures. At least something good was coming from this mess and a lot of doors were opening. How typical that all she could think of was the one that had closed.

If she really looked at it, a whole lot of people were pleased with how things had transpired. What did it matter that her heart was breaking in the process? Just like her leg, sooner or later, it would heal. That was the nature of life. Hearts, like bones, eventually mend.

She still found it surprising Steve would be so unreasonable in his reaction to her column. Maybe if she just picked up the phone...but no. That was his move and if he didn't care enough, then it was a lot better to find out now.

"You probably wants some time alone to sort through this, eh?" said Duff, coming into the newsroom and dropping a bag of mail on her desk. "I'm sending out for coffee and biscuits from Hatty's. Get you something?"

"An intravenous line of Blue Lagoon martinis would be great." She held out her arm hopefully.

"Go on with you. I knows it seems a bit overwhelming, but this'll blow over in a few more weeks. And when things gets back to normal, you'll be missing it. Most of us only gets fifteen minutes a lifetime, but you lucked out. You gets more than the whole of Charlie's Cove combined. I fails to see what's wrong with that. Now, how about one of Hatty's blueberry coffee buns? I highly recommends them."

"A few weeks? You must be joking. This isn't going to blow over in a few weeks. Do you know who I just talked to this morning?"

"Who?"

"Ricky Volcano, that's who."

"Ricky Volcano? A name like that could land you a few fights around here."

"Duff, Ricky is the host of Canada's number one reality TV show, *Live with Ricky*. You can't be serious that you haven't heard of him?"

Duff rubbed his chin and pulled a walkie talkie from his pocket. "Stinky," he said into it.

"Wha'?" came the crackling reply.

"You heardda Ricky Volcano?"

Stinky snickered. "Skylene watches him. Thinks he's something, that one. He wears t'ongs."

"Yes, b'y. Big time, eh? Over and out."

Misty shook her head knowingly and stifled a smile. What Stinky really meant was *thongs*. It just came out like tongs and tongs was the local buzzword for men who may have crossed to the other side.

"I wants a raise if I'm babysitting Volcano," said Duff.

"Believe me now?" replied Misty. "He's coming here and they want live coverage of my interviews with the shortlist. Did you get that? They actually expect me to draw up a shortlist of candidates and select one, right on Ricky's program."

"Sounds reasonable to me." He slipped the walkie-talkie into his pocket again. "So a sticky bun's good?"

Misty pulled a handful of letters out of the bag Duff had given her. "Bring me a dozen. I can throw them at this stack of letters and choose the ones that stick to the buns. Look at this." She began reading off names and flicking the envelopes over her shoulder. "Sandy Currie, Walter Doyle, Avery...*yuck* Sharpe, The Kissing Pi..." Misty released the rest of the envelopes and dropped to her knees to retrieve the one she'd just tossed over her shoulder.

She poked her head up over the desk where Duff was watching her curiously. "God, yes. The sticky bun is good. Perfect. And a coffee."

"You sure is in a state today." He shook his head disparagingly and walked out.

There it was. She clutched the letter in her hand. She hadn't been seeing things. In the top corner in bold, black ink were the words The Kissing Pirate. *This must be some kind of a joke. After what he said to me, he couldn't seriously have taken me up on my suggestion and sent an application, could he?*

She peered over her shoulder expecting to see Tilly or Phonse laughing but there was no one watching her.

He had used a black marker to print her name. Misty Muldoon, c/o *The Yarn*. And up in the corner, equally neat, were the three rather hokey words that meant so much. *The Kissing Pirate.*

It had to be him. Who else would know about that name? It was something private we shared together. She closed her eyes and was instantly transported to her kitchen.

When her phone rang, Misty jumped. She had just passed five minutes without any sense of time or space. Still disoriented, she picked up, hoping her thoughts had radiated directly to Steve. She'd read about things like that.

Her voice was husky, her throat dry as she stammered her name.

"Finally. Getting through to the premier is easier than getting hold of you. Who answers your phone? You should pay her more. She's like the Rock of Gibraltar."

Definitely not Steve. Her hormone levels dropped as she cleared her throat. "Are you referring to her looks or her I.Q.?" Misty asked, thankful her heart had slowed down enough enable her to hear.

"A sense of humour. I'm liking this. You sound like a great interview, Ms. Muldoon. You're stirring up a lot of interest across the country."

"Which goes to show you what pathetic lives most people lead," she replied. "I'm not sure I want an interview." And she meant it, too. If that letter was an offer from Steve, she didn't want any more interviews in her future, none. "Who am I speaking with anyway?"

"Mike Curry, NTV News. We'd like to do a story on you, Ms. Muldoon."

"Misty, please. I may be divorced and desperate but I'm not old enough for the *miz* thing yet."

"Misty it is. Just give me a few clips, a bit of information and then I'll go away. You know what it's like. They send us out to get a story, we really need to get the story." There was heavy emphasis on the last part.

He'd hit her with the truth. She knew exactly what it was like. How many times had she been in his place? "You'll have to excuse me. I'm a bit stressed out these days." *To say the least.* "Here's the deal. I'll do the interview but nothing personal, all right? Just keep it light." *Except for this,* she thought, as she looked at the envelope still clutched in her hand. *This is very personal.*

"How's it going anyway? Find Mr. Right yet?"

"No," she lied. "I haven't found him."

"You'll have your opportunity to tell us all about it. Two o'clock good?"

"If you can meet me at the newspaper office." She had some things to do before he arrived and not much time to get them done.

"A bit of natural habitat. Like it. Well, folks, this is where it all began...Hey, I might even give you my resume."

"Stop!" Misty found the idea disturbing. What she didn't need was another resume. "I'll do the interview, okay? But no resumes. This is strictly business."

"If this is business, Misty, I'd like to see the way you have fun. See you this afternoon." He disconnected quickly, probably sensing he deserved a blast for that last comment.

It's so frustrating. No one will ever take me seriously again. She held the letter up to her desk lamp and peered at it. *But what would it matter? As long as the one man who counts takes me seriously that's all I* need. *Unless...unless,* she thought uncertainly, *he's written to ridicule me. Maybe he would be just like everyone else, brimming with smart remarks and sexual innuendo. What a fool I was to ever write that column.*

She turned the envelope over in her hands. She was actually afraid to open it. Misty Muldoon, petrified of a letter, second guessing every thought and living out fantasies. Never a good sign, not unless you're planning to go crazy.

Hold on, she cautioned herself. *You're not crazy, you're in love. Madly, head over heels in love.* That was the truth. The simple truth of it all. She wanted Steve in her life.

She took a pair of scissors from her desk and carefully cut a small sliver from one end of the envelope. She wanted to keep it perfect. And maybe someday, with her grandchildren bouncing on her knees, she'd pull it out and say...*Oh, for Chrissakes, just read it.*

She gently tapped the envelope against her hand until the paper inside slipped out. As she unfolded the letter, she took a deep breath and held it. At least if she needed to pass out, she'd be halfway there...

Dear Misty,

If I'd thought I'd have to compete with hundreds of other men to get another kiss from you, this would never have happened. I knew procrastination would catch up with me someday, but like this? No way.

A few weeks ago the biggest problem in my life was my work schedule. Now, it's a beautiful auburn-haired woman with the most intriguing copper eyes and a smile that would light up the universe on a stormy night.

My God, he's a poet. This is good. I like poetry. Her face had likely turned a nice shade of crimson...but she still wanted more.

I didn't expect you to issue an open invitation to the rest of the province while I was away. I've never been afraid of a little competition, but this? I guess that's the price I pay for being a fool. But a fool is only a fool if he makes the same mistake twice, <u>which I won't</u>.

He wants me. Ohhhh. Spots began to form before her eyes and she picked up the pace. She was becoming more lightheaded by the second.

I can't get you out of my mind. I'm sorry for what I said. I'm sorry for what I didn't say. Mostly, I'm sorry for the way I behaved. I'll play this game your way if I have to. Misty Muldoon, you're someone I'd like to get to know for the rest of my life if you'll have me.

She let go like a busted paper bag, her heart racing joyously. *His life. He said his life.*

One more thing I can tell you. Salt and vinegar chips just don't taste the same anymore. They're missing a certain spice, an ingredient that's ravishing and very, very addictive. I'm "Misty-fied", if you get my meaning.

Consider this my application.

The Kissing Pirate

Consider this my application? As far as she was concerned, he had the job. But how was she supposed to tell him? Her life was a mess. Out of control. And there was no way to shut it off.

She read the letter again. This was real and it was everything she had dreamed of. Everything she had ever wished for.

But what's the best way to let him know how I'm feeling? Put a sign in the front window of The Yarn? To KP: The answer is yes. Of course, she'd call him but what she really needed to do before that, before anything else, was get some control back into her life and shut down this lottery for her heart. It was more important to her than anything to let him know she was ready to do whatever it took to bring them together.

"Misty, what do you want me to do with these?" Duff was back and with him, the reality of the challenge she faced. She folded the letter, picked up the envelope and slipped both into her purse.

"These were setting by the front door." He had another bouquet in his arms and a paper bag in his free hand. "And here's your coffee and bun." She took the bag first, then pointed to Phonse's desk for the flowers.

"He started this. We may as well let him share in the glory." Hatty's coffee was just what she needed. On top of the way she was feeling, a good shot of hot java would jolt her into warp speed. She checked her watch. Just over an hour before NTV would be here and just enough time to write a column for this afternoon's deadline.

The one thing that would get Steve back on The Rock was a letter of apology and acceptance. And by publishing it in her column, it would serve a dual purpose. In addition to Steve, it would let everyone else know she'd made a decision and put the brakes on this love raffle that was being played out in the media.

"Hatty says she'll send lunch over if you don't feel like going out."

"Great, great," Misty replied hardly paying attention. "It's not food I need, though. It's time." She spread her hands. "I thought you were out of your mind when you said I'd need help but now I'm beginning to agree with you. You were absolutely right. I need all the help I can get and then some."

Especially if I'm going to clear this mess up and welcome Steve back into my life.

CHAPTER 27

Mixed Messages

Misty paused to consider just the right way to approach her column.

Should she mention his name? Would he get the message if she didn't? She felt as though she had a bad case of writer's block. And when this might be the most important column she would ever write, she wasn't much impressed with herself. What she was going to say might mean the difference between a life of regrets or a life with Steve in it and it was certainly no time to be running dry.

Or to be nervous. She took another sip of Hatty's wicked brew and began.

Misty's Misadventures

The Truth Behind the *Mis*

By

Misty Muldoon

You all know me by now. So I'm not going to waste valuable space talking about myself. I'd prefer to talk about human frailty and how one person could, by simply writing a personal letter that was accidentally published, turn her life into an entertainment odyssey for millions of people. Sounds unlikely? I would have agreed with you until I did that very thing.

How does one obscure columnist go from Charlie's Cove to garnering headlines across the country? If I could package the process, I'd make millions. Easily. I swear a boardroom of marketing specialists couldn't have dreamed this one up. Of course, marketing types have never encountered Phonse Penney or Tilly or Avery Sharpe. Be honest now, if you believe in synchronicity or not, a lot of things have come together in ways no simple columnist could ever anticipate.

Thank you for sending me your texts, messages and letters. It's been a boost to my ego, which has been pretty badly damaged in the past few years. I appreciate every one of them and I love every one of you for sending them in. Yes! I really do, but I'm not prepared to marry you. I'm really an old-fashioned girl. I want the traditional things. A man, a moon, and a swoon. And that's just what I had one night late last summer. A night I can't forget.

You know who you are. Our union may be anything but traditional, but it has been grade A in terms of romance. And that's what rings my doorbell.

What happened to me wasn't planned. I didn't set out to undermine your attention. Admittedly, I may have felt a wee bit frustrated. What woman wouldn't, realizing day after day that the only connection to her one true love is email, text, or phone?

But despite all the *mis*understanding, you still submitted your application for my heart. When I read your letter, I knew it had to be you. You may hide behind a funny name but you can't hide your intention. You're asking if you can be the one and only. I'm answering you in the best way I know how. I'm setting everyone straight. You are the one. The only one. KP, what else can I say? Come on home. I miss you. And yes! I love you.

Until next time,

Misty.

There. That was it. Good enough? She wasn't sure as she reread her words. *Why was this so hard to write?* Misty checked her watch. Her deadline was almost up. *Deadline, what a word, especially when these lines had to be anything but dead. They needed to be magnificent.* She closed her eyes and tried to imagine how she would react if she read this column in the paper. How would she feel?

"Hey, you scraggly-assed lottery ticket. That better be a column you're writing. Lemme see."

Misty looked sideways at Phonse, who was craning his neck to read over her shoulder. She immediately minimized the screen on her monitor and turned around to face him. She was acting as though she had been caught doing something illegal. She actually looked guilty and for what reason? If she wasn't ready to let Phonse see what she was writing, could she be serious about sending it across the country?

"What'er you at?"

"Nothing."

"Yes, b'y. Looks like nothing. Give us a gander."

"I don't know. I'm writing a column, but I'm not sure you're going to like it."

"And when did that ever bother you before? Lemme see it." Phonse poked her in the shoulder. "Pull it up. C'mon. I'll give you the truth."

Misty opened the file and waited while Phonse read it. She was afraid he might be upset that she was closing down the contest for her heart. After all, he had taken to calling the whole affair his retirement plan. "Well," she asked. "What do you think?"

"Hmmmm."

She could see the wheels turning.

"KP. Who the hell is that? Kirk, Kenneth, Kirby? Probably some cute endearment like kissy-pooh or something."

"Leave it to you to turn this into something tasteless. KP, for your information, is a very special name for someone very special. The right person knows its significance. It will mean something to him."

"And you're willing to throw it out for the rest of the country to play around with? You takes the cake, you do."

"Are you going to run it?"

"Why not? Makes a nice little tantalizer. We'll have 'em on edge trying to solve the puzzle. You sure you can't be a bit more specific? KP, eh? Give us a little hint, b'y."

"I'm not ready yet. This is it. Take it or leave it. What do you want to do?"

"Send it over. I'd say this ups the ante for everyone. I got a few ideas of me own."

"You can't mess with my column."

"Never said I would. Just that I has a few ideas, that's all."

"Like what?"

"None of your business. See this here?" He pointed to the sign on this desk: Editor-in-Chief. "Until this sign sits on your desk, what ideas I has is none of your beeswax."

She would honestly have to describe the look on his face as a smirk. There was no other term appropriate for someone who looked so piously self-satisfied. She resented her lack of control over the situation but realized she didn't have much choice. "As long as you aren't going to change my column," she said, making one last attempt to impress her concerns upon Phonse.

"What you sees is what you gets," he replied as he walked away.

You sly old bugger, Misty thought as she watched him until he disappeared into the print shop. She didn't trust him one bit but at least he had promised to leave her column intact and that would have to do. She sent it to his computer with a click of her mouse. *Oh, Steve. I hope you understand. Unless I let everyone know that my heart is taken, we don't have a hope in hell of getting together. Maybe now people will leave us alone and we can get on with our lives in private.* She looked up to see Tilly waving at her from the doorway.

"Your interview is here. You wants I sends them in?"

Misty shook her head. "Nope. I think I'd rather do this out front." She'd play the game one last time. After all, what could it hurt? The real story would be out tomorrow and then maybe they'd all leave her alone.

♥

Who's KP?

The headline screamed from the front page of *The Yarn*. Phonse was running a contest with a thousand-dollar reward for the identity of KP. It couldn't have been any worse. Of course, you had to have an appreciation of what a thousand dollars might mean to someone without a regular paycheque.

And that wasn't the most disturbing part. Ricky Volcano had arrived in town late the previous day and was on the phone first thing this morning and wanted to meet with her later. He upped the reward to $5000.00, hoping to entice interest in his weeklong feature on Charlie's Cove and Misty. What she had thought would put a damper on the raffle for her heart had just the opposite effect. It seemed as though everyone was more intrigued than ever and the search for KP was the focus of every talk show across the country.

Misty raked her hands through her hair as she despaired over the way things had been manipulated yet again and even at the risk of sounding like Dr. Phil, she had to admit that her life was once again out of control. And if she felt like this, what must Steve be thinking by now?

"Here." Duff passed her a bag of Purity peppermint knobs. "These was left for you. Wants I tastes one to be sure it's safe?" He took a candy from the bag.

"Safe? I need a food taster now? Don't be silly." She took a candy and popped it in her mouth. It provided an interesting flavour along with her morning coffee.

"Could be a jealous missus out there. You bees taking up a lot of attention."

"If I could just get five minutes alone with Phonse Penney, just five minutes, there wouldn't be any need to worry about me causing any marriage breakups. I'd be too busy explaining why he was charging me with assault and buttery."

"You means battery, don't you?"

"No, actually I do mean buttery. What I have in mind is kicking his butt all the way to the town wharf and then lobbing him into the icy cold Atlantic Ocean. And all of this under the cover of darkness, too."

Duff chucked. "You're all right, after all. You still got a sense of humour."

"Amazingly. Phonse has too many ideas about where this is going."

Duff sucked away on the knob. "You been the best thing's ever happened to Phonse and this paper." He had settled into a chair with his feet up on one of the desks. "Look around sure." He scanned the room with his eyes. "Not much to it, is there? Just a bunch of beat-up furniture, a few phones, and a couple of computers. I'd say you're the most valuable thing in this place. I sees Phonsie's point of view. He's worked all his life and things is finally happening for him."

He was doing it again. Giving her advice in that way he had.

"But, Duff, this is my life here. He's marketing me like the flavour of the week."

"You tell me this, then. If you'd worked here all your life and barely eked out a living, think you'd do it any different?"

Duff's question really irked her. He knew damn well she wouldn't do it any differently. She'd been in the business of promoting widgets and if something like this had ever landed in her lap, she would have danced naked up Barrington Street. She hated that he had to be so right.

"Well?" Duff asked again.

Misty shook her head despondently. "No," she admitted. "I'd probably do the same thing. Maybe even worse. By now I'd likely have posters all over town."

"Yes, b'y. When'd you develop the psychic abilities?" Duff was grinning at her.

"What?" Misty sat up in her chair and stared at him. "You're kidding, right?"

"No, he already done it. You looks good in 'em, too."

She slammed her hand against the desk and made a great show of her frustration, but inside her heart had softened. Duff's summation of the situation was accurate. Phonse was only doing what made sense to him and the more she resisted, the harder it would be for her. Somehow, and it was a big somehow, she had to work with him and try to get him to see things from her point of view. Phonse might be pig-headed and occasionally dangerous, but he wasn't entirely heartless. She felt sure that somewhere in there Phonse had an actual heart. All she had to do was find it.

"You knows this is good for everyone in Charlie's Cove. It puts us on the map and I thinks you owes it to us to give this some thought. When a toilet gets plugged, it ain't always bad."

"Excuse me?" *Where did he get this stuff?*

"She don't get plugged unless the personal processing factory's in good working order. You got to look at things from the right perspective, hey?"

"By golly, you never cease to amaze me."

"Man's got a lot of time to think when he's fishing. Maybe too much." He winked at Misty. "Well, anyway. Give it some thought. There's more than one way to look at this. Could be good for you, too."

The phone rang again. When no one picked up, Misty pushed the candy into the corner of her mouth and answered. "*Yarn* office."

"Put Penney on the line, will you? I need to speak to him. Bugger is hard to get hold of."

Not that she was suspicious by nature, but she was beyond trusting Phonse since his latest twist on things. "Mr. Penney seems to be out of the office at the moment," she lied. "May I take a message?"

"You're a sweet thing. Tell him Wayne Christianson from *Fort McMurray Today* called again. I need that picture of the Muldoon wedding resent. Someone deleted it."

"I'm sorry, he wired you a picture of my wedding to Jake Muldoon?" She looked at Duff, who was wagging his hands, telling her to settle down. She ignored him. "You need the picture, Mr. Christianson? It'll be a cold day in hell. I'll send you Penney's obit instead." Misty slammed down the phone.

She'd been so caught up in what was happening in Charlie's Cove she hadn't even considered the possibility that her past might get dragged into this. Where did Phonse get a picture of her wedding? As far as she knew, there weren't many pictures floating around.

She and Jake had gotten married in Vegas at a drive-thru "I Do." It had been a wild, spontaneous time and all she had were a couple of Polaroids that had been kicking around their house. Just a few in a box that...Misty slapped her hand against the side of her head this time...she'd left in the basement storage closet. Jake. It would be just like him to get into cahoots with Phonse. He loved attention, which was where her marital problems all started, and what better way to get it than ride on her coattails?

"Now, Misty, things happens all the time. Like I told you, Phonse bees just doing what anyone in his place would do. Let 'er go."

She wasn't interested in Duff's perspective anymore. If Phonse ran this story in all the papers that subscribed to her column...it would be way too personal and maybe even harmful to her children. *She wasn't a sweepstake ticket for anyone. Not him, not Jake Muldoon, not Charlie's Cove, not Newfoundland.*

She bit down on the peppermint knob with a fury and exploded. "He's gone too far this time."

"But remember what I told you," Duff said walking over and placing his hand on Misty's shoulder. "Leave him be. In a few weeks this'll all be over."

Too absorbed in her own drama to pay attention, Misty shook him off and continued. "That weasel's got my ex-husband involved now. I'm sure of it. My past isn't going to be the subject of dinner conversations right across this country. I don't need it and my children don't need to be drawn into this, either, which is probably where he's heading." She stood up and stormed toward the print shop.

Duff tried to grab her arm but she deftly sidestepped and slipped away. "Wait, Misty," he called to her. "It don't bees all that bad. Think of the opportunities."

"Screw the opportunities. It's not your life he's playing with. I'm having it out with him now and nothing you say is going to change my mind," she replied, cracking the peppermint knob with her teeth, imagining the whole time it was Penny's head. "Gimme that cowardly little wea...ow." There was a shot of pain at the front of her mouth and she heard a noise that was decidedly different than the crunching of a candy. Something wasn't right. She stopped with one hand on the doorknob to the print shop and another over her mouth.

"What's the matter, Misty?" Duff ran over to her.

Misty slowly ran her tongue over her teeth. There was a jagged edge at the front of her mouth that hadn't been there before.

"My purse," she mumbled, trying to ignore the throbbing pain that had started. She ran to her desk and dug into her purse for her make-up bag that held the small lipstick case with the mirror. It seemed forever before she pulled it out.

The colour drained from her face. Half of her front tooth was missing. Her front tooth. "Ook at 'is," she turned to Duff, her finger pointing to her broken tooth. "My toot. My toot. My toot's b'oken." She was afraid to form her words. Afraid her tooth might fall out altogether.

How would she get her tooth fixed in Charlie's Cove? Today. In the next hour?

Duff cleared his throat and very calmly put his hand into his jacket and pulled out his walkie-talkie. "Ced, you there?"

There was some crackling and Cedric cut in. "What's up, Duffster?"

"My toot." Misty tugged on his arm.

"We got a bit of an emergency, b'y. We needs a ride to Doccy Snow's. The little missus here cracked off her front toot. Nothing that old Doccy can't fix, eh?"

"P-U-L-L." Ced replied. "Over and out."

P-U-L-L? Never. No one is taking out my tooth. Misty ran her tongue over the rough edge. She knew they were trying to reassure her. It didn't work. How could it? Nothing could help when you'd just lost half of your front tooth.

"C'mon, Misty." Duff tucked her purse under his arm and led her to the door. "Never minds your coat. Ced's truck is like the Banff hot springs. I thinks he's on the male change of life meself."

Misty followed obediently behind him. As far as she was concerned, her life was in his hands now. *Here's Misty. She doesn't need a lover. She needs a new tooth.* She could imagine the headlines.

Duff held the door for her. "I feels like I'm living in Hollywood, Newfoundland. Every time I looks at you, I thinks of Ann-Margret."

"I don 'ook anyt'ing 'ike Ann Marg't," Misty mumbled from behind her hand, trying to form her words without using her mouth or her tongue.

"No, b'y, and that you don't. But you sure got the Hollywood thing going on. You gives high maintenance a whole new meaning."

A whole new meaning? Hardly. High maintenance meant facials. High maintenance meant manicures and pedicures. It did not mean being stranded in a small harbour town on the coast of a largely unpopulated island wondering what in the hell you were going to do to get your tooth fixed. *It did not mean that.*

CHAPTER 28

Open-Wide

Duff led the way into Doccy Snow's office. Misty followed close behind, her hand still covering her mouth.

"Duff," said Mavis, looking up as they walked in. "Haven't seen you in here in a while. Dentures giving you trouble?"

Duff smiled broadly and leaned on the countertop. Misty forgot her own predicament for a few minutes as she sized up what was happening between Duff and Mavis. Mavis was about fifty-five years old, Misty guessed, give or take a few years either way. She was a bubbly woman with a ready smile. And Duff, he could be any age. She had figured him for mid-sixties but it was hard to tell with these well-seasoned, salty dogs. After years on the water, they usually looked much older than they really were.

"Nah," said Duff. "Me dentures is perfect. And so's the rest of me."

Misty did a double take. *Could Duff be flirting?*

A little smile broke at the corners of Mavis's bright-red lips as she narrowed her eyes at him. "You just t'inks you're God's answer to bingo, coming in here and acting the fool. Man your age should have more sense in his head." She adjusted her blouse. "And quit looking at me like that."

"I calls it appreciatin' the scenery. Come over for a cuppa tea later."

"I knows you got more than tea on your mind."

Duff looked at Misty and shrugged. "I been asking her out for t'ree years," he said pleading his case. "T'ink I'd be somewhere by now but I tell you, getting into a Protestant's bed is like trying to snoff the queen herself."

"I begs your pardon," said Mavis. "This is a dentist's office."

"That's what I means. I presents opportunity and that'd rather freeze her arse off and be proper."

Duff's love life was interesting and might even make a great column, but at the moment Misty had all she could take of it. "My toot?"

"I bees getting to that."

Mavis stood up, hands on her rounded hips. "My darling," she said to Misty. "I apologizes for the likes of him. What's the matter with your tooth? Give us a look."

"She cracked it off," said Duff. "One of the Purity knobs again."

"There should be a warning on the bag. The business them knobs brings us. Tch, tch, Misty, and you being a Newfoundlander and all. What're you doing biting on Purity knobs? They bees for sucking."

Duff took an audible breath as though he were about to say something until Mavis cornered him with her eyes. "Shut up, you."

Misty admired Mavis's timing and quick wit. No wonder Duff was frustrated. *Now that would be a story. Headline. Gums and Roses: Loving on the Rock.*

"Let's have a look-see. C'mon, my dear. Open wide. I seen everything at least once."

"Dere's some stuff you haven't seen yet," said Duff, seizing his opportunity once again.

Mavis pursed her lips and iced him with her eyes as Misty opened her mouth and removed her hand.

"You did a right good job on that one," she said to Misty. "My, oh, my."

Her concern didn't do anything to ease Misty's anxiety. "Can 'ou fis it?"

"My dear, we fixes far worse than that. You're not nervous are you, my love?"

Actually, until Mavis brought it up she hadn't thought about anything more than getting help. But with the idea planted that there might be something to be nervous about, her tooth began to throb again. "It wone 'urt, wool it?"

"Isn't that sweet?" Mavis looked at Duff and smiled cherubically. "She bees talking like one of us now," she said. Mavis had a motherly way about her, when she wanted to. "No, my sweetheart. It won't hurt. We hauls out teeth by the dozens and you never hears any screaming."

"Don' wan it 'auled!" Misty hadn't realized her eyes could open wider than her mouth. "Jus fis it. Ca' 'ou fis it?"

"Not a problem." Mavis patted her hand. "We fixes teeth all day long. You just have a seat over there with Duff and I'll let Ruby know we got an emergency. You bees some lucky this morning."

Lucky? Misty was having a hard time to see it from that perspective. *If this was luck, what was un-luck. Losing two teeth?*

As Mavis shooed them toward the seating area, Duff watched her with appreciation.

"Sted Grouchie just cancelled short notice," she said. "But see how things works out? Along comes a crisis, right when you needs one."

"Loves that woman," he said as they sat down and Mavis left them alone. "Can't get nowhere with her, though. You bees a specialist at attracting men. Got any ideas?"

"Not 'ike 'is." She pointed at her mouth.

Duff paused in thought. "S'pose it could be my dentures. These old things probably turns her off, wha?" He opened wide and Misty got an eyeful.

Misty nodded in agreement. "Noo den'ures. Goo' idea."

She leaned back in the chair and tried not to think about what was coming. It didn't work, of course. All she could think about was what was coming and what might happen to her poor front tooth. Amazing how attached you get to things like fingers, toes and teeth. Particularly when you're a walking billboard for *Live with Ricky. Nice girl, great legs, love the hair, love the attitude, not bad, really...except for the tooth from hell.*

Why couldn't she be in a city? Doccy Snow looked seventy if he was a day and he was going to fix her tooth? For God's sake, his phone number was "PULL."

By the time Mavis returned to take her into the surgery, Misty's anxiety level, on a scale of one to ten, was a solid twelve and her legs felt unsteady.

"Here you goes," said Mavis taking her by the arm and passing her over to Ruby. "She looks a bit pale, Ruby-doll. I told her not to worry. Doccy Steve is..."

"Dotty Steve?" Misty grabbed the back of the dental chair with her free hand. "Dotty Steve?"

"Now, don't you worry," said Ruby, waving Mavis out of the room. "You knows Dotty...Doccy Steve. Chip off the old block. 'E could do this with 'is h'eyes closed." She pried Misty's fingers from the chair and eased her into the seat.

He was in town and hadn't even called her? Just dropped off the letter and that was it? "'ere's Dotty Sno?" Misty asked, refusing to release Ruby's arm.

My God, the column. He was here and I let that column loose across the country? But I didn't have much choice; I had to set everyone straight. I don't understand, why hasn't he called or returned my calls? What if...

it was unthinkable...the letter as good as told me it was from him. She put her hand to her head and squeezed her temples. Her thoughts were fluctuating faster than a Charlie's Cove weather pattern as she tried to process what this meant. *I opened my heart like a romance novel. He'd read it all by now and hadn't even responded.* Misty swung her feet to the floor.

"Oh no you don't," said Ruby, placing a firm hand on Misty's shoulder and lifting her feet back onto the chair. "You can't be running out on us now."

"But," began Misty, wondering how she could explain why she couldn't, absolutely wouldn't, see Steve now. Not under any circumstances. She was humiliated. Rebuffed.

"No buts. We needs to treat that tooth now, dear." Ruby picked up a chart.

Misty sat back obediently and exhaled her frustration, ignoring a shot of pain as her breath passed over the open nerve in her tooth. Maybe Ruby would leave the room and she could make good on her escape. But then what would she do? See Ricky with a broken tooth and have it splashed over the evening news?

"Any allergies?" asked Ruby, ignoring Misty's agitation.

Only to Steve, Misty thought as she winced from another jolt of pain and shook her head.

"Medications or reactions?"

Same and final answer…only to Steve but she nodded no to Ruby.

Ruby lowered her voice. "Is you on the patch for birth control?"

"Birt' cont'ol? Wha'dat got to do wit'my toot?"

Ruby laughed. "Not a thing, b'y. That one were for Phonse. 'E's scared you're going to get up the stump."

Just the mention of Phonse's name raised her ire again. She still hadn't resolved the problem of her wedding photo or how she was going to shut him down permanently.

"See, now you're relaxing. There's some colour back in your face," noted Ruby as she continued with her questions.

Misty managed to answer everything even as she agonized about the fact she would soon be face to face with Steve. *What would she say to him? Hi, honey, so I see you're back again. No, how about "so exactly when were you going to tell me you blew into town?"*

"Ever had laughing gas?"

"Wha?" she said as Ruby interrupted her scripting.

"You'd be perfect for h'it. I'm not sure I h'ever seen someone so jumpy. The gas'll relax you so much, you won't care if we takes your 'ead off. Sounds good, what?"

"Gim'me da gaz." Little did Ruby realize her anxiety had little to do with her tooth anymore. That seemed the least of her worries. What she needed was something to take the edge off seeing Steve again. Her tooth might be shattered but her heart was in far worse shape. *Why hadn't he called her? At least then she would know-*

"God love you, but you seems some nervous," said Ruby as she wheeled a tank over and sat down again. "I calls this multi-tasking," she explained. "Bet you 'ad no idea I bees a licensed nurse, too, thanks to the retraining incentives. H'if the government keeps closing fish plants, I'll be a brain surgeon by the time I retires."

Ruby reclined the chair and slipped a mask over Misty's nose. "Now, you just breathe, nice and h'easy." She gently brushed her fingers back and forth over Misty's hand. "That's right now. 'Ow's that feel?"

Misty didn't mean to, perhaps it was her apprehension or maybe it was just the general hullabaloo in her life, but her first breath was supersized. And she followed that with several more Olympian intakes until her eyes suddenly crossed. At least she thought they did. There were two Rubys. She smiled at both of them just to be sure. And she giggled. *This feels kind of nice. Sweet Ruby.* Misty took Ruby's hand and kissed it.

"Oh, yeah. That bees better," Ruby laughed. "Just what the doctor ordered."

"What did I order?"

Is that Steve? He sounds so far away, like his voice is coming from a tunnel or drifting across the water. How I love his voice. So deep and mellow. Mmmmm. She closed her eyes and slipped away on the crest of a wave.

"And who do we have..." Steve began, and then answered his own question. "Misty Muldoon. Ah...well...ah...Misty Muldoon. Yeah, well, imagine that. Ruby?"

"Yes, Doctor?"

"You didn't tell me who was here. You might have mentioned our celebrity guest." Steve pulled a mask up over his face. "I see you administered the nitrous. Probably a good thing in this case," he added. "Great."

Misty especially liked the way her name rolled off his tongue. "Miiissssteeee. Mmmmmmmmmmm."

"What, Doctor?" asked Ruby, sounding unsure. "You likes it when I gets things ready, mostly."

"Never mind."

"Don't you be getting a case of the nerves, too," she said sharply. "That's all I needs."

"She seems to have taken to the nitrous, Ruby. Let's have a look. Open wide." Misty opened obediently, her mouth stretched from one ear clear to the other and back again.

"Whoo-ho. No TMJ on this girl. Don't let her bite me, Ruby. I might lose a hand."

That beautiful voice. Misty drifted, floated across the ocean. Up and down. *This is fun.* Up and down she bobbed. *Down and waaaay up and whoa...there he was!* Leaning over the deck of the ship and staring at her, the rogue of the big blue seas, the pirate with the bluest eyes, her very own Kissing Pirate.

"Misty?"

"Here," she cried, her voice bouncing across the waves. "KKKKKKKKKKKayyyyyy PPPPPPPPPPPeeeeeeeee." Misty threw out her arms.

"Careful. Watch her arms, Ruby. How much did you give her?"

"She was right nervous."

"Ruby?"

"I think it was her condition what caused this."

"Oh, KP," Misty sighed.

"Misty? Are you all right? Open your eyes."

Misty dove into the water again. *So deep. So sexy.* She swam toward him. "Itz you. Really you." She reached up and grabbed hold of him.

"Doctor, are you okay?"

Ruby? What was Ruby doing on the pirate ship?

"Ah, it's a bit awkward. Can you give me a hand?"

A hand? She was as light as a feather in his arms. *Why would he need help from Ruby?* "Go 'way, Ruby."

"My magnifying loops are hooked in her bib. She's got a grip on me like a boa constrictor. I'm sure...maybe if I jus..."

"Kizzzz me." Misty pulled him closer and Ruby chuckled.

"Ruby, stop laughing and give me a hand here."

"But, Doccy. I can't 'elp it. She's like an h'octopus. All arms and suckers and she's not letting go."

"I'm going to lose my balance. This chair is going to take off on…"

There was a great crash.

"Land ho," cried Misty. Her eyes flew open and she held on for dear life. "We're goin' down." *Two of him. There were two pirates.* "Oh." She moaned as she tried to get things in focus.

"She got your number, Doccy. You looks some sweet, the two of you," Ruby said.

"Shut up, Ruby. Can't you see this is serious? We've run aground," said Steve, and he began to laugh as well.

"Whaz so funny?" Misty mumbled as she tugged KP closer. He was wearing something over his mouth and she pulled the funny mask off his face.

"She's going for the gold. Look out, Doctor."

It was that irritating Ruby again. "Ge' off tha ship, 'uby," Misty said, then sighed. "Mmmmmmmm, love d'oze lipzzz." She pulled Steve closer.

"Ruby, I may need some help, after all."

"Let me come around, Doctor. Looks like she's coming aboard."

"Uh-oh. Too la…"

Misty planted her lips on his. A wave of ecstasy sizzled through her. Electric. She melted into his arms and looked deeply into his eyes. *There were four. There were two.* His warm breath caressed her face. *Such kind and gentle eyes.* She swam into them and sighed, "KP."

"This is one for the books," laughed Ruby. "Misty, you got to let the doctor go. 'E's gonna fall on you."

"Faw fo' me, 'uby. You goddit w'ong." She was still holding KP in her arms. Those eyes. She would never forget them. Ever. Where was she?

"Misty? This is Steve. Can you let me go?"

She blinked and fluttered her eyes. "Dotty Steve?" Slowly, the world wiggled into shape. She was holding him in her arms and her heart was thundering in her ears. "Who? Wha? Dotty?"

Misty blinked several times in rapid succession. There was Ruby. *Ohmigod!* She pushed her way through the haze that covered her brain like impenetrable fog. *Her tooth.* Slowly, she began to remember. *Doccy Snow. No…not Doccy Snow but…*she looked at Steve who was now leaning over her.

"KP?" she asked.

"Misty, is you all right? This bees Dr. Steve, Doccy Snow's nephew. 'Member? You broke your tooth." Ruby looked concerned. "She thinks you're KP, Doctor, the one she's looking for in the paper."

"But," Misty began and then shut up. What had she done? Better yet, what had she said? Her face burned and she knew she was turning the most vibrant shade of red. No one in town knew the extent of her involvement with Steve and now Ruby had seen her falling all over him. Literally.

"I'm so sow'y. I...I donn unnerstan' wha' happen'd. I mean, itz been re'lee crazze and I jus'...I donn know." She looked at him and tried to smile. "I...I'm so emba'azzed." Her voice was barely a whisper.

"For adding a good bit of fun to our day? Absolutely not. Hey, Ruby, you remember what happened?"

"'oo me? Not a thing."

"Good," said Steve. "Neither do I. Some people have unusual reactions to nitrous, especially if they're tired or stressed."

"Or maybe 'aving 'alf the men on the h'island chasin' you," added Ruby. "The doctor's single, too. 'E's good to go."

Good to go? If you only knew. He's more than good to go. He's it.

"Let's have a look at that tooth."

Misty opened her mouth. It was probably the widest it had ever opened in her life. She wanted to disappear into it, under it, behind it, and right off the face of the planet, if truth be told.

"And the good news is," he said as he leaned over her. "We can fix you up."

Is there a special message in that? Misty wanted to talk to Steve but there was no opportunity at all.

She hadn't seen him since the night they'd spent at her house. And suddenly, all those feelings she'd experienced with him then descended upon her, bringing with them vivid memories of his touch and even, she admitted, his scent.

As she stared into his eyes, for a moment it was though they were alone, isolated in a private enclave for two. No Duff, no Mavis, no Ruby. And in that brief instant, as quickly as she might extinguish a candle, a silent transmission of thoughts and feelings passed between them. When Steve began his work, Misty simply closed her eyes and tried hard not to think about either him or her tooth. On both accounts, she failed miserably. Every touch of his hands, every subtle brush against her cheek was a tender reminder of their time together. The effects of the nitrous left her logy and she gently drifted in and out as Steve continued his restoration. Occasionally, their eyes met and her body responded in ways entirely inappropriate for someone in a dental chair, but she couldn't help it.

"There," Ruby finally said. "All finished. H'earth to Misty. Quick switch. Close your mouth and h'open your eyes."

Misty blinked. She had no sense of time, wondering how long she had been there. The lights were so bright. She looked over. Steve was still sitting next to her.

"'ave a look-see." Ruby passed her a mirror. "Some job, what?"

Misty held the mirror to her face. She took a deep breath and slowly parted her lips. She saw two teeth. Two perfect front teeth. *How did he do it?* Her broken tooth looked just like the twin sitting next to it.

"Whadidisay? 'E's a h'artist."

"Amazing," said Misty getting the feel of her new tooth. She spoke tentatively but the excitement in her voice at seeing the miracle of Steve's work wasn't tentative at all. She was very grateful. "It's perfect. I can't believe it. Thank you. Thank you so much." She looked at Ruby and then at Steve. Above his mask those wonderful eyes regarded her warmly.

After a few minutes and a few adjustments, she was finished and Ruby removed her bib. Steve looked down at her. "It was very nice to see you, Misty." His eyes conveyed unspoken humour. "Keep an eye on her, Ruby. She might be a bit unsteady on her feet. You're not driving, are you?"

"Uh, no. Duff's waiting for me. I don't know how to thank you," she said. "I have to meet Ricky Volcano this afternoon and, well…it would have been terrible with half a tooth."

"You may still find it terrible, but at least you'll look nice."

She wanted to say something to him about his letter but how could she? Ruby was hovering over them like she expected Misty to assault Steve again. And no wonder. Not every patient wraps her arms around the doctor and then fastens herself to his lips in a manner requiring surgical separation.

If they could just have a minute alone, maybe then...

"Well, duckie," Ruby interrupted her thoughts. "You sure got your fan club." She was waiting for Misty to follow her.

"Good luck, Misty." Steve offered his hand to her. "I'm glad I could help."

Misty placed her hand in his. "Thank you," she said and gave him a crooked, half-frozen smile. He had taken off his surgical gloves and his hand was warm and soft and strong.

"Are you feeling okay?" he asked. "You just went a bit pale." He tightened his grip on her hand.

She felt so trapped. Maybe she could run away and hide. For about six months. Quite possibly a year. Except that wouldn't solve anything and it certainly wouldn't heal her heart, if there was any chance at all that it could be healed.

"Excuse me," Ruby said. "You 'as another patient in the next room, Doctor."

"Right." He released her hand and Misty tore her eyes away from him and followed Ruby. She wanted to look back but dared not. *What if he was looking at her? What if, well, what if he wasn't?* What was she supposed to do now? She was so afraid she'd blown it. *Oh, KP, will you ever forgive me for...for...*she didn't know where to begin or end. *Just give me a chance.*

"Good h'as new," Ruby broadcast across reception to Duff, who stood up and walked over.

"Ricky Volcano just arrived at the office. We got to get you right over there," said Duff pushing her toward the door.

"But...but I don't want to." Misty passed her debit card to Mavis who promptly passed it back.

"Doc says it's on the house, Misty. Not every day we gets a celebrity in here."

"She already paid, sure," Ruby added, not even cracking a smile. "She paid with a big, fat kiss. Doc's not h'over it yet." She chuckled as she waved good-bye. "You leave h'our doctor alone, Misty. 'E won't h'ever come to work again."

"You kissed him?" Duff and Mavis said in rhythm.

"It's not like it sounds," said Misty.

"Oh, yes it is," said Ruby, who was still hanging on. "I thought I was in the middle of *The Young and the Restless*. Talk about h'action. Whoo-eee."

Misty felt herself blushing under the scrutiny of Mavis and Duff. She wished that annoying trait of hers came with an off button. "Honest," she said. "It really wasn't my fault. Ruby administered too much nitrous. I was out of it."

Duff seemed to ponder what she'd said before he turned to Mavis. "S'pose I kissed you like that, then that wouldn't be my fault, either?" he asked.

"Don't even t'ink it, you rascal. She's a celebrity. Anything goes with her."

"Will you two give me a break? This has been bad enough."

"She's gonna put this place on the map, Mavis," Duff added.

"But I..."

Duff looked at her. She saw the frustration on his face. "This bees the best thing what's happened in years, Misty. The ship's finally docked and we're all counting on you."

It was true. Everyone in the Cove was looking at her now. She had single-handedly created so much interest in the small community that there was no stopping it without disappointing them all.

The last thing she wanted to deal with was applicants for her heart. It would all be a lie. As far as she was concerned, the deal was done. Her heart was taken. A fact confirmed by the fierce ache she experienced as Duff held the door for her and she walked out and away from Steve.

"There's Ricky and his crew," Duff pointed out as they turned into *The Yarn* parking lot a few minutes later. "This is your lucky day, Misty. You is really going to be hot now."

And bothered, Duff. Hot and bothered with no immediate relief in sight. She traced her tooth with her tongue and thought of Steve one last time as she stepped out of the van and straight into Ricky's warm embrace.

"Misty Muldoon," he said as he picked her up and swung her around. "Welcome to *Live with Ricky*. I'm doing what a lot of men across this country have been dreaming about." And he planted a kiss smack on her frozen lips.

T'ongs be damned, thought Misty, as he slipped his hand on her ass. That, she hoped, wasn't on camera for Steve or anyone else to see.

CHAPTER 29

The Right Stuff

"Smile, Misty. Here, let me put a dab of powder on your nose."

Misty was fed up with powder dabs and mike clips and camera flashes. She'd been running on high octane for two days straight. Since the hunt for KP had started, she hadn't had a minute's peace.

Last night she'd tried to call Steve and talk to him. The only number she had for him in Charlie's Cove was his cell phone and the message manager picked up. The first few times she hung up, but after the third attempt she had left a message for him to call her. She'd lain awake for hours with the phone in her hand, hoping and wishing he would call but in the end she had fallen asleep without hearing from him.

She was so confused. By now, he had seen her acceptance in *The Yarn*, so why wouldn't he call? Maybe he'd changed his mind and decided he couldn't handle things. She had a strong feeling he wouldn't want his life played out in the media and she had complicated things more than ever by her last column.

And what made matters worse, Ricky Volcano had finally nailed her for *the* interview. She was about to be featured from coast to coast on *Live with Ricky*. Ricky was making a final pitch for the identity of KP. Misty cringed and hoped Ruby hadn't been thinking about what Misty had called Steve the other morning. She cringed when she recalled the way *KP* had sailed off her lips several times. If Ruby put two and two together and thought there was more to it than just a mistake, then Steve's life was on the verge of turning into a circus as well. He'd never forgive her.

So caught up was she in her misery, she scarcely realized where she was, let alone what she was doing. And adding to her discomfort was the fact a fierce wind was ripping into Charlie's Cove and she was having what she called a wild hair day.

Volcano resembled his name, if you could believe it. He had a shocking cap of bright red hair that was a cross between Don King and Lyle Lovett. If Ricky wanted you for an interview, there was no getting away from him.

Misty had been up early, sneaking out her back door, hoping to get to the office before the Cove woke up. She'd been doing a pretty fair job of blindsiding Ricky Volcano, who seemed to be entertained by interviewing everyone she had ever had contact with. But when she stepped out, she was blinded by a flood of light that caused her to lose her footing and bounce down the steps on her backside.

It was Ricky.

He nabbed her and carted her off into town where they were shooting the closing scene for live coverage of "A Mate for Misty."

"Ricky always gets what he wants, honey," said Ricky's assistant, Monet. "He was hired for a number of things. I've heard some of them are in his pants but most of what I see is above the neck. You didn't stand a chance."

That was Sue-Lee's opinion, too. Sue-Lee was their make-up and wardrobe girl. She'd befriended Misty in five minutes flat. She'd also stuffed her inside a parka trimmed with pink fox and placed a matching fox-fur hat on her head. "You have to look the part. Everyone expects the wild, wild north here so I'm providing authenticity."

"If it's authentic," snapped Misty, "why not let me wear my Columbia jacket?"

"Sweetie, you've been around TV long enough to know we never do authentic like that. Any baby seals on the ice?" She was yelling at one of the crew.

It was all Misty could do to contain herself. She shuffled over to sit on the trailer steps in her matching pink mukluks. Someone passed her a steaming hot cup of coffee and it fogged up her sunglasses. Which were pink, of course.

"Move over."

Misty shuffled blindly to one side and made room.

"Trying to get a private moment with you is like trying to get an audience with my uncle, the absent dentist."

Misty choked on her coffee. It burned her mouth and she began to cough. A sharp pat on the back settled her down.

"And coffee stains your teeth, by the way."

It was KP. Here. In the worst possible place. His timing was quite possibly worse than hers. "You gave it to me," she said, trying to sound much cooler than she felt. "What are you doing around here? Are you nuts?"

"I'm trying to blend in with the crew."

Misty stared at him. The only thing visible was his eyes. Today, they looked icy blue like the reflection of the sky on the water. The rest of him was bundled under a wool hat, scarf, and heavy overcoat with the collar turned up.

"I wanted to see you," said Misty with just a bit of desperation in her voice. "But we can hardly talk now. Do you know how many times I've tried to reach you?"

"Probably about half as many times as I tried to reach you," he replied as he dismissed her complaint. "How's your toot?" He laughed as he saw the expression on her face when she smiled and boldly displayed his work. "Fine, I see. You can close now. I tried to call, you know, but your answering service was full. Tilly wasn't taking any more messages. I was afraid to show up at *The Yarn* or on your doorstep in case someone shot at me with either a gun or a camera. So this is my final resort. I rescheduled my morning and decided to track you down. It wasn't easy given that you're disguised as a flamingo."

He decided to track her down? The butterflies set up camp again and she didn't need the coffee for warmth anymore; she was generating more heat than a wood stove and oil furnace combined. She looked around cautiously to see if anyone was looking at them and relaxed a bit when she saw everyone was busy getting ready for the hit.

"You've been looking for me?" she asked, sounding somewhat surprised. "I thought you were avoiding me."

"I was doing what the situation required—keeping a low profile. But I was definitely looking for you. I wanted to check on you and then that tooth. I can't guarantee my work if I can't get close enough to examine it personally." His eyes were a dead giveaway to a smile she knew was buried behind his scarf. "And stay away from the knobs, at least until this racket settles down some."

"I've learned my lesson," she said. "You really were looking for me? After what I did? All this and everything? You're still interested in me?"

"You're the only woman who's ever kissed me in the chair."

"Is that a body part? Because if it is, I'm not familiar with it." Misty laughed for the first time in several days.

"And I love your sense of humour. Do you realize I've never had one normal moment with you?"

"Okay, we're ready. Get Misty," someone yelled across the lot.

"I have a feeling that's not about to change in the short run," Misty replied. "Andy Warhol's fifteen minutes have morphed into a long-term engagement. Will you be here when I finish? Maybe we can sneak off somewhere for a few months."

"Nice." Steve smiled. "I may take you up on that but first you should know I didn't get in this outfit to deliver coffee. I'm actually in charge of making sure the cables don't freeze to the asphalt. Don't you see Hollywood in these eyes? I had to pay Stinky Pelley twenty bucks for this opportunity and I plan to get my money's worth."

Misty's butterflies picked up the pace and her stomach rolled over with the anticipation of having Steve nearby when she was being interviewed. "You're actually going to be watching me? I'm nervous enough without you watching me."

"Front row centre, sweetheart, so don't say anything you wouldn't want me to hear."

"Oh, creepers. This is bad enough and I can't be held responsible for what Ricky makes me say. Or do, for that matter. He pushes everyone's buttons. That's what he does. He's deadly."

"Misty, I've seen you do your thing. You're the most charming misadventure on two legs. I know you can handle it. Just don't give my spot away. I'm still in the running, aren't I?"

"You still want to be? After what I did? I just thought...maybe you thought I was crazy."

"Because you want someone to love you?"

"Well, that, but mostly the way it all happened. I'm not as desperate as it looks."

"I never, ever thought of you as desperate. Vulnerable, possibly desperately beautiful, but just plain desperate? Not hardly."

Misty's heart simply ached. There was no other way to describe what she was feeling.

"Misty! We're waiting." It was Volcano's assistant. "Ricky's getting cold."

"Then Ricky needs thicker blood," she yelled back, wanting to jump into Steve's arms and run away. She looked at him again and he gave her a thumbs up and pulled on a big pair of gloves. He followed her across the parking lot and as she stood in front of the camera, he settled in by the side of the cameraman.

"Why would anyone ever live here?" Volcano was shivering in his mukluks and parka. He was holding a mike in a hand swaddled in a big fur mitten. "We need a voice check. Say something, Misty."

There was actually a shiver in his voice.

Misty obliged. "I'm not getting into my personal life and all questions about sex are off limits, Ricky."

"More," he said. "Keep talking."

If her comments were having any impact on him, he wasn't acknowledging it, so she continued. "No questions about my preferences and definitely nothing about favourite positions. I've seen your interviews."

"That's good." He stared at Misty and his eyes were calculating. "But just you remember, a volcano is hot, hot, hot."

His voice shot up on the last two hots and she wanted to pull Ricky's touque down over his face. She looked to see if Steve was watching, which he was. She hoped he couldn't overhear the conversation and that he had no ability to lip read. The wind was whipping around them and she was counting on it to smother her exchange with Ricky.

"Okay, Ricky. In ten." The floor director counted down, ending silently with three, two, one, as they went to air.

"Live with Rick-ee. Heeeey, Canada! Ever seen Charlie's Cove? Don't blink your eyes. You might miss it."

Misty listened to Ricky's intro with a twisted little smile. Only a few months ago she would have been saying the same thing. Now, she found his tongue in cheek rather offensive.

"Meet Misty Muldoon, the lady looking for love. Think you'd like to curl up in front of the fire with her? Think you're the one? We've been interviewing candidates all week long and we have a stack of applications here that would take us a year to go through, so we're going to take it to the max today. We're going to find out exactly what this woman wants, if that's ever possible."

There was a drop of snot hanging off Ricky's nose. *Not tough enough.* He definitely wasn't getting on the shortlist, if there even was one. She sneaked a peak at KP. He was squatting behind the camera guy. His nose sensibly hidden behind his scarf.

"So, Misty, tell us, what exactly are you looking for? Marriage material, a lover, a boy toy? The country is waiting."

If he hadn't added that last little qualifier, she might have been all right. The thought of the country listening gave her a sudden attack of nerves.

"Ah...ah," Misty stalled as Duff's words ran through her head. *We're all counting on you. You're the best thing that's happened to Charlie's Cove in years.* "Marriage," she blurted out and immediately blushed.

"That's big. We're talking marriage material with a capital M. So, men, KP especially, if you're not prepared to commit, don't send a resume. Should cut out about half the prospects, wouldn't you say?"

Misty wondered if KP could hear their conversation from where he was crouched down with the cables. Hopefully not, the way the wind continued to howl.

"What's he gonna look like, Misty? Give us a glimpse. We've got men wondering if they should waste the time buying a stamp. Full head of hair, washboard stomach, ginger, blond, brown, grey? Tall, short? Professional or blue collar?"

"He's tall," she said.

"Tall," encouraged Ricky. "All the short guys are boycotting your column as we speak. What else?"

"Well, he's got blue eyes."

"Blue eyes. Hear that fellas? That just cut out a whole segment of people descended from the Basques. And?"

Misty took a deep breath. "And he's got great teeth."

"Teeth?" Ricky was squealing. "She likes nibbling, boys. Crank up the wattage on your smile. What about below the belt, Misty? Looking for anything special there?"

Misty giggled. *Sweet Ramona. She actually giggled.*

"Well, that hit a hot button. Don't apply if you don't got the zoom." He did a little razzle-dazzle with his hips and in his parka he looked like a walrus doing the hula. "What else, Misty? This is your chance to do what a million girls dream of—run an ad for the perfect hunk of testosterone." He looked around and gestured to his floor director. "Let's get some local colour in here. Get us a real live specimen from the local rack. Something to stimulate her imagination." He pointed at Steve. "Why not that strapping big boy? He'll do. Get him up here and let's hope he's got good teeth."

Ohmigod! Not Steve. Misty turned the colour of her hat. This couldn't be happening. She watched in horror as the camera focused on him. There was a furtive discussion between Steve and the floor director, all of it on camera. *He'd say no. Of course he would.*

He didn't. He walked over to Ricky and the camera followed him.

"Live in Charlie's Cove on The Rock. We're going to dissect a local chappie and see what it is Misty Muldoon is really after. Hey, big guy. Whoa-ho, blue eyes. Hey, Misty." Ricky jabbed her with his elbow. "He's got blue eyes and he's tall."

Ricky didn't give her any opportunity to comment. He slipped the mike under Steve's nose and upped the ante. Steve tugged his scarf away from his mouth and smiled.

"It's hot and it's happening. He's got the teeth. Look at that set of pearly whites. Boy, you must have been raised on raw meat. What's your moniker?"

"Steve," he said.

"What do you think, Misty? Like the name? Steve. Good, manly name. Do you prefer one syllable, two? Or three?"

"Two," said Misty. *KP.*

"Stephen, then. Sorry, Steve. It's got to be Stephen. All right men. We just eliminated anyone named Todd, Ike and James. Take off that hat, Stephen, and let's have look at the hair."

Steve slipped off his toque and the wind whipped across his head, pulling his hair back, and giving everyone a good look at his hairline and chiselled features.

"Hmmmm, not bad. But what does she say? Preferred colour, Misty? Stephen's got brown hair."

"Brown," said Misty weakly, wondering when Ricky was going to figure this out.

Ricky did a little dance. "We may have found Mr. Perfect right here in Charlie's Cove. Put your hat back on, Stephen, and open your coat. Let's see what you've got going in there."

"He will not," cried Misty.

"What's this? You can't be getting shy on us now, Misty." A crowd had gathered around them. "What'll it be, sweetheart? Washboard?"

"Washboard," she replied and the colour in her cheeks intensified.

"Right. C'mon, Stephen. You've got the country tuned in. Show us if you've got what it takes."

*He would not do this. He couldn't. He......*Misty watched him lower the zipper on his jacket.

"Make it fast, Stevo. You don't want any essential parts freezing off. Tight shot, Denny. Get in on the abs. Give us the goose."

Steve opened his jacket and pulled up his shirt. At the sight of rippling muscles and a dark line of hair that disappeared into his jeans, she almost passed out. Ricky was screaming in an English accent. "He's got it. By gum, he's got it. Give us the go, Misty. Like it?"

Misty fanned her face and pursed her lips. *What else could she do? It was perfection.*

Steve lowered his shirt and started to close his jacket.

"Uh-uh." Ricky stopped him. "Not yet. We've got one more test. Make it quick, Misty, before this boy freezes his necessities. How does it look down there?"

Misty put her hands over her eyes.

"We'll take that as a yes. The lady is overcome. Do up your jacket, Stevey, with two syllables. How about it, folks? Need to see more?"

The crowd cheered. Misty saw Wince Newhook with his camera.

"What about chemistry?" Ricky stepped between Misty and Steve and put his arms around them. "What happens when two molecules interact?"

There was a roar from the bystanders.

"Baby, it's cold outside. Let's raise the temperature. Wanna see it?"

The camera scanned the crowd. Misty saw Pansy with the girls. *How much had they seen? What a fine example of morality she was.* There was Phonse. And Duff. The whole town was there. Watching her. Their hopes and dreams for a little bit of fame and notoriety clearly visible on their faces.

Misty watched it all in slow motion. Ricky stepped back and pushed her toward Steve. She looked into his eyes. He placed his gloved hand under her chin and raised her mouth toward his.

Their breath clouded in the frosty air. She could see each fine line at the corners of his eyes where the skin folded softly. His eyes were cool now, a baby blue so translucent and clear she felt she could see her reflection in them.

Her toes tingled and like a thermometer set in a glass of hot water, she felt her mercury rising. Only inches separated his lips from hers. She no longer heard the cries of excitement from the crowd. She only heard the gentle sound of Steve's breath and felt it upon her face.

Slowly, he lowered his lips to hers. Misty melted into him as he lifted her to the tips of her toes. She wrapped her arms around his neck and pressed against him. His kiss swept over her and she forgot about where she was and all the people who were watching them.

It was heady. It was thrilling. It was amazing, this magical electricity that passed between them.

Somewhere in the background she could hear Ricky cheering them on as he orchestrated the crowd for the biggest reaction. When

Steve finally stopped kissing her and set her back on her feet, she swayed unsteadily. Thankfully, he didn't release her. Instead, he cradled her in the curve of his arm and hugged her to him. The strength of his body next to hers felt so unbelievably right. And if he wasn't holding her so closely, she felt sure she would have collapsed in a heap. She could blame it on the fact she was nervous, or the fact she hadn't eaten but she knew it wasn't anything like that. She was feeling the full effects of being in Steve's embrace in front of thousands of people, those right here in Charlie's Cove, and the rest in their kitchens and living rooms across the country.

Whistles and hoots of laughter and cheers shot into the air like fireworks. Ricky was providing play-by-play commentary for his audience. Misty tuned in again and a smile broke across her face. Her heart was filled with the kind of joy that was hard to explain. She hoped Ricky wouldn't ask.

"The Volcano just blew, folks. I hope you didn't miss it. If I were you, and this is just my opinion, I wouldn't bother to send in an application. I think love just arrived in Charlie's Cove. The temperature here went up five degrees to minus ten. Throw out the long-johns. Open the windows. Give these lovers a hand. You saw it happen live on Ricky Volcano."

Steve suddenly pulled her to him again. He delivered another passionate kiss, then turned to the camera and smiled.

"'E's KP,'" someone screamed. It was Ruby. She was running toward them, her arms waving wildly, a copy of the paper in her hand. "It's 'im, Doccy Steve. 'E's KP."

Steve looked at her. "What do you think, Misty? Wanna stay around?"

Misty's shook her head. "Not a chance."

"Then c'mon."

Steve grabbed her hand and she had no choice but to follow. The camera chased after them as far as it could go but Steve didn't slow down. He pulled out a set of keys and with a blast of a horn, the engine in his SUV roared to life.

"In you go, missus." He opened the door and helped her up into the vehicle, then ran around to the other side. He backed up and peeled out like he was going to a fire and not running from one. Misty got up on her knees and looked back at the scene they'd left behind them.

It looked like total pandemonium.

"I can't believe you did that," she gasped. "You should see what's going on."

"I am, honey. That's what rear-view mirrors are designed for." Steve was laughing.

"Looking back at the sights?"

"At the same time that you're moving forward."

Misty turned around, sat back down in her seat and fastened her belt. "There's a lot in what you just said, you know."

"I'm sure you'll tell me." Steve took her hand, placed it on his leg and covered it with his.

"Coming back here was like going back in time for me. It was probably the lowest point in my life."

Steve nodded and waited for her to continue.

"But it wasn't, really. It brought me back to where it all began and everyone around here was so wonderful and supportive, all in their own unique ways. So, it was like looking back and moving forward all at the same time. And then I met you."

"Don't stop now," he encouraged her. "This is the best part."

"And fell in love."

"Uh-huh." He was alternating between watching the road and looking at her.

"It's been the most wonderful experience of my life."

"Mine, too," said Steve. He put on the blinker and turned into a side road.

"Where are we going?" she asked him.

"Forward."

He turned off the vehicle and pulled her into his arms. As he kissed her, she managed to do one last thing. She pulled the rear-view mirror out of its slot and threw it into the back. It landed like an exclamation point on the leather seat.

This would be her best column yet.

Printed in Canada